D1193312

HIP

A Novel

Dr. Bob Bell

PUBLISHING

Hip, A Novel
By Dr. Bob Bell

Copyright © 2019 by Dr. Bob Bell

All rights reserved. No part of this publication may be reproduced, distributed, or transmitted in any form or by any means, including photocopying, recording, or other electronic or mechanical methods, or by any information storage and retrieval system, without the prior written permission of the publisher and author, except in the case of brief quotations embodied in critical reviews and certain other non-commercial uses permitted by copyright law.

Crescendo Publishing, LLC
2-558 Upper Gage Ave., Ste. 246
Hamilton, ON L8V 4J6
Canada

GetPublished@CrescendoPublishing.com
1-877-575-8814

ISBN: 978-1-948719-18-6 (P)
ISBN: 978-1-948719-19-3 (E)

Printed in the United States of America
Cover design by Abdo_96

10 9 8 7 6 5 4 3 2 1

Dedication

Hip is dedicated to courageous patients, to my talented partners, and to my darling wife Diann and our family who forgave me for spending so much time at the hospital.

Endorsements

"Dr. Bell capitalizes on his expertise as a surgeon, academic and administrator to produce a book that is highly entertaining and enjoyable. The details of orthopaedic treatment, scientific methodology and health care infrastructure are all accurately portrayed."

Dr. Peter Ferguson
Chair of Orthopaedic Surgery University of Toronto

*"Like a surgeons' knife, Dr. Bob Bell cuts through the personal, ethical, and career dilemmas facing medical staff in our leading healthcare institutions. Seldom do patients get an insider's view of the conflicts, ego and power politics of the medical practitioners who provide their care. Dr. Bob Bell was a "surgeon's surgeon" who operated brilliantly during his long career before heading up a large complex medical system as CEO. Bell is a gifted story teller with a true insider's tale to tell. With 400,000 Americans undergoing hip replacements annually and nearly 1 in 2 of us facing a cancer diagnosis in our lifetime, **Hip** will connect with readers with taut authenticity."*

Paul Alofs
Award Winning Author of *Passion Capital:*
The World's Most Valuable Asset

"Loved the book – I did not want it to end! Very impressive – a nice quick read and really well written!"

Marnie Escaf
Health Care Executive

"Great read. Locked myself in a room to get to the end. Well done."

Ed Clark
Senior Business Leader

*"Just finished **Hip**. What a great read! Couldn't put it down once I started."*

Catherine Booth
Senior IT Consultant

*"From the first chapter, **Hip** draws the reader into the complex world of medicine, research, and pathology by weaving an intriguing story that is instantly relatable. Author, Dr. Bob Bell, offers a compelling storyline of what it means to be true to the Hippocratic oath and the challenging and competitive environment of medicine and patented technology. **Hip** will not disappoint readers as a 'page turner'!"*

Julie Drury
Patient Partnership Leader

"I liked it! It's fast and intriguing."

Tom Kennedy
Senior Financial Executive

*"I really enjoyed reading **Hip** and found the author's knowledge gave the book credibility much like Michael Crichton and John Grisham. It's a great story with mass appeal. The storyline was gripping and did pull me back to the book."*

Dr. Sherif El-Defrawy
Surgeon and Health Care Leader

"This is going to be a big hit."

Dr. Alan Hudson
Neurosurgeon and Health Care Executive

*"**Hip** is a great read!"*

Dr. Rafi Hofstein
Medical Innovation Executive

"I loved the book! Couldn't put it down once I got started!"

Ralph Shedletsky
Organization Development Executive

"What a page-turner! What a great way to use all the author's expertise. It was such a delightful read."

Patti Cochrane
Health Care Executive

Table of Contents

Chapter 1

Andrei Kovalov, PhD
April 28

I was at home when Sam called. I'd finished one drink and was pouring my second when the phone rang. By the end of the call, I knew I'd need a one-way ticket out of here. And soon.

Up until that moment, things had been so good. We were just weeks away from the Initial Public Offering (or IPO, as the financial guys called it) that would bring me the payday I'd worked for my whole life. Dr. Hendricks was raising more money than I thought possible, promising hundreds of investors that the *super-B.I.G.,* the new hip replacement I'd created along with Hendricks, was going to be "stronger than your own hip." Thanks to him and that tagline, I was going to end up with at least $25 million from the IPO, with royalties to follow.

For an immigrant who had arrived in America with nothing—working day and night to finish my PhD and then slugging away in the lab trying to find a marketable product—I was looking at a well-deserved payday. And I would make sure my damn ex-wife who'd kicked me out of the house and kept me from seeing my daughter wasn't going to see a penny of this money.

"I'm sorry, Dr. Kovalov," Sam was saying on the other end of the phone. "You know that our team has been short staffed in the pathology lab. This new dog bone cancer work that Dr. Maloney is doing with Dr. Gershwyn has just stretched us to the limit. Everyone wants their specimens prepared in days, and bone specimens are really very time consuming to prepare properly."

I swirled the ice cubes in my drink, wanting only to relax and plan my new life. Why should I listen to Sam telling me about his problems?

"Yeah, I know, Sam. You guys are always getting asked to do more work 'cause you do it so well." This was the truth.

We'd tested the mechanical strength of the *super-B.I.G.* bonding to dog bone in Meredith McClintock's lab. We'd been trying it out in arthritic dogs for the past few years to test how well it would perform in humans. Through her lab analysis, Dr. McClintock had shown that the molecular biolayer I had designed to coat the metal *super-B.I.G.* hip replacement doubled or tripled the strength of the attachment between bone and metal. It meant our prosthesis was at least as strong as the patient's own hip.

I took a sip and tried to guess why Sam was calling. We'd sent some samples over for testing with Sam's group at the pathology lab—he was the chief technician there—but it was just backup testing. Nothing crucial, everyone thought, just routine. So, I wasn't quite sure why he needed to call me after hours.

"You know that we appreciate doing your work, Dr. Kovalov," he stammered. "I was just saying that we were short-staffed because— well, I am phoning to say that we mixed up one of your *super-B.I.G.* specimens with one of Dr. Maloney's cases."

I could hear the anxiety in his voice. What was going on? "Dr. Kovalov," he said, "somehow we got one of your specimens mixed in with Dr. Maloney's slides."

"Okay, Sam, I appreciate you letting me know," I said. Why did he keep calling me Dr. Kovalov? We'd been on first-name terms for ages. "We are almost finished sending you *super-B.I.G.* specimens anyway, Sam. We will be in market soon."

"Ah, well…there may be a problem, Dr. Kovalov. Dr. Maloney has looked at the material already and realized that the slides were from a dog that had received the *super-B.I.G.* implant. And… Andrei, Maloney says there is a lot of bone cancer in this specimen, all around the *super-B.I.G.* prosthesis."

Fear sobered me immediately and I stood up with the phone held rigidly to my ear. "That's impossible," I said, trying to sound relaxed. I faked a chuckle. "Hip prostheses don't cause bone cancer. Maloney is no pathologist. He doesn't know what he's talking about." I switched the phone to my other ear. "Listen, I'll take a look myself just to make sure. But I know he's mistaken. Have you got the specimen back from him, Sam?"

"Yeah, I got it back, Dr. Kovalov."

"Keep it there. I'll be down soon."

I paced around my living room. This could ruin everything. If it were known that my IGF biolayer—the molecular coating on the prosthesis that stimulated amazing bone bonding to the implant— also caused cancer, the device would never be allowed into the market. This would be an absolute disaster, unless I could figure out a way to neutralize Maloney.

Luckily, I was the only one who knew that this was not the first time a dog had developed cancer around the *super-B.I.G.* implant. In fact, this would be the fourth case of cancer arising in the fifty dogs who had been examined after receiving our hip implant. I had destroyed the evidence of cancer in the first three cases without anyone else knowing. But Maloney could prove difficult.

If it became known that four *super-B.I.G.* dogs had cancer in their artificial hip joints, my big payday would be gone, and my career would be finished if people discovered that I'd been hiding the evidence. Right now, the idea of taking the money and disappearing back to my homeland after the IPO was sounding better and better. With enough money, I could do just that. Going home with all that hard currency would promise me a secure and very pleasant life.

Because if four dogs in fifty got cancer in only two or three years after getting the *super-B.I.G.* hip replacement, it meant that patients would almost certainly develop cancer after getting their hips replaced. And I would not want to be around when people realized

3

that my wondrous biolayer not only created a great hip replacement, but it also caused cancer. After the risk of cancer with the **super-B.I.G.** became apparent, everyone would want to know how much I'd known and when I'd known it. The fact that I had disappeared would probably tip them off.

To protect my money and myself, I would need to go into hiding—possibly for the rest of my life. Where I grew up, I could do that easily with $25 million. But disappearing would mean not seeing my daughter ever again. And if she knew what I'd done, what would she think about me?

I knew her mother told her all sorts of things about me that weren't true, or that I didn't want her to know. Soon, my daughter could also know me as the evil scientist who gave thousands of people cancer.

On the other hand, it was Hendricks' face all over the **super-B.I.G.** public relations. He starred in the promotional videos. He was the blue-eyed, silver-haired surgeon who rich investors and clueless regulators trusted. He would be the one having to explain why patients were stricken with incurable, untreatable cancer as a result of his miraculous product.

With a little luck, everyone would blame Hendricks. I would just be a forgettable footnote in the history of hip replacements.

And then, maybe one day, I would be able to connect with my daughter again.

Chapter 2

Dr. Patrick Maloney
February 15

*W*hen I started my run near Longfellow Bridge, I realized once again just how out of shape I was. I tried to lengthen my stride, but my muscles and lungs held me back like elastic bands stretched across my thighs and chest. I remembered the sense of lightness I'd once enjoyed while running. That was just three years ago. Three years that had made me into a surgeon, but handicapped me as a runner.

I had been using the Charles River bike path for my daily run since moving to Boston six weeks ago. Most hockey players weren't runners. I was a grinder on the ice, however, and had needed the stamina that running provided. In juniors and university, I'd been known for working every moment on the rink. Most of our opponents had known I was always willing to go hard into the corners and drop my gloves if needed.

Before starting work in the cancer lab in university and med school, playing hockey had been my main pressure release valve during my teens. It had kept my mind off my family—my dad, my sister.

Although I had travelled plenty for hockey, I'd never lived away from home before. Hard to believe that I was here, 130 miles by road and a light-year in prestige from Solway Mills. Graduates of my orthopedic residency program typically did not end up working here. My colleagues from Solway looked forward to a small-town orthopedic practice in rural New England, fixing broken bones and arthritic joints and providing advice to minimize the effects of aging on the skeleton.

Completing surgical training with a "finishing school" fellowship at the hospital here in Boston was a gateway to surgical prominence and wealth. But those prestigious fellowships were generally reserved for surgeons graduating from the world's leading hospitals and universities. Heads of state and their family members, celebrities, and elite athletes—all sought treatment here. It was the gold standard of world-class hospitals.

I liked running on the concrete bike path around the Charles Basin. Although it was still winter, I looked forward to watching sculls launch from the university boat houses as spring arrived. This was Boston's intellectual heartland at MIT, Boston University, HBS, and Cambridge Square.

This evening, Boston was enjoying a preview of spring. The Charles was ice-free, and the ridges of previously cleared snow that defined the path in winter had melted away. I had been improving my pace in the six weeks since I'd gotten back to running, but I was no match for the younger and fitter undergrads who inevitably passed me on the path. I could hear footsteps approaching and knew I was about to get smoked once again.

The young woman passing my left shoulder was a vision in mauve engineered fabric- tights and a form fitting sweater top- and she was breathing easily as she drew even with me. I tried to pick up my pace to save my ego, but to no avail. Her shoes flicked on the pavement and she passed me easily with a little glance of acknowledgment. My heart was pounding out of my chest and I needed to slow down to a trot.

As the runner pulled away into the early evening darkness, her gait made me think about the patient we'd operated on earlier in the day. I had only been working with Dr. Gershwyn for a few weeks, and this was the first time he'd left me alone in the operating room. Of course, Gershwyn being Gershwyn, I'd received comprehensive orders in the boss' unmistakable New Jersey accent.

"She has a big bone cancer in the back of her knee. It didn't shrink much with chemotherapy, and there is not much space between the cancer and her main leg artery. Expose the inner side of the knee and start taking down the blood vessels to the cancer. Remember she'll have a tourniquet on, so don't waste time."

Gershwyn was the country's leading specialist in bone cancer treatment, and this patient had been referred from California. Sarah was sixteen, with parents who had successfully invested in serial tech start-ups. She was born lucky—intelligent, precocious, and very athletic, like my little sister. But she was also the only child of wealthy parents. And now, she had bone cancer in her leg.

Fortunately, the cancer growing from the back of her thigh bone just above the knee had not spread elsewhere in her body. She had received several courses of chemotherapy—all covered by her parents' insurance, of course—and was now ready for the cancer to be surgically removed from her leg. The likelihood of a cure was probably about 70 percent. But her cancer was large and located in a difficult spot behind the knee, close to the large artery that supplies the lower leg and foot with blood supply.

I knew the surgical dilemma: cut too close to the cancer, and cancer cells would be released into the surgical site, which would result in the cancer re-growing and spreading. Cut too close to the artery, and the patient could lose her leg from a damaged blood supply. There was little or no room for error with this operation.

I had started the surgery that morning at 8 a.m., preparing the case for Gershwyn's arrival. Wrapping the sterile drapes and tourniquet around the thigh, I fell into that mental space I was accustomed to when undertaking difficult surgery. Time stopped and my attention tunneled into the surgical field in front of me. Nurses had told me more than once that they could set off a firecracker beside me and I would not hear it—but I would react instantly if the anesthesia heart monitor changed its chirping rhythm.

Working with a physician's assistant, I'd been able to move things along quickly, dividing tissues to expose the blood vessels behind the knee while leaving a thin layer of normal tissue covering the cancer to prevent cancer cell spillage. Inevitably, bone cancers release proteins that cause new blood vessels to grow into the cancer, as well as increasing the size of existing arteries and veins to enhance the cancer's blood supply. The first stage of this surgery required division of these larger than normal blood vessels to allow us to separate the artery gently away from the cancer.

By that point, I could hear the taps running in the scrub basin outside the OR and knew Gershwyn would be coming in to take over the surgery. Distracted, I spread my dissecting scissors too aggressively and, to my dismay, saw that I'd ruptured a blood vessel. A normally small artery at the back of the knee had grown large and delicate under the protein stimulus of the cancer, and I tore it in half—right where it attached to the main artery. Just as Gershwyn entered the room, the carefully controlled surgical site filled with blood.

Gershwyn was known as an occasionally profane surgeon, and the situation really called for profanity. The delicate, crucially important cleavage plane between the cancer and artery had disappeared, and the structures were obscured with blood. But it was pretty obvious to me where the bleeding was coming from, and I knew that I could fix this quickly.

"What the fuck happened here, Patrick?"

"Not to worry, boss. I just nicked a vessel over the cancer, flush with the main artery—all the veins and arteries are double normal size." I had asked the nurse for a tiny blood vessel suture in a needle driver clamp, which was already grasped in my right hand. My left hand exposed the leaking vessel.

Gershwyn was known for his growl. "We will need to get a vascular surgeon in to fix this mess. Dammit, we're going to be all day fixing this."

I knew we didn't need a vascular surgeon. I had fixed this kind of injury in lots of trauma cases in Solway. "Boss, by the time a vascular guy gets here, we will lose twenty minutes of tourniquet time."

While I spoke, I rotated the needle driver a few degrees at a time, passing the suture through the edges of the gaping hole in the torn main artery. After three passes of the needle through the margins of the hole, it was straightforward to gently spin a knot down onto the surface of the vessel. The bleeding stopped as quickly as it had started, and I could feel tension dissipate in the operating room.

"All yours," I said. "Sorry I tore that vessel."

Gershwyn rolled the repaired artery over and examined it through his loupes—surgical magnifying glasses. "That's as neat a job as I have seen from any vascular surgeon," he grunted. "Where did you learn that?"

"Where I trained, the nearest vascular surgeon was a helicopter ride away," I said. "When we had gunshot wounds or torn vessels with fractures at nighttime, there were lots of opportunities for fixing damaged arteries."

Gershwyn grunted again and took over the job of removing the cancer. Fifty minutes later, the end of the thigh bone was removed with the cancer intact. To punctuate the removal of the cancer, someone switched on Gershwyn's "closing music" on the Bluetooth speaker in the OR. As usual, Springsteen's percussive opening to "Born to Run" led the shuffle. And, as usual, the boss quietly sang along with the other Boss behind his mask.

The staff in the OR brought new instruments into the room, and we began the implantation of the cancer-replacing metal prosthesis that would rebuild the last six inches of Sarah's thigh bone and provide her with a new knee joint. All being well, she would be walking on her new leg within forty-eight hours.

Gershwyn left the OR after we inserted the implant, and I completed the surgery with the physician assistant. Forty-five minutes later, I was entering post-op orders on the computer in the anesthesia recovery room while Gershwyn spoke to the relieved parents.

I could see Gershwyn's hand on Sarah's foot, checking the pulse that depended on the blood flow in the artery that I had repaired two hours earlier. He looked over and nodded briefly, letting me know my artery repair was working fine. Then, he abruptly pivoted away and headed back toward his office.

I'd been running through MIT campus on the Cambridge side of the river while replaying Sarah's surgery in my mind. It was dark by the time I crossed the Boston University bridge, and I figured I should be getting home.

As I jumped off the stairs leading down from the bridge, crossing to the Boston side of the river, I heard voices up ahead. The path was poorly-lit in this section, but I could make out three figures along the path and recognized the young woman in mauve who had so easily passed me twenty minutes ago. Two young, beefy guys were standing in front of her, sniggering as she approached.

"Hey, babe, I love that shirt and them yogi pants," the shorter one said in a broad Southie accent. "They really stretch nice, huh?" The other one laughed.

She took a step to the left to run around them, but they mirrored her movement to block her path. She tried to pivot to the right to sprint past, but they grabbed at her arms to block her.

I had to say something. "Hey, guys, that's enough, huh? Let her finish her run."

"Are you her fuckin' white knight?" The bigger one, who had the build of an out-of-shape linebacker, leered at me. "You better have a horse ready to take her away."

They both turned their attention to me, lining up to block my way. The woman stepped around them and jogged down the path.

I had learned three things in various confrontations in my hockey days. First, you look for the biggest guy in the pack, because when you bring him down, the other players tend to leave you alone. Second, you make sure you always take the first shot, aiming somewhere soft that doesn't bust your hands. Finally, you make sure to immobilize your opponent's arms so they can't do you any damage.

I didn't say anything, but jogged straight at the bigger Southie, the one who'd called me a white knight, and launched my left fist at his face. When he leaned back to protect his nose, I rotated my hips and shoulders quickly and launched a short right hook that landed just below the rib cage at the top of his abdomen. As my fist hit his soft belly, he crumpled forward, sucking for air. I grasped the bottom of his jacket and pulled it up over his head, pinning his arms so I could topple him onto the ground, where he lay gasping like a landed bass.

The other guy watched this with his mouth open, no longer grinning. I left the two of them there and ran down the path to where the mauve jogger stood. She looked somewhat astonished at this rapid turn of events.

"Was that absolutely necessary?" she asked.

"To be honest, I'm not sure. But if it was necessary, it needed to be done quickly without stopping to ask. And that guy will be fine in five minutes—believe me, I've been at the other end of that punch back in my hockey days." I reached out a sweaty hand. "My name is Patrick."

She didn't take my hand. "I think I've seen you around the hospital, right?"

"Yeah, I'm working for Albert Gershwyn. Are you there as well?"

"I operate the lab for Jon Hendricks." She took my hand and shook slowly. "I didn't like you punching that guy. I run here every day. I can deal with this kind of stuff without a goon show."

She lifted a large whistle that hung around her neck. "One toot on this and those guys would've been gone."

She lifted a canister from her belt. "And if the whistle isn't enough, the pepper spray does the trick. But it sounds like you're new here. You'll need to learn some things about Boston."

And that is how I met Dr. Meredith McClintock.

Chapter 3

Dr. Patrick Maloney
February 16

I looked around at the leather couches and chrome end tables in Gershwyn's office as I joined him for a new consultation the next morning. Here, patients were booked at a stately pace—enabled by Gershwyn's substantial consultation fee—and the waiting room rarely held more than one family. The consultation room was outfitted with digital screens to facilitate discussion of pathology results, X-rays, or scans.

Privacy in Solway had been an abstract concept. The clinics had been crowded, with curtains separating stretchers that patients laid on to be examined and then sat on to hear what the doctor had to say. With eight examination stretchers in a 500-square-foot space, every spoken word could be heard by anyone occupying the other seven stretchers. Orthopedic consultation is usually not delicate or personal; however, issues regarding return to work and disability deserved a private space that was never available.

Most of the patients who gained access to Gershwyn came well prepared for the discussion about their condition. Gershwyn had just completed examining Randell Prentice, a twenty-one-year-old college student from Manhattan now attending Yale. Randell had a six-week history of shoulder pain and was referred with X-rays and an MRI of his shoulder. Gershwyn had described the tests to Randell and his parents, pointing to the images on a digital screen.

"Randell, I'm sorry, but everything about your symptoms and tests suggests that we are dealing with a cancerous bone tumor. That's the bad news."

Gershwyn looked from Randell to his parents. "The good news is that your lung CAT scans and other studies show no evidence of the tumor spreading. It seems to be confined to the shoulder bone. And, it's not a huge cancer—it's mainly contained within the humerus, which is the arm bone that forms the lower part of the shoulder."

Again, Gershwyn paused. The Prentices remained silent. "I won't patronize you and suggest that this is a good cancer. There is no such thing. But I will say that if this is cancer as I suspect"—here, Gershwyn lifted his steady gaze from Randell and locked eyes with Randell's mother— "it is curable with today's treatment. We will be able to give you the exact likelihood of a cure after we do the biopsy and review the pathology and genetic changes in the cancer."

He gestured to me. "This is Dr. Patrick Maloney. He's my fellow, which means he's my right-hand man. He's going to describe to you everything that's going to happen in the next week, and answer all your questions based on what we know today."

He reached out and grasped my shoulder. It seemed a bit corny, but I actually felt pretty good to be referred to as Gershwyn's right-hand man. "After we get the initial biopsy results, Patrick will provide a preliminary discussion of treatment, which won't start until we have all the results back, and that may take up to a week. But before we start any treatment, I will personally answer any other questions you may have."

Randell's mother had been writing every word in a leather-bound folio. She now opened the folio to a different tab, revealing pages of handwritten notes, likely from previous consultations.

"Dr. Gershywn, Dr. Hugesson in New York suggested that Randell likely has a Ewing's sarcoma. Do you agree with that diagnosis?"

"I agree with Dr. Hugesson," said Gershwyn, nodding slowly. "Based on the X-rays and MRI, Ewing's is most likely. The biopsy will confirm the diagnosis."

"Forgive me for asking," she said. "I don't want to sound like I'm testing you. Dr. Hugesson mentioned that identification of a genetic translocation is necessary to diagnose Ewing's. Will you be doing that test?"

Gershwyn twisted to look directly at Randell's father, who had been silent to this point, looking simply distraught. Gershwyn reached out and took one of the father's hands and one of the mother's hands.

"I understand you both want to ensure everything possible that can be done for Randell will be offered to him. This hospital has more experience with these types of bone cancers than anywhere else in the world."

He nodded at the word "anywhere" as if to emphasize the point. Randell had been staring at his hands in his lap and now looked up at his parents, looking as though he were more worried for them than about his cancer.

Gershwyn, still holding their hands, continued. "And the resources that we offer patients include the research potential at the university, where all of our team has appointments. So, our care is based on the latest understanding of cancer, including the genetic origins of the disease and treatments that may develop from cancer research. We'll talk again in the next week when all your tests are back, and I will personally share those results with you and provide you with my advice as to how we should proceed."

After one firm shake, he let go of the Prentices' hands. "I need to leave you for now. Dr. Maloney here will take over."

The Prentices all looked at each other and nodded appreciatively, probably assuming Gershwyn was off to save another life. I knew that he was actually going to meet with the university's investment advisors. I'd heard his department's funds had been underachieving in the market recently, and he wanted an explanation.

He laid a card on the table that included an email address. "This is our team's secure website. Patrick will describe how you can download an app from that site, which will provide you with private messaging to our team. Even after you talk with Patrick, I know you'll have a hundred questions you'll want to ask."

He pointed to the folio in Randell's mother's lap. "Record your questions in your notes and then email them to us. We'll answer within twenty-four hours. That's my guarantee."

I had a momentary flashback to another consultation, eighteen years ago. I was at Solway, on the other side of the desk, holding my mother's hand when a surgeon had simply announced that my little sister had a cancerous tumor in her leg and would need an amputation. It couldn't have been more different than what I'd just witnessed. At no point had the surgeon given us a chance to ask any questions. And though chemotherapy would have been standard treatment for my sister's condition, it was never mentioned to us as an option. Neither was the surgery I'd performed on Sarah just yesterday. And nobody had referred us to a specialist, a cancer surgeon like Gershwyn.

The doctors who'd treated my sister at Solway had either moved on or retired by the time I'd started medical school there, so I'd never had the opportunity to question their decision-making. I knew that my sister had a very aggressive cancer that spread to her lungs from her knee, and that chemotherapy may not have helped to save her life. But maybe the doctors would've considered other options if they'd thought we could afford it, or if our insurance coverage hadn't expired after Dad had died. It had taken Mum ten years to pay off every penny of my sister's treatment.

Gershwyn lifted himself from the chair and shook three hands, leaving Randell's mother until last and assuring her that he would take good care of her son. And then, he was out the door, continuing on a jammed schedule that rumor suggested began at 4:45 in the morning. I had heard that he started with a workout in the gym in his home, and I knew that many nights, he finished with a dinner with donors that could go on until 10:00 or 11:00 p.m. He was nearly sixty, recognized as one of the world's most expert surgeons, and I had rarely seen evidence of fatigue in the six weeks we had worked together.

As Gershwyn left, I slid into my boss' chair. Mrs. Prentice glanced to the door, as though wishing Gershwyn would return.

Randell leaned forward, perhaps sensing a peer in me, someone closer to his age. Perhaps they were waiting for some sort of formal introduction. Instead, I plunged right in.

"The most important test we will do in the next couple of days is a needle biopsy of the bone," I said. "Randell, you'll have lots of freezing at the site of the biopsy, and our nurses will also give you drugs that will relieve any pain and make you drowsy, almost asleep. The doctor who's doing the biopsy will actually work inside a CAT scan machine—so she'll be able to see the inside of your body as she operates—to ensure that she is biopsying the right area of the tumor. It will take about forty-five minutes, and you'll probably remember nothing."

Mrs. Prentice was taking rapid notes. Randell watched, looking glad to be addressed directly. I imagined most doctors had usually spoken to his parents up until now.

"After we take the biopsy, a number of tests will be done on the sample removed from the bone. The first test is to look at the tumor cells under the microscope. This will point us in the direction of further testing, which is mainly focused on understanding the genetic changes that occur in cancers."

I went on to explain the likely options for treatment, including chemotherapy and surgery. I promised we'd know more about the best way to proceed once the biopsy was done. Then, Gershwyn's office manager, Justine, took over while I booked the CAT scan biopsy for the next day. Justine handed the Prentices hospital brochures and explained where they'd be going tomorrow and what to expect.

Before I left, I shook hands with the three of them, and noticed Randell gripped my hand more enthusiastically than he had Gershwyn's. I then headed for another part of the hospital.

As I walked down the increasingly familiar corridors, I thought back to all the doctors I'd observed over the years. People often speak of empathy as being key to how doctors communicate with their patients. Doctors who are more direct and blunt are sometimes seen as cruel. But in my experience, insensitive doctors were not bad people. They were often just less confident in their skills, and their lack of confidence translated as abruptness to their patients.

This lack of confidence also did not necessarily mean they were not capable. Some surgeons felt inwardly confident that they would provide the patient with the best care possible—even in the worst of circumstances. These surgeons seemed to bond with their patients, offering them a partnership that promised full disclosure with sympathy and trust.

Surgeons who lacked confidence, no matter how skilled they were, seemed afraid of creating that human bond—possibly because of the emotional risk of what would transpire if the patient had a poor outcome. I hadn't entirely figured out Gershwyn's approach yet. He seemed to be able to build trust in his patients while remaining a bit distant and brusque.

I was absolutely determined to figure out how to be both capable and caring. I was enjoying being at the center of the intellectual world of bone cancer. But one of the most important things I had learned as I'd watched my sister succumb to that same disease was how crucial it was that doctors remember they could just as easily be in their patients' shoes.

Chapter 4

Dr. Albert Gershwyn
February 16

I was fifteen minutes ahead of schedule when I left the office after meeting with the Prentices, and all I could think about was how damn lucky I was to have landed that Maloney as my fellow. That artery repair he'd done in the OR yesterday was outstanding. And the patients seemed to like him. Mrs. Prentice didn't mind me leaving. If he was capable of looking after patients both in the OR and in my office, my life was going to be much, much easier.

Word had spread already that he was a superb surgeon, and even Hendricks had heard about him. He'd sounded envious as well as curious when I ran into him in the elevator this morning. Wanted to know where I'd found this "Mahoney" guy. "He found me," I'd told him. I wouldn't give Hendricks my secrets.

It was actually about twenty months ago when I first met Patrick. I spent about six Saturdays a year going to smaller training centers in New England to describe advances for treating bone cancer at our hospital.

I only got to Solway once every three or four years—it was a bit out of the way. I figured these tours were part of my responsibility as the regional leader in the field. And the educational visits also ensured that referrals of new patients kept coming to me from all over New England.

I'd worked out a successful schedule for these weekends. I would arrive Friday night for a medical dinner organized by the local surgeons so everyone knew that I was in town. Usually, there were a few too many drinks at the dinner and lots of compliments to our hospital. Saturday morning, I would give an interview to the local media about advances at the hospital and university that would invariably run on the local Saturday evening news and appear on the local paper's front-page Monday morning. Then, I would spend Saturday with the residents, showing them various cases and quizzing them on their approaches to complex problems.

At Solway, most of the residents slept through the Saturday session. I knew from past experience in Solway just how difficult it was to engage these dullards. They were overworked and constantly fatigued. I even wondered whether I should stop coming to this backward training program. But on that one visit, there was one young resident who stood out. He knew a lot about bone tumors, and obviously enjoyed testing wits with me. He was well prepared and inquisitive. Even called me out when I slipped up on a diagnosis.

I took a break for a coffee mid-afternoon, with just another hour left in the day. Justine had booked a dinner that evening with a fellow Jersey boy who had consistent success in the markets and wanted to give something back. Hopefully I could convince him that he would gain a higher place in heaven by giving to our program at the hospital.

The coffee was like dishwater. *No wonder those residents can't stay awake*, I thought as I checked my phone. There was an urgent message from Justine—it just said, *Call me*. It wasn't like her not to give details. I reached her while she was at the gym. She wanted me to know right away. The surgical fellow I had accepted to come to Boston eighteen months from now had called to say his wife refused to move, and he was going to accept another position in Chicago.

I remember snorting at Justine. Nobody turned me down like this. He would probably regret his decision. But now, I had a problem. I needed a full-time young surgeon to work with me as a fellow for a year or two at least, to allow me to do everything else my job required besides surgery.

I always had lots of helpers—residents, visiting surgeons, physician assistants, and nurses. But I needed a surgeon who could consistently cover for me in the operating room and in the clinic. Someone who was recognized as high potential from his residency. The young guy from Chicago had been highly recommended by his chief, and now, he had gone elsewhere.

When I finished with Justine, I turned around to find Bill Sloane, the chief of the Solway residency program, hovering by my table.

"Sit down, Sloane," I told him, pulling back a chair.

"What do you think of the guys this year, Albert?" he asked, taking a seat and crossing his arms nervously.

"That kid in the front row seems bright."

Sloane nodded. "That's Patrick Maloney—a local kid who finishes in December next year. He is smart, and also one of the best natural surgeons we've ever trained. As you know, the residents here get a lot of time on their own in the operating rooms at the county hospitals. Patrick is a great young surgeon. He's super smart and patients love him."

I took a sip of that dishwater, trying not to sound too interested. "What is he doing when he finishes residency in eighteen months?"

"Oh, you know how it works. He's from around here, so he'll probably start helping out with clinics in the smaller communities and start working at one of the county hospitals. You know—a general practice, fixing fractures, doing joint replacements, that kind of thing." Sloane was probably describing the start of his own career twenty-five years ago.

"If I pay for his travel and board, can you give him a three-week elective period in Boston in September?" I am an absolute believer in fate. I knew that I would never land another all-star as my fellow with only eighteen months until the job started. All the known stars would have jobs already.

An hour later, I took Patrick aside and offered him a three-week elective with me in Boston—an offer he eagerly accepted. Already he was smarter than that Chicago moron. When he arrived in Boston two months later, two things were obvious. He stood out like a poor country cousin compared to the sophisticated Ivy Leaguers who held most of the training positions in the hospital. You could always pick out his junker in the resident/fellow parking lot beside all the German rides. But he was also a remarkably skilled surgeon for his limited years of training.

I was absolutely delighted. After a couple of weeks, I realized this kid was a workhorse with not a shred of the entitled, prima donna personality evident in many of our hospital's trainees. And he was so excited to be offered a fellowship in Boston that he signed the contract without even checking on the salary.

He had even done some pretty decent research on bone cancer while in undergrad and med school in Solway. I wanted him to work with our research team and had made sure Justine booked some time for him to meet Roland Barnes after finishing clinic today. *This kid could be special*, I thought. But I wasn't about to let Hendricks know too much about him just yet.

Chapter 5

Dr. Patrick Maloney
February 16

*J*ustine had told me to go to the eighth floor for my research meeting that afternoon, and I was eagerly anticipating the visit. Although the hospital was home to more than sixty orthopedic surgeons, there were really only two surgeons who counted when it came to research, and their two labs shared more than 80 percent of the eighth floor.

At the far end of the corridor, Gershwyn's laboratory was directed by Dr. Roland Barnes, a fiftyish cancer scientist who had collaborated with Gershwyn for more than twenty-five years, coming with him when he moved to Boston. Barnes had completed his PhD supervised by Gershwyn and then, during his post-doctoral studies, established his independent career with two major publications that were key to understanding the genetic origins of bone cancer.

Finishing his post-doc, I had heard that he'd considered offers to join a selection of top scientific institutes. However, Gershwyn had apparently offered him several unbeatable advantages—better compensation, more guaranteed research funding. Barnes would have a university appointment, which allowed him a rich selection of students and post-docs to work in his lab. And, unlike university appointees on a tenured stream, he would not need to spend countless hours teaching. He could focus all his energy on research.

The Barnes/Gershwyn partnership was known to be a very powerful engine for generating funding from national granting agencies like the National Institutes of Health. With his extensive practice focused on bone tumors, Gershwyn provided the lab with an endless source of rare human cancer specimens for genetic analysis.

Gershwyn also provided a clinical context for the scientific experiments that the duo proposed in grant applications. Many scientists working solo without a clinical collaborator could propose that their experiment would result in better patient care. However, that claim was much more credible when made by a research partnership that included one of the country's premier cancer surgeons.

Over the years, their partnership had defined many of the genetic alterations found in bone cancers. Despite these discoveries of gene abnormalities, Barnes was still pursuing his holy grail—a genetic change in cancer that could be used to design a new targeted drug treatment.

If a new form of therapy could target only the molecular changes that led to cancer, avoiding damage to normal cells that did not have the cancerous genetic changes—that would change everything in cancer treatment.

Last week in the OR, Gershwyn had mentioned that the lab might be approaching a new targeted therapy that would make use of a small molecule called IGF in bone cancer. Ironically, I had done work on IGF and bone cancer in the little cancer lab at Solway.

Like many cancers, bone cancers are often damaged by chemotherapy drugs. These drugs could be given before surgery to assist removal of the cancer and also to prevent it from spreading to other parts of the body. However, the drugs are also highly toxic to the patient and don't work in every cancer.

That means that the chance of survival in osteosarcoma (the most common bone cancer) is about 60 to 70 percent. I knew many cancer scientists were focused on developing precision or targeted cancer treatment that would target a specific abnormal gene in the cancer without damaging normal tissues. But not all of them had Gershwyn and Barnes' seemingly infinite resources.

I was intrigued by the lab. From its publications, I knew it was much better equipped than the facility that I had worked in at Solway. But Gershwyn saw a potential match. He'd instructed me to meet Barnes and determine whether the work I'd done in Solway might fit with work in Barnes' lab.

I walked into the lab and introduced myself to Barnes. Unlike Gershwyn's office, Barnes' space was purely functional. His desk was covered with papers, and there were countless files stacked in various piles.

"So, welcome," he said, waving me into a chair across from his desk. "Albert has told me about your interest in our work. And I already knew the papers you produced in Solway. Pretty impressive for a small facility."

"Well, thanks, I appreciate that. But this is a different league." I looked around the lab, where at least fifty people were busy at a variety of tasks. A large group was clustered around two cabinets the size of compact refrigerators.

Barnes noticed my gaze. "Those are the world's fastest genome sequencers. This is a big advantage of working here—Albert's grateful patients and other donors are extremely generous, and we are able to continuously upgrade our technology."

"We use those sequencers to analyze the genes of every cancer that Albert removes in the operating room. With his continual supply of rare cancers and our ability to sequence the genetic changes in the cancer, we are creating new science with every case he operates on."

I was impressed. "So, how do I help—apart from making sure the boss has time to get away for fundraising dinners and meetings?"

"Albert told me about your work on IGF and bone cancer in Solway. He thought that you might be interested in our IGF work."

"Yeah, I examined various bone cancer cell specimens and found that many bone cancers produce IGF and IGF Receptor. I did some experiments implanting human tumor cells in mice, showing that if you lowered IGF, many of these cancers grew much slower."

Barnes nodded. "Yeah, that was nice work. We've been working on something similar, and we think we're ready to take it to the next level. Albert told me to talk to you about it."

"Well, I am very curious to hear more."

"Unfortunately, before I can explain that project, I'll need to get our lawyer to come up here so you can sign a non-disclosure agreement. The work is being done at Sumner Veterinary Hospital and there are various commercial interests involved. Could you come back in about an hour, and I'll get our lawyer to bring the appropriate papers for you to sign?"

"Yes, of course. Now, I'm *really* curious. And impressed that you can get a lawyer here in an hour."

I walked out into the corridor, letting it all sink in. I could be helping to find new treatments for bone cancer. Whatever it was Barnes needed me to do, it would be incredible if I could contribute to better treatment for the disease that killed my sister.

Chapter 6

Meredith McClintock, PhD
February 16

I'd just finished going through the morning's emails and was thinking about getting another coffee before starting my data analysis for the day. Dr. Hendricks had at least three investment meetings scheduled that week, and I knew he could always use fresh data to bolster his pitch. This had occasioned several late nights in the lab, and I needed a caffeine boost.

I'd also had an impossible time falling asleep the night before. Those creeps along the bike path had bothered me, partly because they seemed bolder than the usual goons I came across. However, I was even more upset that it had turned into a fight with some random guy thinking he needed to protect me.

I could look after myself. Part of me, however, had to admit I was pleased that guy Patrick had come along when he did. And *that* was almost worse.

To my surprise, as I walked down the corridor looking forward to a latte, the very same Dr. Maloney stepped out of Roland Barnes' lab entrance thirty feet down the hall. "Well, if it isn't the middleweight champion," I said. "Have you assaulted anyone since I last saw you?"

His cute Irish face blushed as he recognized me.

"Aw, you can't really call that an assault," he said, trying to put his hands in his pockets and missing them. "Just a poke in the tummy for a guy who deserved it. How are you?"

"What brings you to my floor?" I asked, avoiding his question.

"I'm visiting Dr. Barnes in his lab, and he just sent me away for an hour. So, you're on this floor too?"

"I run the lab down the hall for Dr. Hendricks. And I checked on you this morning. It turns out you're the mysterious surgical prodigy the nurses in the OR are talking about."

His ruddy complexion got even redder. His hands had managed to find his pockets now, but somehow failed to give him the appearance of a casual stance.

"So, Dr. Maloney, do you like science?"

His answer sounded like it came out of a surgery textbook. "Most of surgery is applied science of one sort or another—so yes, I am very interested in what you do up here."

"If you have an hour to kill, let me show you our lab," I said, glad for a reason to put off data analysis for a while. "Dr. Hendricks' research always directly applies to his surgery, so I think you'll find it fascinating."

I was also proud of the organization that I had brought to Dr. Hendricks' lab and enjoyed showing it off to visitors. It had been a mess when I'd started here—like other labs had just dumped their unwanted furniture in the space. I'd managed to clear most of it out over the past couple of years. So, when I led Dr. Maloney into the lab, he entered into an open, uncluttered space with minimalist furnishings in clean neutral wood tones.

Unlike most medical labs that were crowded with benches laden with chemical reagents and analyzers, this part of the lab was organized around individual desks and computers. I could see Dr. Maloney checking the screens, which were open to image analysis applications for measuring bone in-growth in the new *super-B.I.G.* prosthesis.

I led him to a large screen in a conference area at the back of the lab and launched a presentation from the nearby laptop. "Okay, Dr. Maloney. Get ready to see the past, present, and future of hip arthritis surgery presented by my boss, Dr. Jon Hendricks."

Nobody was better at explaining what we did in the program than Dr. Hendricks. And this video was designed for fundraising for the *super-B.I.G.* program, so it was done very professionally. He'd recruited a startup film studio out of New York that had won Emmys for producing a couple of new Netflix dramas—and conveniently enough, one of the producers there was our lead donor's niece.

The video opened with a gently smiling Dr. Jonathan Hendricks appearing on the screen, looking his patrician best. He had reassuring silver hair and his eyes crinkled as he smiled. He rarely wore that face in person; it was usually reserved for public talks and investor meetings. Dressed in a crisp white lab coat, he looked exactly like the kind of person you would *want* to operate on your hip. The soft introductory score ended, and Hendricks began his presentation looking directly at the viewer. The entire setting and his demeanor in this video said, "Trust me."

"My friends," he began, "more than fifty years ago in England, Sir John Charnley implanted the first successful hip replacements in patients suffering from the pain of severely arthritic joints. Those initial artificial joints were glued to the bone with bone cement. These first cemented hip replacements were designed to allow elderly arthritis patients to get out of wheelchairs and start walking again."

A picture of an X-ray of a hip replacement appeared on the screen beside Hendricks, and he pointed to it. "Here is a solidly fixed cemented hip replacement shown shortly after surgery in an active sixty-five-year-old woman who wants to dance, play tennis, hike, and garden. Fortunately, she is still active and wanting to do these activities fifteen years later—but her hip has not kept pace with her."

The X-ray changed to show the hip components dramatically tipped over from their original positions. "More accurately, the cement has not kept up with her. It has fractured, allowing the metal components shown in this X-ray to become loose within the bone. She is now suffering a lot of pain.

"In our laboratory, we have worked to perfect the design of hip replacements. We call our innovation the Bone Ingrowth Hip— or B.I.G., for short. It allows bone to directly attach to the metal implant without cement. It actually makes the metal hip replacement part of the bone."

The picture beside Dr. Hendricks changed again to show a close up of the thigh bone part of the hip replacement prosthesis, covered with what seemed to be wire mesh. "The mesh you see attached to the surface of this implant allows bone to grow into the implant. It makes a very strong bond between the prosthesis and thigh bone."

The picture changed again to show this coated part of the implant covered in white bony material. "How can we prove that? We, of course, cannot generally take a hip replacement out of our patients to see how well the implant is attaching to the bone. However, we had an unusual and sad case of a patient who died from an unrelated heart attack five years after he got a hip replacement. We were able to recover his implant with the family's consent. And you can see that the implant is totally covered in bone. But unfortunately, most of our patients are not able to give back their prostheses for analysis."

He broke into another smile. "That's fortunate for them! But that is where our lab work comes in. For years now, we have had a strong relationship with Sumner Veterinary Hospital. That's New England's largest animal hospital. Sumner has developed an international reputation in treating dogs suffering from hip arthritis. This is a very common disease in large dogs. It is just as crippling for these poor dogs as it is for our patients."

I looked over at Patrick and could see he was engrossed in the video. His eyes never left the screen.

"Doing a hip replacement on a dog is an expensive undertaking. Many pet owners simply cannot afford the cost. However, using donations that we obtain from grateful patients and philanthropists as well as granting agencies, we can provide the dogs with a joint replacement. And all this at about one-third the normal cost. We pay the remaining two-thirds cost to Sumner through our granting program. We help these dogs return to running normally instead of limping. In return, we ask two things of the owners. First, they must allow the veterinary surgeon to use our specially designed B.I.G. prosthesis in replacing the dog's arthritic hip joint.

"Working in dogs, we can modify things like the metal composition of the mesh or the pore size of the mesh. And we are starting to coat the mesh with a biological substance to improve performance. That way, we can test these changes in dogs before we introduce them in humans."

At the words "biological substance," I could see Patrick nodding slowly, as though something had just dawned on him. I wondered if he'd heard of this work before.

"These prostheses have exactly the same coverings as our human prostheses," Hendricks went on as an animated graphic showed dog and human prostheses side by side. "The shape of the prosthesis is modified for the dog hip anatomy, but is otherwise the same as what we will be implanting in our human patients three years from now. In other words, we are testing dog prostheses several generations ahead of the implants we use in human patients.

"The second condition for owners to get access to this special program for their dogs is that they must let us remove the prosthesis after their pet passes away. They call us when the dog passes, and we bring the dog back to Sumner Vet Hospital. There, we carefully remove the prosthesis from the hip and then return the cremated remains—if they wish—to the owners.

"In this way, we are able to rapidly evaluate changes in our design of the **B.I.G.** prosthesis. There are several advantages to this system.

"Dog lives are shorter than humans, of course. We see the results of our design modifications within two to four years rather than following humans for fifteen to twenty years. And we avoid the moral distress of doing surgical experimentation on *healthy* animals.

"These dogs need and benefit from their surgery. And our human patients benefit dramatically from what we learn from our research on hip implants in dogs."

Hendricks paused and refocused on the camera. He was just so good in this video. "I am a dog lover and could never experiment on healthy animals for the sake of improving treatments in humans.

The **B.I.G.** program allows pets whose owners otherwise might be unable to pay for surgery to get access to the best treatment possible at Sumner Hospital.

"Now, I want to introduce you to Garry Richards and his buddy, Zeus." The video faded to a beautiful green meadow, where a man was jogging in a blue track suit with a large Alsatian, who was running and jumping alongside him as though anticipating a treat.

"Three years ago, neither Garry nor Zeus could walk, let alone run. Zeus was confined to lying around the house. Garry was limping with a cane. Both of them had arthritis in their hips. Within a month of each other, Zeus received a B.I.G. Mark 14 canine prosthesis and Garry received the Mark 11 design for human patients. As you see in this video, they are both enjoying the outcome of their surgeries."

In the video, Garry pulled a ball out of his pocket and threw it into the field for Zeus, who took off after the ball like he was jet propelled. Hendricks' voiceover continued. "We have now implanted the B.I.G. Mark 14 in 100 dogs. The results we are seeing are just amazing. We are calling this, our latest prosthesis, the *super-B.I.G.* It is very similar to the B.I.G. prosthesis. The federal food and drug regulator has already provided market approval for the *super-B.I.G.*, so we know it's safe for everyone.

"Based on our work with dog arthritis, we are getting ready to offer the *super-B.I.G.* to our human patients. In fact, I expect that if Garry needs his second hip replaced, he will get the same *super-B.I.G.* implant that Zeus is enjoying today."

The screen faded to a woman in an impeccable blue suit sitting on the corner of a desk. She introduced herself as the CEO of the Hendricks Foundation. "Thank you, Dr. Hendricks, for the outstanding work you do for our patients suffering from arthritis and for our pets," she said to the camera. "Viewers like you can help Dr. Hendricks continue to improve the **B.I.G.** hip replacement with the experimental work he is doing in his Boston laboratory. This work is certainly not cheap. It requires constant funding to pay for the dogs' surgery. We also fund the scientists who are developing the next generation of improvements for the implants, as well as the engineers who test the implants.

"This is remarkable and important work. Dr. Hendricks needs your support. Consider visiting the website shown at the bottom of this screen to make a donation online. We need and are grateful for your help. To learn more, connect with us through email, Twitter, and Facebook. And thanks for helping Dr. Hendricks ensure that he can help people and pets, just like Garry and Zeus, in the future."

As the video ended, Patrick turned to me. "Wow," he said, sounding impressed. "That's a great fundraising pitch! I know that some people refuse to donate to research because they are afraid that their money will be used to experiment on animals. This turns the tables completely. If you are an animal-lover, you would want to contribute to help those poor dogs get their hips replaced."

I nodded. "Our fundraising has increased dramatically with two things. One is the focus on talking about helping dogs who desperately need it get access to the best surgery. The second is pushing this message across social media, where it bifurcates into two communities—people who want to contribute to improving outcomes in arthritis, and people who want to help dogs. I've been really surprised how big that second channel is."

"I'm supposed to be helping on a cancer project in dogs that Gershwyn and Barnes are running at Sumner, but I haven't heard any details yet. Will I be working with your team there?"

"No, Gershwyn and Hendricks keep their programs very separate." I grinned. "They are—they're sort of 'frenemies,' in a way."

Patrick nodded thoughtfully.

"We are finishing the evaluation of an amazing new approach that we are calling the *super-B.I.G.*," I told him. "Hendricks hints at it in the video. I could tell you more about it, but then I would need to kill you—and that would be a shame."

Patrick considered that comment and then checked his watch. "Meredith, I have another twenty minutes. Without breaking state secrets or putting my life at risk, can you show me what you do in all this other space?"

"Follow me, Dr. Maloney, and I'll show you where we test the future of hip replacement."

I opened the door to our mechanical testing area, where visitors always remarked that the air was cooler and there was a notable background hum.

Patrick recognized several machines that were commonly used in bone research. "These are material testing machines, right? Designed to test the strength of mechanical bonds by pushing or pulling on materials to tear them apart. You must be using them to test how firmly bone has bonded to your B.I.G. metallic implants, right?"

I nodded. He was a quick study. I then spread out my arms to encompass the mechanical testing machines and other consoles Patrick did not recognize. "This is the product of my PhD thesis and the start of my time working for Dr. Hendricks. When I started with him, he was having a lot of difficulty testing whether or not modifications to the B.I.G. surface were improving bone fixation or not.

"I had my master's degree in biomedical engineering, and part of my thesis described a new method for cutting through metal using high-speed diamond grit rotary saws. Dr. Hendricks had read my thesis before he hired me—which was an incredible compliment. And then, he encouraged me to continue my interest in this area and do a PhD with him.

"The problem we were facing was that the high-speed water-cooled diamond saw was very good at cutting through metal. But it was damaging to the bone and tissue that connected to the prosthesis."

Patrick nodded. I realized he probably understood the challenge from his orthopedic experience.

"Eventually, our breakthrough was to realize that we could use two different methods for cutting through the bone ingrowth into metal mesh and the solid metal of the prosthesis. To cut through the bone and the titanium mesh bone ingrowth tissue—that's the part where the bone and the metal prosthesis connect—we developed a narrow high-pressure water jet supplemented by fine grains of sand in the water. It gives a very clean, non-destructive cut down to the surface of the titanium prosthesis."

I walked down the aisle between machines and countertops to a large white console that was delivering a subdued hum. "This is the product of my PhD thesis. We call it a sequential cutter."

I pushed a button on the touch screen monitor that swung over the machine on a retractable arm, then punched a second command on the screen. The top of the console retracted. Inside the machine, a segment of dog thigh bone was held in a clamp within a clear plastic enclosed hood that was covered in water and a fine grit. On one side of the bone was a nozzle that was also wet.

I pointed to the nozzle. "That is the water cutter. It sprays a very fine and exact jet of water and cutting sand. This clamp rotates the bone under the spray, and the water cuts a thin line through the bone and the underlying B.I.G. mesh that contains ingrown bone. When the mesh is completely divided, the resistance to rotation in the clamp drops dramatically since the water spray is now striking a shiny, smooth titanium surface."

Patrick was carefully following my words and looking down at the nozzle. I continued, "We realized we could know when the water jet had completed its work by measuring resistance to clamp rotation. Once resistance dropped, we knew we'd successfully divided the bone and the mesh.

"That was the eureka moment that turned this from a graduate student's project to a useful experimental method. Using nanosensors on the clamp rotation motor, we could figure out when to stop using the water cutter and bring the diamond cutter into action to work on the titanium stem."

I pointed across the hood to a covered wheel on the other side of the bone. Patrick seemed intrigued and followed my gesture to the wheel.

"We needed an even finer cutter so the diamond cutter could fit inside the cut made by the water jet without causing further damage to the bone. Getting a diamond cutter that fine was difficult. And it was impossible to get one forged so it could cut through a titanium hip stem without fracturing." I'd spent about six months destroying hundreds of diamond cutters. None could go through an entire titanium stem with as fine a cut as we needed.

"The next eureka moment," I told him, "was when we realized we could use several cutting wheels for each stem cut. What we needed was a signal that would tell us when each cutting wheel was close to the breaking point."

Patrick had been leaning forward to inspect the machine. When he looked up at me, the light inside the cabinet seemed to accentuate his freckles.

"Once again, the answer was nanosensors. We learned that the earliest sign of cutting wheel failure was a pattern of subtle vibration that predicted the wheel would break within about two minutes. We developed a system in which we could switch out a used wheel for a fresh one so we could go through a whole titanium implant without fracturing a cutting wheel."

Patrick was now looking squarely at me with a concentration that was somewhat disconcerting. "It can take between two and five wheels to cut through, depending on the specimen. The wheels in this console are the most expensive part of the whole process—about $1,500 each. We need lots of donations from Dr. Hendricks to keep that part of the program going."

"What do you do with the specimens after you cut the slices?" Patrick asked. Usually, people's eyes glazed over when I told them about the machines, and only refocused once they heard the price tag. But Patrick seemed genuinely interested in the work.

"We test the effectiveness of the B.I.G. prosthesis in three ways. We take the first slice cut from the specimen and use it for mechanical testing. That's why it's so important that each slice we take with the water jet and diamond cutters is exactly the same thickness."

There was a recently cut specimen at the side of the console, and I handed it to Patrick. Like everyone seeing a slice for the first time, Patrick turned it on end to marvel at how thinly the specimen was cut—about half the thickness of a quarter.

"We put the slice flat on a special mounting and then measure it in the mechanical testing machine by pushing on the central stem and recording the energy needed to push the stem out of the B.I.G. bone ingrowth. This is called 'push out load.'"

He nodded. I knew all orthopedic surgeons had at least a general understanding of mechanical testing.

"We also take an adjacent slice of the specimen, embed it in plastic, and polish it in preparation for scanning electron microscopy. This produces highly accurate images of how much bone has grown into the mesh surrounding the B.I.G. prosthesis. We use those scanners and computers from the room at the entrance to quantitate bone ingrowth into the B.I.G.

"Then, we finally take a small number of very thin slices embedded in clear plastic and stain them using normal pathology methods, just to ensure the bone cells look okay.

"And that, Dr. Maloney, is the summary of how I have spent my last five years. Three years completing my PhD and designing all this equipment, and two years running Dr. Hendricks' lab and testing all the various versions of the B.I.G." I wondered if his twenty minutes of concentration were up.

"What is your testing showing? Is the B.I.G. getting better? And what do you see with this *super-B.I.G.* implant Dr. Hendricks mentioned in the video?"

Guess he still had remaining concentration. "Yeah, the current *super-B.I.G.* version is really quite amazing," I told him. "One of the guys from Sumner came to us four years ago with a novel idea that has provided a giant leap forward in bone ingrowth, leading to the *super-B.I.G.*

"The results we are getting with this new implant are two to three times stronger in mechanical testing, with similar increase in bone ingrowth. Dr. Hendricks is getting ready to make a big change in what he is offering human patients because of what we are seeing with dogs in the lab."

"What's the new secret sauce?"

"Nice try, but I'm afraid I can't tell you about it. We all sign non-disclosure agreements, and Dr. Hendricks is really a stickler for confidentiality. But actually, the guy who came up with this new model worked with Gershwyn and Barnes until Dr. Hendricks hired him as a junior scientist. So, you might meet him at some point. He's now directing the biology part of the program. Dr. Andrei Kovalov is his name."

He checked his watch. "I apologize for taking so much of your time. It's been a terrific tour. You mentioning Dr. Barnes just now reminded me that I'm due back at his lab."

I smiled. I'd been having fun. "I always provide a special tour for fellow runners."

"Speaking of running, I'm going out again tonight. I'll try to go a bit earlier so I'm back before the night demons come out. I'm just getting back into shape after three years away from the track, so I'd be slowing you down—but it would be great to have some company."

I winced internally. He seemed so genuine. "Well actually, tonight is just a stretch run for me—nothing at fast pace," I said. "And hopefully it will be an easier run for you too, since you won't have to go postal on anyone like you did last night."

He looked down. "Hey, I'm not a thug, honest," he said. "It's just that those two guys might have been seriously dangerous, and when it's two against one, you don't have the luxury of waiting to find out."

I considered his invitation to run. I had so many reasons to stay away from the hospital's fellows.

"I will be at the south end of the Longfellow Bridge around six," I finally said. "If that works for your schedule, I would be happy to have your company."

He nodded, smiled, and thanked me again for the tour as he walked out.

Chapter 7

Meredith McClintock, PhD
February 16

I watched Patrick's gait as he strode down the hall. He had a tiny bit of a gut, but he also had a hockey player's powerful legs. I liked his quiet calm and that choir boy's face—the faint freckles and blush that reflected the Maloney name. He just seemed interesting. And, he was interested in my work—which was more than I could say for most of the male surgeons here, who considered me inferior because I didn't carry a scalpel.

But I couldn't get closer to him. At least, not beyond running together. I'd fallen for an orthopedic surgeon before and had promised myself that it would never happen again.

David had been confident, and I'd been drawn to him. But that had turned out to be the confidence of a con man. He had come from the West Coast to work with Dr. Hendricks for a year. I'd met him down in the OR when I'd gone to show some results to Dr. Hendricks.

After a few weeks of flirting, he'd asked me out for dinner, and I accepted against my better judgment. I never dated guys from the hospital, and especially never orthopods—it was just too close. But this guy was an irresistible Californian: blond, blue-eyed, muscled like a Venice Beach surfer, and reserved in an almost mysterious way. I just fell hard. Within weeks, he was practically living at my place.

I had been involved in relationships before, but never with this sense of abandon. It seemed to affect everything. Music was more intense; colors were brighter. Food tasted better. Sex with David was incredibly liberating.

Work was going extremely well, and I had conquered most of the gremlins in my specimen preparation work. Hendricks seemed very happy with me and the results we were achieving. He started bringing donors into my lab to show off my research. I knew Hendricks wasn't easy to impress, so that meant something.

I just began to feel a glowing warm excitement that powered me through the day. At work, my friends noticed.

"What is up with you?" one of them asked when a few of us went out for drinks one evening after work. "You're looking amazing. You always do, but there's something different about you now. You're more open. A month ago, we couldn't drag you out for drinks. You would've said you needed to go for your run. But now you're here, you're having a beer, and you haven't looked at your watch once. So, what's happening?"

After a few minutes of denial, I finally told them that David and I were seeing each other and I thought that he might be very special to my future. My friends were delighted. They promised they'd keep it quiet; everyone frowned on relationships with colleagues at the hospital. But from then on, they'd occasionally flash me knowing smiles when we passed each other in the hallways.

Even though David worked with Hendricks, I thought we had kept our relationship secret from him. But one afternoon, Hendricks asked me to meet him in his office at end of day. When I joined him, I could see he was uncomfortable. Usually, he was pretty rigid and extremely polite when we met together. Now, he was even more rigid and could not look me in the eyes.

"Dr. McClintock, some people have suggested to me that you are seeing David socially," he said. He did not look happy.

Like an idiot, I immediately thought that I knew what was troubling him. Hendricks was worried that when the rest of David's fellowship year was over, he would ask me to marry him, we would return to the West Coast, and Hendricks would lose me as his lab leader.

It hurt even now to remember how stupid I was. I thought that if Hendricks were that worried, then maybe he would offer David a permanent job in Boston and I would not have to leave the lab behind to be with David.

"Meredith, has David told you that he is engaged to be married in eight months, shortly after he goes back to California?"

I couldn't breathe. My diaphragm wouldn't move. I actually gasped for air.

"His fiancée is a successful venture capital investor in Silicon Valley from a very wealthy family," Hendricks continued, still staring at a spot somewhere above my shoulder so he wouldn't have to look at my face. "David has a lucrative position in a private clinic in San Jose that has been supported for generations by his fiancée's family."

I so wished that I would have simply said nothing. But of course, I couldn't believe that of David. I insisted that it couldn't be true, that David would never do that, that we had something special together. Throughout my rant, Hendricks sat silently. When I paused for air, he leaned forward and placed a hand on my forearm.

"I am sorry to say this, but you have been deceived," he said. "David has told me about his wedding plans and the advantageous situation he will have in California. You do not seem to figure into his plans after he leaves Boston."

Humiliation then replaced all other emotion. Hendricks was a blue-blooded New Englander with a ramrod sense of morality. I knew he would disapprove of David's duplicity. However, he would equally deplore my recklessness in falling so quickly and completely for a real cad. I'd worked so hard to gain his trust and respect. How could he take me seriously now?

"I am going to have a serious talk with David. I would like you to take a week's vacation and stay away from the hospital. I will speak to you after your week off." He stood and walked me to his office door without looking at me. I left his office feeling like a social leper.

I called my best friend that evening. Shanice and I had grown up together in the hospital, and she knew exactly what I needed. She came over equipped with martini makings, and after several drinks and a confessional catharsis, I slept soundly. As I nursed a hangover the next morning, I reserved a B&B in Nantucket and disappeared for a week. When I returned, David was gone. I later learned he had been turfed out by Hendricks with a day's notice and a threat to disclose to California if he did not leave quietly. I never heard from David again.

Fortunately, my nerdy buddies in the lab were generally too socially unaware to know that anything had happened. Hendricks came to my office the first day back and confirmed David was gone. He wanted to get back in the rhythm of our mutual work on the *super-B.I.G.* prosthesis.

After that, he never mentioned anything about David, and I was so relieved that our interaction immediately returned to the productive professional relationship that we had enjoyed for more than four years.

In the moments after Patrick left my laboratory, I felt that buried sense of humiliation recalled like a burning blush in my cheeks. Sure, this new guy was different. But I was absolutely convinced that I would never again date someone from the hospital—and never, ever hook up with an orthopod.

Chapter 8

Dr. Patrick Maloney
February 16

I walked up the corridor toward the Barnes lab, but my mind was definitely back in the lab down the hall. Meredith was brilliant, lovely, and entirely in charge.

I hadn't dated in a while. I had been working so hard for so long that I was starting to feel like a monk.

Most of the people I interacted with were staff in the hospital. Surgical residents spend countless nights sleeping in the hospital, and our call rooms can serve purposes other than surgical call. However, dating at work would often become a problem, and in general, I preferred not to be considered a jerk at work. So, I simply swore off relationships with colleagues.

Back in Solway, I was so busy that any relationships I tried to pursue turned out to be short-lived. I was simply working too hard to get deeply involved during residency, and when the Boston opportunity came up, I was gone as soon as I could leave.

But I was thinking about nothing but Meredith's brilliant green eyes as I re-entered Barnes' lab and walked into his office.

Barnes was there with the hospital lawyer, who introduced himself as Charles Schwarzman. As I sat down, Schwarzman opened his briefcase and pulled out a folio of papers.

"These are standard non-disclosure agreement forms," he said, pushing papers at me. "They're commonly referred to as NDAs. And these are confidentiality papers that describe the ground rules around what can be discussed and disclosed."

"These papers describe that the NDA and confidentiality extend to all activities undertaken in the employment of Dr. Gershwyn both here at the hospital and Sumner Hospital, and any and all activity related to the Gershywn/Barnes lab. Furthermore, these documents bind you to maintain confidentiality for all activities in the hospital or its affiliates. You can sign here." He handed me a pen and pointed to the line on the documents where I would sign.

I shook my head quietly. This was crazy. "This is really too broad," I said. "I can understand maintaining confidentiality for everything in this lab and the work we may do at Sumner. But asking me to maintain confidentiality for everything I learn in the hospital is crazy. That would suggest I could not teach residents in other training programs anything that I learned here. That doesn't make sense."

Schwarzman smiled at Barnes. "They are smarter these days, aren't they? Dr. Barnes, you are the client here. Will you be satisfied if Dr. Maloney only signs the NDA and confidentiality agreements for the Gershwyn hospital work, your lab, and work supported by Gershwyn at Sumner?"

Barnes nodded. "I get what Patrick is saying. Confidentiality around everything that he learns at the hospital seems too broad and silly. Sure, let's limit the NDA to our lab and the Sumner, as well as Albert's practice."

I signed the appropriate forms after reading them carefully and writing in my own hand the limitation that I was insisting upon. I handed them back to Schwarzman, who tucked the papers into his briefcase and stood up to leave.

"Wait a second, Mr. Schwarzman—you need to counter-sign the sections that I changed, limiting the extent of the NDA. And how do I get a copy of the document?"

"You're kidding, right? I've never given anyone a copy of an NDA."

"Well, I guess this will be a first time, Mr. Schwarzman," I said. "I never sign any agreement without getting a copy."

The lawyer looked at Barnes. He was in a rush and I was ruining his afternoon schedule. He signed the handwritten note that I had appended to the NDA, agreeing to limit the extent of my confidentiality. "Do you have a photocopier?"

"Of course," said Barnes. "Give me the papers and I'll be right back." He returned momentarily and handed me the copies, which I reviewed. The lawyer then left in a much worse mood than he arrived in.

"He's really not a bad guy," said Barnes as we heard the ding of the elevator outside. "He's responsive and gives reasonable second-tier intellectual property advice. But, of course, we eventually always get IP specialists involved when we want to protect something significant. Anyway, you made no friends with Mr. Schwarzman. Gershwyn told me you are easy to get along with. I'm not sure Charles would agree."

Barnes' smile let me know that I hadn't burnt any bridges with him. I had a feeling that the scientist had secretly enjoyed what he had witnessed. "Let's get down to the interesting stuff. Have you got some time to talk about curing cancer?"

Barnes leaned forward as I nodded. "Patrick, Albert tells me that he expects you to get involved with our Sumner Vet Hospital dog work, which is essential to the future of our research here. It will be a lot of work, but it gives us an amazing way to test new treatments on dogs that need our help and have cancers that are very similar to human bone cancers. And we think we are starting a very promising new set of experiments that will require an expert surgeon."

"And, by coincidence, the new treatment protocols are based on IGF, which we have both been working on."

I nodded. It was hard to believe this lab and the little facility I joined in Solway were working on the same question.

"As you know, large dogs get bone cancers more commonly than humans, but the genetic changes we are seeing in dog bone cancer are much the same as in humans. The most common bone cancer in dogs is osteosarcoma, just like in adolescent humans, and it responds to chemotherapy just like human cancers respond in most cases.

"You know how complex it is to treat osteosarcoma in humans. Well, it is just as complex in dogs. Until about twenty years ago, most dogs that got osteosarcoma were just put to sleep. Then, a veterinarian surgeon out west started providing dogs with the same treatments humans receive.

"It turned out the dogs responded to treatment similarly to people. Albert and I started talking about this finding years ago and thought that if we are going to use our understanding of the genetic origins of cancer to influence treatment in human patients, we might start by testing genetic treatments in dogs first."

I couldn't believe what I was hearing. Hendricks was treating dog hip arthritis at Sumner while Gershwyn was trying to cure dog bone cancer at the same vet hospital. Did these guys talk to each other?

Barnes continued. "When we described our thoughts to the surgeons at Sumner, they were incredibly enthusiastic. They are the major referral center for New England and receive more than a hundred cases of dog osteosarcoma annually. The problem, of course, was the cost.

"Giving several cycles of chemotherapy and then even a simple surgery like an amputation would cost tens of thousands of dollars. And using a replacement metal prosthesis after tumor removal to replace the cancer and save the leg rather than amputate it—well, that would cost over two hundred thousand dollars."

I really did not know much about healthcare costs, but remembered that my sister's bills cost about one hundred thousand dollars. But then, she'd only had an amputation and no chemotherapy.

"And that is where Gershwyn's genius for fundraising came in. He realized that if he approached donors and told them he was going to learn how to save young people with bone cancer by curing dogs with the same cancer—well, he would have a story that appealed to dog lovers as well as people who wanted to cure cancer. And suddenly, he was raising twice as much money in his Foundation's campaigns, and we were ready to launch a dog bone cancer program at Sumner."

I couldn't resist. "You know, Dr. Barnes, I heard exactly the same story about Sumner from the woman who runs Dr. Hendricks' laboratory down the hall. Except Hendricks is curing hip arthritis in dogs and humans."

"Oh, you were talking to Meredith in Hendricks' lab?" His face lit up. "She's terrific, huh?" Then, seeing my surprised look, he blushed and chuckled. "I mean, she's a great scientist. She has really moved their lab to a new place with her methods to test their dog hip replacements as they introduce new models of implants.

"I guess that is similar to what we are doing, now that you mention it. But Albert and Jonathan wouldn't agree that they were copying each other. They are pretty competitive—you'll notice after you've been here a while.

"Anyway, back to my story. Albert started offering to pay from his research foundation for treatment in dogs with osteosarcoma if the veterinary surgeons would treat them for free. But none of the veterinary cancer surgeons had experience in bone cancer surgery.

"So, Albert thought that maybe his fellow might be able to do the surgery, but I guess from what he's said, surgery on a dog with osteosarcoma is maybe even more difficult than surgery on a human. His last two fellows just couldn't do it."

I was beginning to understand the role I was going to be playing.

"And that is a real shame, because we have discovered the same genetic changes in IGF that you noticed in human osteosarcoma are also very common in dogs. I think these IGF genetic changes may offer some powerful new treatments for the cancer, and I am really eager to try it out in dogs. But the treatment will still require removing the cancer with surgery, and we need a bone cancer surgeon to try the new treatment.

"Gershywn knows about the lab work that you did on IGF, and he told me confidentially that he thinks you are a pretty good surgeon for your stage of career. He thinks you might be the guy who could get this program going."

I didn't know whether I was being sweet-talked, but found the concept of trying new bone cancer treatment in dogs appealing.

After all, if my family had had access to new treatments, maybe I would still have a little sister.

"Well, it sounds very interesting. I would like to learn more about these therapies. I suppose that is why I had to sign an NDA?"

"That's right. There's a lot of biotech interest in what happens at this hospital, and Albert has engaged a small biotech with some interesting molecules related to IGF. We think there is a great chance to test new IGF cancer treatments in dogs.

"The pharma business has changed, and I think this will work to our benefit. It used to be that no companies were interested in rare diseases like osteosarcoma. They called them 'orphan diseases' in contempt, because the rare disease meant there were no profits to be made. That is all different now. The federal drug regulator has an orphan disease strategy that gets treatments for rare diseases to market much faster and with less regulatory requirement.

"If the disease has no effective treatment, then a new, useful treatment gets rapid approval. And the company can charge just about whatever they want to charge, especially if the treatment is for a young adult or child—like with osteosarcoma. The insurance companies will pay any price."

"Okay, Dr. Barnes, I'm very interested. What is the next step?"

"I'll talk to Albert about this conversation and we will likely arrange to get together at Sumner. I'm sure that I'll see you there soon."

I left the lab and rushed home to get changed so I could reach the south side of the Longfellow Bridge by 6:00 p.m. Changing into my running gear, I thought with dismay that it needed a wash. I was not going to be an impressive sight. Then, I also remembered how fast Meredith had been passing me last evening and realized I was probably going to vomit somewhere along the banks of the Charles that evening. That would also be unimpressive.

Chapter 9

Ms. Justine O'Donnell
February 21

*W*hen he was in Boston, Albert Gershwyn always began his day on his elliptical in his home gym at 5:30. By 6:00 a.m., he would take a water break before doing some weights. He would call me every morning at 6:00, and we went over his schedule for five minutes. The call ended when he hung up on me. It wasn't rude; he was just efficient with his time.

I'd worked for Albert Gershwyn for twenty years.

I got married just before starting with Albert. My husband, Dennis, was a good guy. We'd known each other since high school. He worked in a warehouse in our old neighborhood. But somehow, after I'd worked in Albert's office for a few years, Dennis just seemed so limited and we got divorced. We didn't have anything in common anymore, and work seemed much more interesting than being home with Dennis.

When I first started, I was just out of secretarial school and did some scheduling and typing in the office. But after the divorce, I spent more and more time working for Albert, and he gave me more and more responsibility—booking his travel, organizing departmental meetings in the hospital.

And then, seven years ago, Albert created the office manager role for me. He put me in charge of hiring and firing the fifteen or so staff that worked for him and the department. But most importantly, he put me in charge of his schedule.

Albert Gershwyn was one of those overachievers who hated to waste a single minute in the day. Every moment was scheduled from the time he climbed onto a cardio machine in the morning to the time that his driver delivered him home after a fundraising dinner late at night. It was my job to make the most out of his day.

Some of the scheduling was pretty routine. Departmental meetings, meetings with the president of the hospital and the dean of the medical school, operating room cases and clinics—these were slotted into the schedule for some time to come. But it was the other stuff that was interesting.

A big part of my role was to help Albert with fundraising. He was a fabulous fund raiser, and our hospital, research programs, surgery programs—well, just about everything relied on Albert's ability to coax money out of our many well-heeled donors. The hospital and the foundation had professional fundraisers, of course, and they would provide us with leads sometimes.

But Albert flew in so many interesting circles—in Washington with advisory roles, in New York with investors in biotech and healthcare, in Silicon Valley with ideas about IT investments in healthcare. It just seemed that everyone who was anyone in America knew Albert and would call him for advice.

And, of course, Albert looked after all of their families' and friends' health problems. He was brilliant at arranging referrals to the hospital, and everyone knew that care at our hospital was better than treatment just about anywhere else in the world. That's how Albert collected favors from wealthy and powerful people.

And when those people were going to consider philanthropy, Albert was the first person they called. Albert had explained to me that it was necessary to take this role very seriously. And this was the most important part of my job.

"Justine, I figure that anyone smart enough to make enough money that they can give some money to the hospital is smart enough to want to hear an intelligent pitch for what we are going to accomplish with their generosity. Whether it's a new operating room, a new wing for the hospital, research support for bone cancer—whatever it is, I have to approach them with the right opportunity, and that takes time and thought and effort."

I would try and learn about the prospective donor Albert was working with. Sometimes, I would meet the donor in the office. Sometimes, it was just a Google search. I tried to figure out where Albert should go for dinner and tried to understand how Albert would describe the need for a philanthropic gift.

People sometimes whispered behind our backs that maybe Justine and Albert were too close, spent too much time together. But he had been married for years, and his wife worked as a marketing executive and had her own schedule to manage. She had zero interest in his socializing or fundraising, but she did like their place on Nantucket. Albert ensured religiously that I made time in his schedule for his wife, kids, and grandchildren. More than once, I had cancelled a major work event for Albert so he could get home for a grandchild's concert or graduation.

He was very committed to ensuring that he could do everything, and there was certainly a lot he wanted to do. And I was challenged and pleased to make sure he could get as much done as he wanted to accomplish.

One of the most important variables in my life keeping Albert organized was the quality of our fellow. After my divorce, I would flirt with the fellows, and they often hit on me in the early days. I had some fun with a few of them. That hadn't happened in a while, not since I became Albert's office manager. And maybe it was because most of them were now ten years younger than me.

If the fellow was a great surgeon, Albert could leave him alone for a few minutes longer in the OR while he made two extra phone calls. Albert always knew when he needed to be in the OR. If he considered his fellow to be reliable, he could afford to spend a bit less time with him.

The same was true in the office. If the patients trusted the fellow, Albert could spend a bit less time with each patient and leave more of the clinical information gathering and explanations to the fellow. Albert was always available if the fellow needed him. But it sure was easier if the fellow could cover for him.

It usually took at least six months for the fellow to get up to speed with the hospital, our bone cancer practice, and the way that Albert liked things done. So, we liked the fellow to commit to at least a year, preferably even eighteen months or two years. When a good person had been here for eighteen months, he could essentially run the practice and really help Albert to accomplish everything he wanted to do. I had even noticed that I could correlate the amount of fundraising Albert was accomplishing with how long the fellow had been in Boston.

But this new guy, Maloney, was really something else. Patients in the office loved him, and I could tell that Albert had a ton of confidence in his surgical skill. And he was cute as hell. He made me remember the days when I had less responsibility and could afford to play around with the fellows. But, of course, those days I was ten years younger—and Patrick would have been a college freshman or sophomore.

Today, the boss had a couple of meetings with the hospital leadership about getting more resources for his program. With the aging population, everyone needed orthopedic surgery and we needed increases in beds and OR time. Albert had been instrumental in achieving over two hundred million of the funding for the new clinical wing at the hospital, so he did not expect too much trouble in ensuring the wing had a big commitment to our department.

Because the meetings around the new wing would require careful analysis of architectural drawings, Albert asked me to schedule a light day in the OR and office. Patrick had done a couple of small cases in the OR and had seen a couple of new patients in the office. Albert was always available if Patrick needed him, but increasingly, he was leaving things up to this very capable young man.

This afternoon, Albert was headed over to Sumner with Roland Barnes. I knew that a big focus of Albert's fundraising over the past year had been to find money to support finding new cures for dog cancer at Sumner. I think he had about ten million committed to the dog work. And I knew Albert was also expecting Patrick to get engaged in the Sumner research.

Patrick was finishing putting orders in the computer for our last consult of the morning when I caught his eye and waved him over to my desk. I could not help twisting a bit so I showed a bit of thigh as he sat down in the chair in front of me.

"So, we are going to be partners—you and me, Patrick," I said as he settled into the chair.

He just stared back. He obviously had no idea what was coming next.

"It looks to me that you may be that one very special fellow Albert can rely on as much in the OR and clinic as he relies on me in the rest of his life. I can tell he is much more relaxed with you in the OR than he was with the last few guys. He was always rushing away to check up on them when they were operating. Now, he is more sanguine. You must be a good surgeon."

Patrick shrugged. "Glad to hear that. I am enjoying myself."

"Patrick if you can keep him relaxed around his clinical practice, we can accomplish great things. I know he is really excited about the lab work right now and thinks that he needs to increase funding to his Foundation to support the lab work at Sumner. If you can manage to free up his time from practice and keep his patients happy, I can arrange to increase the Foundation money flow. All that takes is his time and presence. So, if you and I can work together, we can really get things cooking here."

Patrick rose from his chair and bowed at the waist in my direction. "Justine, I look forward to working closely with you. It will be an honor and a pleasure."

He smiled at me and wandered toward the office door. I pushed my chair over to the younger secretary next to me, who typed Gershwyn's letters. "Have you noticed that Patrick has lost weight since he first got here?"

The secretary looked up. "Yeah, he's got a nice butt for sure," she commented, and went back to her dicta-typing as I wished I could wind the clock back.

Chapter 10

Dr. Patrick Maloney
February 21

I left Justine feeling a bit disconcerted. I almost felt that she'd been hitting on me. She was an interesting woman, and looked like she had been a fox in her time. But now, she was totally committed to Gershwyn and making sure he got everything done that he needed to do. I knew that it would make my life easier to be on Justine's good side.

I headed for the OR. I needed to check on one of the extra jobs for the hospital's orthopedic fellows. About once every three weeks, each fellow was responsible serving on the trauma team. The hospital was not a major trauma center, but its position in downtown Boston meant that trauma cases occasionally found their way to the ER because of proximity rather than expertise.

Trauma care was not the lucrative sub-specialty practice that attracted surgeons to the hospital for further training. Fellows came to this hospital for the finishing school that prepared them to do total joint replacements, straighten crooked spines, repair deformed hands or feet, perform arthroscopy of frozen shoulders, and look after professional athletes.

These were all lucrative specialties, and a fellowship at this hospital promised a stellar career of private practice with well-insured patients. Gershwyn's bone cancer surgery was not lucrative at all. Income in cancer surgery was less than half of what other orthopedic specialists made. The few surgeons who were drawn to the specialty were attracted by bone cancer's intellectual and technical challenges.

Trauma surgery often involved long and tedious management of damaged arms, legs, and spines in patients who had made poor decisions in their lives. Poor decisions often led directly to their injuries—drinking and driving, riding a motorcycle in bad weather—and poor decisions often left them poorly insured or uninsured.

The staff surgeons at the hospital avoided trauma care whenever possible, and subsequently had little skill in managing complex injuries. Most of the fellows in sub-specialty programs came from upper-class surgery training programs that avoided trauma patients. So, there was surprisingly little expertise in the hospital in looking after badly broken bones.

I had been on trauma call several times since arriving in Boston, and nothing very exciting had occurred. I was on call again tomorrow, and therefore was on second call today in case multiple trauma patients arrived simultaneously. I knew that a trauma patient had come to the operating room earlier that morning. Since I was leaving the hospital to go to Sumner later in the day, I wanted to make sure that the fellow on call would be available and not stuck in the OR unable to respond to a new case.

I changed into greens and went into the trauma OR. As I entered, I immediately sensed the atmosphere that attends the rare occasion when a surgeon is out of his or her depth.

The tension was palpable. There was no music playing in the background, no relaxed chatter—just an aggravated voice belonging to Anson Shaw, the on-call orthopedic trauma fellow for the day, who was complaining that he couldn't see where the bleeding was coming from, and the irritated voice of the anesthetist, saying, "Well, you better find it and stop it, or the blood bank is going to run dry, damn it."

I checked the record on the computer. This patient had been hit by a truck four or five hours ago. He was a casual laborer—possibly an undocumented worker. He'd been brought to the hospital in shock with a falling blood pressure. The general surgeons had taken him to the OR immediately, correctly anticipating a ruptured spleen.

They had tried to preserve the organ by repairing the laceration. He'd needed six units of blood before the general surgeons gave up and removed the spleen. As the general surgeons closed his wound, they'd called for the orthopedic trauma team to deal with his badly damaged left knee and femur.

The truck had hit him on the left side, breaking the knee and thigh bone into multiple fragments. While the general surgeons had been working in the belly, the leg had been swelling with internal bleeding. I could see that the anesthetist was concerned; he had provided enough transfusion to deal with the blood loss in the belly, but was still having difficulty keeping the blood pressure stable.

I looked at the anesthesia monitors and saw the blood pressure was falling and the pulse was racing. I looked at my colleague across the table. Despite the mask, I could see nothing but fear in Anson's eyes.

Anson Shaw had finished three years of training in an Ivy League program with minimal exposure to trauma. He was now completing his fellowship in sports medicine prior to returning to the same Ivy League university. There, he would start off treating the basketball and baseball teams while working his way up to the football team. He was also looking forward to a seven-figure practice.

I had met Anson at a cocktail party two weeks after I'd arrived in Boston from Solway Mills. The evening had got off to a bad start for me. Like an idiot, I had not thought to enquire about a dress code at the Faculty Club where the event was held, and had arrived in khakis and a sweater. The butler at the entry desk sneered that a jacket and tie were required and that he "might be able to find something in the cupboard."

I ended up in a tweed jacket cut for someone twice my size and a garish yellow tie. Walking into the cocktail party, I noticed the barely disguised smirks of the fellows already in the room, all turned out in well-tailored suits and blazers.

Anson came over to introduce himself, directing one such poorly disguised grin over his shoulder to his colleagues. "You must be Patrick Maloney—Dr. Gershwyn's new fellow, huh? I hear that you were able to fill in on short notice when his first choice cancelled. I think you're the first fellow to ever come here from Solway, right?"

I felt like taking the arrogant son of a bitch up against the wall, but kept my temper in check. The evening went downhill from there. Everyone in the room seemed to know each other except for me. The conversation was full of stories about well-known professors that I had only read about, future jobs that guaranteed remarkable incomes, and tailors that could be relied on for bespoke suits. When the discussion turned to what brokers offered the best investment services to young surgeons, I wandered out into the entry hall, returned the jacket and tie, and hailed a cab.

Chapter 11

Ms. Shanice Brown, RN
February 21

*W*hen we all realized that the orthopedic trauma fellow on call was Anson Shaw, our hearts sank. He had a reputation for dilly dallying and not being a decisive surgeon. And the one thing this patient needed was decisive.

I'd been scrubbed since the case began, working with the general surgeons getting rid of that busted spleen. I knew the anesthetist was relieved when the general surgery team turned over to the orthopedic trauma surgeons. But when he saw Anson, the anesthetist immediately dialed the blood bank and ordered "six more units of packed red cells to OR 12."

From previous experience in the trauma OR, we knew that Anson Shaw had finished his training with minimal exposure to trauma. And we knew that he was certainly not prepared for what faced him here today. Working with a junior and senior resident, Anson had reviewed the computer images of the fracture. I heard him describing just fine to his residents what needed to be done to fix this fracture. But I had a strong sense he had no idea how to do it.

Just as Anson's team had finished opening the outside of the thigh, Patrick Maloney came into the room with hands scrubbed and requested a gown. The anesthetist was pumping blood as fast as he could, and the blood pressure was still falling. You weren't supposed to lose healthy young men from a ruptured spleen and a leg fracture, but this man was at risk of coding. "Hey, guys, you gotta get the bleeding under control. I can't get the pressure up."

"Hey, Anson, my schedule's light this morning—mind if I join you?" Maloney sounded much calmer than I was feeling at this moment.

"Sure," said Anson, sounding pompous. "This is an interesting C3 fracture. I've seen several presented at rounds. Feel free to scrub in and observe."

Maloney quickly gowned and gloved. "What's the pressure?"

"Seventy over forty," answered the anesthetist. "You guys gotta get moving here."

And then, amazingly, I could not believe my eyes. Maloney just took the knife out of Anson's hand and extended the incision ten inches toward the hip. I could have just about cheered.

"Anson, we need more exposure here," said Maloney. "Let me start off and I will turn it over to you once it is exposed." I could sense that he was entering that zone that great surgeons move into in critical situations like this. He was quick and efficient, with no wasted motion and complete focus on the surgical field.

The heart rate from the anesthesia monitor was tripping along way too fast as Maloney explored the leg that was now swollen to three times its normal size and tense as a sausage left in the sun. As he exposed the quadriceps muscle, that sweet, coppery smell of active bleeding filled the room. The normally flexible quadriceps were a turgid gelatinous taut mass. I could see that retracting this unyielding massively swollen muscle to get access to the bleeding was going to be real difficult.

Despite the tension, Maloney sounded calm as he talked to the residents while working relentlessly at separating the muscle from the bone.

"There are usually four 'perforating' vessels that wrap around the back of the bone from the deep femoral artery. It looks likely from the X-rays that the third and fourth perforators are both ruptured. Bleeding from these vessels can be really difficult to control."

The anesthetist was becoming frenzied as all his monitor alarms started sounding simultaneously. The heart rate was too high, blood pressure was too low, and blood oxygenation was falling.

"We are going to lose this guy if you don't stop the damn bleeding," he said, wiping the back of his neck.

I handed Maloney large rake retractors. He positioned the retractors for the senior and junior residents and had them pull the unyielding quadriceps muscle forward off the femur. Just then, the bleeding that had been pouring from the fracture slowed perceptibly.

The anesthetist swore. "Shit, I'm losing him. You gotta stop and pack the wound; he has no blood pressure. I can't get the pressure up. I can't get any pressure at all. Get ready to call the arrest team."

Maloney kept on working, and I could hear him say to the residents, "With no blood pressure, the bleeding will slow down or stop for a minute or two before cardiac arrest occurs. There, you see? We can visualize the wound much better." He then slid a retractor over the femur and continued working rapidly toward the knee, separating muscle from bone, looking for the bleeding site.

"Damn it, I said stop operating," said the anesthetist. "We got no pressure. Pack the wound and stop operating."

"You'd better stop," suggested Anson, now sounding far more nervous. "He's going to die."

But Maloney ignored the comments. And suddenly, we could all see the torn section of the perforator artery slowly leaking residual blood.

He slipped a clamp around the vessel and said to Anson, "Pass me a 2-0 tie." I handed Anson a silk tie, but his hands were shaking so badly he could not place the ligature in Patrick's instrument.

"Give it to me on long forceps," he told me, and with his hand still controlling the clamp, he managed to pass the tie into the jaws of the grasping instrument.

He slipped the tie down on the bleeding vessel and stopped the flow entirely. "That's one," he said to the anesthetist. "What's the pressure?"

"It's up to 40."

"Keep pumping blood. We got one more big one, and then it should stabilize," Maloney ordered as he continued pulling the inelastic quadriceps muscle off the bone.

"Just get it done, for Chrissake."

I could see him slide his instruments down the femur to where he sensed the fourth perforator artery should lie. He seemed to be working on instinct when he slipped a retractor over the broken femur and handed the retractor to Anson. I could feel the vibration of Anson's shaking hands on the entire wound as he held the retractor. Maloney then guessed roughly where the vessel should be in this badly damaged thigh and handed a newly placed retractor to the junior resident.

With the muscle retracted under tension, we could all see the telltale squirt of the ruptured artery. Again, Maloney sounded remarkably calm when he said to the residents, "The fourth perforator looks like it's been completely torn in half by the fracture. It's bleeding freely, hidden behind the broken bone. We are not going to be able to expose the vessel from this side of the femur. We're going to need to control the bleeding with blind suturing."

"Pressure's down to 30 again. How long 'til you control it? He's going to die if you don't control that bleeding in the next minute." The OR was filled with the smell of blood mixed with the acrid odor of surgical sweat. The anesthetist's monitor continued to trip alarms as the heart rate and BP were outside normal limits.

Patrick didn't answer. "2-0 silk on a needle."

I passed him the suture, but as he took it, he kept his eyes on the spurt of blood coming from behind the femur. He passed the point of the needle deep into the muscle, hopefully encircling the end of the vessel he was visualizing, and pulled the suture through, gently holding it with the index finger and thumb of his opposite hand. He passed the suture into the muscle again and again, obviously following the image of the vessel in his mind. Having passed the needle three times, he gently tied the suture down, cinching the end of the vessel in his mind's eye as he tied the knot.

"Should be better now. What's his pressure?" Patrick did not lift his eyes from the wound. Cutting the first suture, he held his hand open for another stitch, which I laid into his palm on a needle driver. He continued to place and tie stitches in the muscle, visualizing where both sides of the ruptured perforators would rest, and hopefully stopping their flow.

"What do you mean should be better? You haven't done anything…wait—pressure is at 60—keep on doing whatever you are doing, man, he's coming back."

Maloney continued his measured suturing. "That should have it. Let's expose the femur and we'll do the fixation."

"I don't know what you did, but his pressure is 100. Whatever you are doing, keep it up, man."

Maloney took a quick look at the computer and again spoke to the residents. "There are two large fragments that will likely come back to normal position if we pull on the tibia."

Taking a drill, he placed a large screw into the shin bone beyond the knee fracture and attached a clamp to the screw that he handed to the junior resident. "Get ready to pull on this clamp when I tell you."

He estimated the length of the fracture and softly said to me, "Get us a 12-hole Condylar Locking Compression Plate." The metal plate was immediately opened on the table, and Patrick inserted it alongside the shattered femur, sliding it under the quadriceps muscle, which had stopped accumulating blood.

"Pressure's great, 110. I think you stopped the bleeding." The anesthetist had stopped silencing his alarms as the pulse rate, BP, and oxygenation had returned to normal.

Maloney held the plate against the femur and touched the first resident's hand, which held the screw in the tibia. "Get ready to pull that screw about four centimeters toward the foot."

Then, he rapidly placed three screws through the plate, attaching it to the bone well above the fracture line. He asked for a guide wire next. "Pull hard," he told the resident holding the tibial screw. Patrick slid his left index finger inside the knee to feel the broken bony fragments in the knee joint. "That's enough traction. I can feel the joint fragments returning to normal position."

Within a few minutes of distracting the fracture, Maloney had the knee fragments pretty well aligned and solidly fixed using locking screws. "Okay, team, this is looking pretty good. Let's remember that 'the enemy of good is better' and accept what we have here."

Dr. Maloney then completed attaching the plate to the bone above the fracture, and the knee joint was progressively attached to the thigh bone. Suddenly, the terribly damaged thigh and knee was looking like a leg, completely straight with the knee bending like normal.

The bleeding that had turned the quadriceps into a tense sausage had stopped, and the muscle was starting to return to a more normal size.

Anson spoke for the first time in forty-five minutes, directing an order to the anesthetist. "We are looking really good here, we'll be done soon. Make sure you're maintaining his blood pressure and get ready to wake him up."

The anesthetist grunted in return. His opinion of Anson was pretty clear.

Anson didn't say anything else for the rest of the case. After finishing inserting the screws through the plate, Maloney put down the drill and turned to the two residents. "I am supposed to meet Dr. Gershwyn at Sumner Hospital in forty-five minutes. Do you guys mind closing?"

Anson was standing near the foot of the bed examining his hands. The residents agreed that they could finish off and Patrick left the OR table and walked toward the door, stopping to remove his bloody gown and gloves. Everyone in the room stared at him. Sure enough, his surgical scrubs were bone dry, not a drop of sweat. I was pretty sure that Anson would be soaked with sweat under his gown. I was also pretty sure he would not live this down for a while.

As Patrick Maloney left the room, I released a gentle sigh and exclaimed to the room, "Well, that was something, huh? Thank God he was here."

Chapter 12

Dr. Patrick Maloney
February 21

I *am going to need to do something about this car soon*, I thought, driving the five miles to Sumner Vet Hospital. My eleven-year-old Subaru Legacy wagon was a great favorite in the backwoods of New England. The car was perfect for hauling around hockey gear, and was terrific in the snow with its four-wheel drive. But it was getting pretty rusty and sounded like a tank.

I walked in the front door of Sumner and checked my phone for the location where I was meeting Gershwyn and Barnes. Although I could hear barking and squawking, the hospital was orderly and spotless. I ran up two flights and entered a hallway, where I saw the Gershwyn/Barnes names prominently displayed over the door. Walking into the room, I was greeted by a large golden retriever whose leash was held by a tall woman dressed in surgical scrubs. She looked up from patting the dog. "Are you Dr. Maloney?"

"Sure am. Sorry I'm a few minutes early. I wasn't sure how long it would take to get here from downtown."

"No problem," she said, extending her free hand. "I'm Kate Benedict. I'm a veterinary surgeon working in Oncology. And this may be your first patient, from what I hear. Dr. Maloney, say hi to Philbert."

She leaned over and patted the dog's head, putting a hand under his right front paw. Dutifully, the dog raised his paw in my general direction. I leaned over and shook the offered extremity while Dr. Benedict smiled.

Kate pulled on Philbert's leash and he stood up from his sitting position. "His name kinda fits, huh?" She scratched Philbert behind the ears. "He is the friendliest dog—just a real suck when it comes to attention. He can't get enough. Do you like dogs, Patrick?"

"Sure do. Had one all my life until the last three years or so."

"That sounds like residency," she said. "You just finished?"

I nodded while scratching Philbert under the chin.

Kate continued, "People think our residency isn't as tough as yours in people medicine, but it's still an exercise in endurance."

There was chatter in the hallway and Gershwyn and Roland Barnes entered, accompanied by another man dressed in a white coat.

"Hey, Patrick," said Gershwyn, interrupting the others. "I see you found Dr. Benedict. Let me introduce Dr. Roger Nabers, the Chief of Veterinary Care here at Sumner and pretty much the top vet in America."

Nabers showed no sign of disagreement with Gershwyn's introduction, but had the good grace to at least smile. "Nice to meet you, Patrick. As you have probably already figured out, that comment means Albert wants something from me. I see that you have met Dr. Benedict and Philbert."

Gershwyn took over. Crouching beside Philbert's right hind leg, he gently ran both hands up and down the extremity and focused in on the knee. "Yeah, Roger, I see what you mean. It's probably perfect for us."

He turned to me. "Have a feel here, Patrick. Poor old Philbert has an osteosarcoma in his knee."

Crouching beside Gershwyn, I noticed a small bandage. "He's already had a biopsy?"

Gershwyn nodded. "Yeah, it confirms osteosarcoma. But Roland has the really interesting results. We're going to look at them today to see if Philbert will be able to enter our study as your first patient."

I felt that the muscle and skin moved easily over the cancer; the tumor was not that large. Even without an MRI, I was pretty sure that we could readily remove this cancer. And looking at the size of poor Philbert's thigh bone and shin bone, I also figured we could use a small human cancer replacement prosthesis and reconstruct the dog's leg after removing the tumor.

I wasn't sure what Gershwyn and Barnes had in mind for a new therapy, but I was pretty sure we could probably treat Philbert exactly the same as a human and achieve a pretty good outcome.

As I stood up, I noticed that Kate was observing me closely.

"Do you think that we can save the leg?" she asked. I thought that the "we" was interesting. Did that mean we would be working together? It would be great to have a full-time veterinary partner if we were going to start operating on dogs.

"I think so. Has Philbert had an MRI?"

"Yes, we tend to do the MRI when we do the biopsy—because, of course, we need anesthesia for both," she said. "I'll show you the images before you leave. His CAT scan, bone scan, and PET are all clear."

I smiled. This suggested that the cancer was still localized in the knee and had not spread elsewhere.

Gershwyn looked at Nabers. "Is there somewhere we can sit and look at the results that Roland got for Philbert's cancer?"

Nabers led the way to a boardroom behind the examination room. "I also want to describe to Patrick what we are planning to do, so everyone knows what we expect of him. Kate will help with the care of patients on the trial if we agree to start, but she does not have the surgical experience necessary to do osteosarcoma surgery. For surgery, we will be depending on you, Patrick. Albert assures me that you've got what it takes, but I want to be very clear what we are planning."

"Our patients are as precious to us as yours are to you," Nabers continued, leading us down a hallway. "Neither can be second-class if we are going to proceed."

I nodded, but did not really know what I was agreeing to. I was, however, pleased with the idea that whatever Nabers was planning, Kate was going to be helping.

"Okay, let's get this show on the road. I need to be leaving in forty minutes," Gershwyn growled. I smiled to myself. My boss was never a patient man.

"What do we do with Philbert?" Barnes wondered.

"Well," suggested Kate, "it's him we are talking about, so maybe he should come with us." As she opened the door to the boardroom, Philbert walked in with a slight limp and waited to see where Kate was headed. When she sat down, Philbert immediately curled up at her feet under the table.

Nabers started the discussion and aimed it directly at me. "Patrick, Albert and I have wanted to start a combined treatment approach for osteosarcoma in dogs and humans for five years now. Osteosarcoma is more common in dogs than humans, and we get hundreds of referrals here at Sumner every year. Many of the cancers would be appropriate for human therapies. We think that there is so much we can learn in dogs that may be applicable in humans, but there are two fundamental problems.

"The first, of course, is cost. In order to treat an animal with chemotherapy and surgery without going absolutely broke, the hospital needs to charge about $200,000 per patient. That's really not much cheaper than human therapy."

"Most owners don't have that kind of money to invest in their dog, and pet insurance doesn't cover it because the insurers say the treatment is experimental. But then, along comes Albert's foundation. He has raised ten million dollars for this project—enough to allow us to treat about fifty patients."

Gershwyn was slumped in the chair at the head of the table, tapping his toe irritably and checking his watch.

"I am amazed," Gershwyn commented, "but since we have started talking about saving dogs' lives—well, the donations to our 'Cure Bone Cancer Foundation' have nearly doubled. And not all the new donors are even dog owners. People love dogs."

Gershwyn was anxious to learn about Philbert's biopsy. "Tell us about Philbert's genetic tests, Roland. Will he qualify?"

At the sound of his name, Philbert raised his head and then rubbed his neck several times up and down Kate's leg.

"Before I give you Philbert's result," Barnes said, "I want to explain to Patrick what we are doing."

He turned to me. "Patrick, you likely wondered like we did why osteosarcoma usually occurs in humans between the ages of about thirteen and nineteen. A similar observation is that not all dogs get osteosarcoma—it occurs almost exclusively in big dogs."

Philbert certainly fit that description. He was a very large golden.

"The thing that links these observations together is Growth Hormone and Insulin-Like Growth Factor, or IGF, which I know you researched back at Solway. In normal humans and dogs, Growth Hormone secretion from the pituitary gland increases markedly just before puberty, which is what causes teenagers to grow so rapidly in such a short time.

"The way it works is that Growth Hormone stimulates the liver to increase production of another hormone called Insulin-Like Growth Factor-1, or IGF. The IGF is secreted by liver cells into the blood, and this molecule then circulates to the growth zones of teenage arm and leg bones. It works the same way in big dogs."

"The IGF hormone stimulates those growth centers to start cells dividing and bones growing. It's this rapid cell division that gives teenagers their growth spurt. The more IGF in the blood, the more the bones grow and the taller the person will become." I could hear Gershwyn's fingers drumming on the table.

"The way IGF works," Barnes continued, "is important to this discussion. Most cells in the base of the bone growth zone produce a protein called IGF-Receptor, or IGF-R. When an IGF molecule in the blood encounters the IGF-Receptor on the cell surface, it binds to its receptor. The combined molecules then send a signal to the cell to divide to form two new cells. There is a lot of IGF-Receptor in bone growth centers during adolescence. The receptor level drops after adolescence concludes. At that point, the production of Growth Hormone also drops, which means less IGF. Bone growth stops."

"What he's trying to say," Gershwyn cut in, "is that IGF gets your cells to divide so your bones grow. High levels of IGF and you've got cells dividing under control. You can see where Roland is going with this."

I nodded. Cancer is caused by cells dividing out of control. Unlike normal human bone growth, which stops at the end of puberty, bone cancer cells won't ever stop dividing as long as the patient is alive. I knew all this already, but I also knew better than to interrupt.

"That's correct," said Barnes, looking unperturbed. I could see he was accustomed to Gershwyn. "Many bone cancers, both in humans and in dogs, show overproduction of the IGF-Receptor in the cancer cells. And I know you found similar results for IGF production in your research. All this suggests that the development of osteosarcoma bone cancer, in some cases at least, may be a perverse mimic of normal human growth."

"Fortunately," he added quickly, "bone cancer in adolescents is a rare event. But it appears that the normal stimulus for human bone growth may have a role in the uncommon development of bone cancer in teenagers."

Gershwyn was twirling a pencil and continued to tap his foot against the table. "Enough with the biology course, Barnsey. Patrick isn't an idiot."

"Patrick, I don't know how you put up with your boss sometimes. Anyway, we are getting to the interesting part.

"What does all this discussion mean to our patients? Several companies, including the one we're working with, have produced antibodies that block IGF-Receptor and stop it from stimulating cancer growth. We have tried these antibodies in one human study to determine if that antibody itself will stop cancer from growing simply by blocking IGF-Receptor. The answer is no. By the time the cancer is fully developed, blocking IGF-Receptor is not enough to slow down or stop cancer growth.

"Now, we want to try something different. We want to try to kill cancer cells outright by improving the effect of chemotherapy on the cancer using IGF.

"Most chemotherapy drugs require the cancer cell to be dividing in order to kill it. You'd think that might be easy, since cancerous cells divide more than normal cells. But in virtually all cancers, only a portion of the cells are dividing rapidly. Many cells are dormant—

which means they're not dividing—at any given time. Dormant cells resist chemotherapy.

"One way to potentially improve chemotherapy is to 'synchronize' cells to divide actively, all at the same time, just when you are ready to give chemotherapy. We think that the more cells in the cancer that are dividing when we're delivering chemo, the more effectively chemotherapy will kill the whole cancer."

Gershwyn twirled his hands in the air, signaling for Barnes to get to the point.

"Okay, Albert, relax," said Barnes. "It's important Patrick understands what we are proposing."

"For dogs with cancers like Philbert's, we are going to try and synchronize cell division before we start chemotherapy. So, on day 1 through day 5, we will starve the cancer cells by giving very strong drugs that block IGF-Receptor. On day 6, we stop this IGF starvation treatment and wait twelve hours for the blocking drugs to disappear. The blocking drugs we are using get degraded rapidly."

Barnes slapped his hands together gently for emphasis. "On day 7, we give the patient very high doses of IGF to stimulate the cancer cells, which are now starving for IGF. That injection of IGF gives them the stimulation they need, and we hope that they all start dividing. This is the synchronization effect. We have tried it in cancer cells in Petri dishes and in mice, and it works very well."

He waved his arms around like a freestyle swimmer. "It's like synchronized swimmers all doing the same movement at the same time, except we're using the IGF molecules to get as many cancer cells to divide as possible. And then, with all the cells dividing, we give the patient standard bone cancer chemotherapy, which is very effective in dividing cells. This works beautifully in mice, and now we want to try it in an animal more similar to our human patients.

"What we are proposing is that all of our dog patients be measured for IGF and IGF-Receptor in the tumor at diagnosis. The measurement of these proteins will be done on the biopsy sample like Philbert just had." The scientist paused for a moment for the news that his colleague Gershwyn was waiting for. "And the exciting news is that Philbert has very high levels of IGF in his tumor and also high levels of IGF-Receptor, suggesting that his cancer may be responsive to IGF stimulation. This makes him a great candidate for our new treatment."

I remembered what Meredith had told me about Gershwyn and Hendricks being frenemies. But I still couldn't believe they didn't collaborate more. Sure, we were looking at bone cancer and Hendricks' lab was focused on hip replacements for arthritis. Still, there was bound to be overlap, especially since both were working on dogs.

Maybe part of the problem was that they had to compete for funding. *Or maybe*, I thought, glancing at my boss, *Gershwyn likes frenemies better than he does friends.*

"As long as the dog is doing okay, we repeat the Synchro Therapy with chemotherapy three times over seven weeks prior to surgery. Three weeks later at surgery—and Patrick, this is where you play the key role—we remove the cancer and repair the leg, so the dog will still be able to walk if possible.

"And that brings us to our patient right here," said Barnes. Kate smiled, peeking down at Philbert, who was now snoring against her leg.

"We'll send in the Trojan horse," said Kate, rubbing Philbert behind the ears. "Starve the cancer cells of IGF, then bait them with a huge injection of it. They'll start dividing like crazy. And that's exactly what we want. That's when we zap them with chemo."

"Well put," said Barnes, chuckling. "Then, we use a variety of techniques to measure cell death in the cancer and determine how successful treatment is. Our preliminary work suggests that IGF synchronization seems to be well-tolerated by the few dogs we've tested so far. Now, we want to test this treatment on fifty dogs. And if it's effective, we'll have a big enough sample size that we may feel confident trying Synchro Therapy with some human patients."

Gershwyn jumped up. "Okay, team, it's decided. Philbert's going to be our first patient and Patrick will be his surgeon. Patrick, this is your chance to create history."

He picked up his coat and started putting it on. "And now, I am going to take off and leave you intellectuals to talk about Synchro Therapy while I go and work on the donations that will allow us to treat more Philberts. Patrick, walk out with me for a moment. See you guys later."

Gershwyn had a car waiting outside and took me by the arm as we walked toward it. "Patrick, James Beattie called me today to lodge a complaint against you."

I had to raise my eyebrows. Beattie had done his residency at the hospital and was staying on to do a hand surgery fellowship; he had been named Chief Fellow. He was one of those patrician prep school boys who thought that someone like me should not be contaminating the fellowship program. I had tried to talk to him on a couple of occasions, but Beattie generally ignored me.

"He said that you were extremely rude to Anson Shaw during a trauma case. Beattie and Shaw say that you took over Shaw's case and degraded and humiliated him."

I could not say a word. I simply stared at Gershwyn.

"Well, Patrick, what do you say in your defense?"

"Well—not much, boss. I'm sorry that Anson's feelings were hurt, I guess. It was a pretty tense case."

"I thought that the whole thing sounded kind of strange, so I checked with the scrub nurse who was in the room. I have known Shanice Brown for fifteen years and I asked her about the case. She told me that you saved the patient's life and that Dr. Shaw was totally incapable.

"She was very complimentary about your skills, Patrick. Bottom line, it was a good thing that you were there today. But you didn't make any friends with the preppy fellows."

With that, Gershwyn opened the back door to climb into his car. "Now, if I were you, I would get back in there and start making plans for Philbert with Dr. Kate. And try not to piss anyone off."

Chapter 13

Meredith McClintock, PhD
February 28

I glanced over my shoulder. "How you doing? Is the pace okay?"

"Great, just great." Patrick was barely able to talk as he trailed me on the running path. "Maybe slow down. Just a bit. Or. I catch up. At bridge."

I smiled and slowed down a bit. "How's that?"

"Better. I think. Thanks. How was your day?"

"Not bad. Yours?" I really did not know why I was putting up with this guy. I'd made a promise to myself that I would not date another orthopod, so there was no reason I should be wrecking a perfectly good run with this guy running so slow.

It was actually kind of embarrassing. His running gear was a mess, and he really could launder those old hockey jerseys a little more often. I could see people watching us who knew me as a runner, and I knew they were wondering what I was doing with this slowpoke who looked like an unmade bed.

And the fact that people had seen us running together a few times meant that sooner or later, people from the hospital would start talking. David and I had gone running together pretty frequently. But nobody ran by David without taking a second look over their shoulder at him. He was always perfect in his running gear, and he had that shock of blond hair that no one could ignore. He was in unbelievable shape, and I'd always had to push to keep up with him.

And maybe that should have been a warning for me. David would run at his own speed and would never really pay attention to how I was doing.

Anyway, stupid to compare this guy Patrick with David. David looked like and acted like he owned the world. And Patrick just did not have that sense of being so special. I knew he was from some little place in northern New England and I had heard some of the fellows talk behind his back, saying that he was only here because someone dropped out of Gershwyn's fellowship at the last moment.

Funny, though—even though people were talking about him behind his back, it didn't seem to bother him. Shanice really liked him. She'd done a trauma case with him a week ago and told me that he'd saved a patient's life when he took over the case from another fellow.

"Gershwyn's keeping me busy," said Patrick, panting. "Is the bone ingrowth. Work. Still making progress?"

"Yeah, we're getting incredible results for the **super-B.I.G.** in dogs. The bone and the hip implant are just totally welded together somehow. We've never seen bone ingrowth like this. Never. The data is helping Dr. Hendricks raise the money we need to start a new company to produce the **super-B.I.G.** for human patients."

"That's. Amazing, Meredith," he huffed. I could see his hockey jersey was soaked. "It's incredible. That. Is going to help. Patients. So. Much."

We were running east on the Boston side toward the Longfellow Bridge. I had a feeling Patrick would be very relieved when this run ended.

And then, I looked over my shoulder and he wasn't there. I stopped and turned back. There he was off the track, bent over the side of the trail and retching. I shook my head. *This is crazy*, I thought. *I have to stop this.*

But then, as I turned to start running back down the trail, I heard feet behind me. Patrick smiled that incredible choir boy smile as he caught up to me.

"Ah, there. Feel much better now. Thanks for waiting for me."

I knew that it was wrong, that there was no reason to run with this guy. But that grin was infectious. I tried to hide my own smile as I took off down the trail.

"Dr. McClintock," I heard him wheeze behind me. "Do you think this is funny?"

"You bet I do, Dr. Maloney," I called back.

"Terrific," he said. "I am so pleased to be able to entertain you."

Chapter 14

Dr. Patrick Maloney
March 14

*I*t was a miserable Nor'easter. It had been raining for hours, and now the snow was starting as day turned to night. The snow was horizontal from the east and the running trail led directly into the force of the wind and snow along the Boston side.

I had called Meredith in her lab at the end of day to see if she wanted to cancel, but she'd said that she had been working straight the past couple of days and nights. She wanted to run one lap of the Charles even if the weather was terrible. "I just need to get out there and run to clear my head. I know it's terrible out, but I need a physical break," she'd told me.

She was working at home and I jogged from the hospital over to her part of town. As I approached our meeting place on the waterfront, I could hardly see her through the blizzard. She had just arrived and was stretching and doing burpees to warm up.

"Jeez, Meredith, it's unbelievable out here. Are you sure that you want to run?"

She smiled and the storm seemed milder. "What's the matter, hockey boy? A little snow and ice too tough for you?"

I returned her smile. Actually, in Solway, this was normal spring weather. The Charles bike path was slippery from the freezing rain that had been falling through the day. But the snow falling was starting to provide more reasonable footing on the slippery concrete.

Looking across the Charles to Cambridge, the five story buildings on the MIT campus appeared like ghostly sentinels in the storm.

"Just watch your footing. It's so easy to twist an ankle."

"You look after yourself. At least you're not likely to find anyone to punch out tonight."

We started off. She was still ragging me about that first night we met, when I'd hit that big Southie guy who'd been bothering her. I would have done exactly the same thing again. Those guys could have been seriously dangerous. I respected that Meredith could look after herself, but didn't think she entirely understood how bad some guys could be.

As we started off on a loop that I thought would take about forty minutes, I was pleased with the new running gear that I had purchased a week ago. The four-season trainers provided much more traction than my old running shoes, and the lightweight track suit was surprisingly warm over my new turtleneck.

I was especially pleased to find that I had shrunk two sizes since arriving in Boston.

We both picked up pace. "Hey, Patrick, you're moving pretty well. It must be that new outfit you got."

In my experience, getting back in shape was not a linear event. Sometimes you could experience a "leap forward" after several weeks of desultory training. I wondered if this could be one of those days.

"How are you finding working with Gershwyn? He has quite a reputation around the hospital."

"He sets an unbelievable standard. He works so hard, he has so many interests, and he's a great surgeon. Unbelievable role model." That was the most I had ever been able to say to her while running. I was a bit surprised that I got it all out.

She nodded. "He and Hendricks are both so successful, but different as night and day. Hendricks makes me think of blue-blooded royalty and Gershwyn just seems street smart. I know they respect each other and probably are both a little bit jealous of each other's success."

I could just about see her green eyes through the snow. "I feel some connection with Gershwyn, you know," I told her. "He isn't one of the Ivy League set. He comes out of a middle-class community in New Jersey, grew up the hard way, and works for everything he's got."

We were moving at full pace now, and I slowed down my words. "It's quite amazing. That he got to be professor and chief. At the hospital and university. He's not from the same background as Hendricks and most of the other New England surgeons in the department." I had fully depleted my oxygen with those few sentences.

"Yeah, I know what you mean," she said easily, as though she were simply out for a stroll. "Sometimes, I am sure that Hendricks resents Gershwyn being chief. Hendricks is the perfect guy with the perfect background—prep school, Ivy League undergrad, med school at our university, and fellowship at the hospital. It's amazing that his lab coat never shows a crease or a wrinkle. I hear he can go through two to three white coats a day to keep them pristine."

"He's more than that, Meredith. He has done more than anyone. On the planet to advance hip surgery and hip replacement. And with the little I learned from you. That first time I visited your lab. This new *super-B.I.G.* hip is going to be huge."

"Yeah, I know." We had turned out of the wind to run in front of the storm through Cambridge. With the wind behind me I was feeling stronger and stronger. Meredith continued, but her voice started showing the strain of the pace we were keeping. "The *super-B.I.G.* is going. To be a massive change. Normally we do not expect. That a new prosthesis. Will start with a large market share. It's almost pleasant running. With the wind at your back. After starting off. Running into the storm."

"What do you mean about the market being large for. The new prosthesis?"

"Right now. The original B.I.G. is the. Biggest selling hip prosthesis in the world. I don't understand the. Fine points of marketing. Patrick, do you mind. If we slow down a bit. So, I can talk easier?"

I couldn't believe my ears. Maybe I was getting closer to her fitness level after all. "Of course." I cut back my stride.

"Everything that is planned for the *super-B.I.G.* is based on the success of the B.I.G. The name, obviously. And the goal will be to get everyone using the B.I.G. to switch over and then capture new market share as well. The tag line for the *super-B.I.G.* is 'stronger than your own hip.'"

We were making the turn and heading back into the wind. Tacitly, we picked up speed and stopped talking. And about twenty minutes later, we were cruising by Meredith's turn off in the Back Bay.

"Patrick, thanks for that. I really needed a workout and might not have come out alone in this weather." And then she scooted up the hill to her place, leaving me to start up into the storm running the last mile and a half to my place.

I looked at my watch. I had figured the loop we ran would have taken about forty minutes, especially given the weather. But my watch said thirty-three minutes. I smiled and leaned into the wind as I ran home.

Chapter 15

Dr. Patrick Maloney
April 1

Gershwyn had been exceptionally busy, operating three or four days a week for the past three weeks. I knew he was going to be away for a couple of scientific meetings in the next few weeks, so he was obviously ensuring he was getting caught up before leaving.

Of course, you could not delay surgery when looking after cancer patients. You needed to ensure that your surgery schedule met the patient's schedule in terms of their chemotherapy or radiation treatments. I found myself working closer and closer with Justine, booking the patients into the boss' schedule. It was complicated, but Gershwyn loved working hard and, as he frequently mentioned when we were discussing scheduling, "We'll get it all done, Patrick. We'll get it all done."

Meredith had been away at a scientific meeting out west in the Rockies, and we had not run together for four days. I tried to get out every day no matter what. I was enjoying feeling fitter and also enjoyed watching winter fade away around the Charles basin.

On this evening, there was a fine rain falling as Meredith and I met outside the hospital to warm up running down to the Longfellow bridge. The temperature was in the 40s and it was really quite pleasant jogging, despite the misty rain. You never forgot that Boston was on the seacoast when you ran regularly in this town.

The clocks had sprung forward a couple of weeks before, and there was plenty of light as we started our run. The soft glow of evening lit Meredith's face.

"The meetings out west went so well." She was obviously excited coming back from the conference. "Hendricks wanted us to have all our papers in a single forum showing the success of our new testing methods, and also showing the results that we are achieving with the *super-B.I.G.* I had five different presentations over two days, and people were so positive about what we are doing."

"Just slow down a bit, Patrick," she added. "I'm not used to talking this much running. Yeah, that's better. People were positive and really excited about our results. And Hendricks was really pleased with the presentations. I thought he would do one or two himself, but he left them all to me—which was quite an honor. But what about you? You told me Gershwyn was going to be incredibly busy in the OR. Did everything go well?"

As I described some of the highlights of the past week, I realized how much I had missed her while she was away. I was alone in Boston. I had never really been away from Solway except for hockey trips. During university, med school, and residency, I had lived away from my mum, but often went home on weekends—and, of course, knew everyone in the community.

But here in Boston, my one connection was Meredith. And somehow, in the midst of telling her about Gershwyn's surgeries, I heard myself say, "I really missed you, Meredith."

Her head swiveled. "Huh?"

Having uttered these words not from my head or lips, but obviously from somewhere deeper inside, I felt more than a bit vulnerable. But the words were absolutely true. I had asked Meredith on numerous occasions to join me for dinner or something else that might be considered a date, but she'd always mumbled something about not seeing people in the hospital and refused.

So, I looked forward to our runs. They were the best part of my days. I decided that nothing further could be lost after my ridiculous exclamation.

"Meredith, I missed you while you were away. I just don't know that many people here in Boston, and I really look forward to our runs. I know this must sound pretty lame, but I missed seeing you."

She ran in silence for a minute or two, then looked over at me. *Those green eyes.* "It sounds like you and Gershwyn are getting along really well. I've heard he eats fellows for breakfast. I know that a couple of guys he hired as junior partners left him pretty quickly."

"Yeah, he can be pretty demanding. But I am getting to know how he likes things done—and usually, when he is demanding, it's to get a better result for the patient."

We just continued on chatting about our work and our bosses for the remainder of the run through the Boston mist as though I hadn't made that stupid remark. Usually when we got to her turn-off in the Back Bay, she just waved and ran across the bridge to her street.

But on this evening, she stopped for a moment and looked at me strangely. Then, she pivoted and ran over her bridge, leaving me standing in the rain feeling like a complete idiot. It was April Fool's Day, I remembered when I glanced at my watch. But I didn't really care how long our run had taken this time. All I knew was that I just felt the fool.

Chapter 16

Meredith McClintock, PhD
April 17

*S*omehow, Patrick's words kept echoing in my mind. They stayed with me even though he hadn't repeated them, and I hadn't asked him about them. We had run quite a bit together, almost daily in the past two weeks.

I'd been almost embarrassed by how out of shape he was initially but, wow, that had changed fast. He'd looked like such a schlump in his old hockey gear when we first started running, but with his new running gear and new stride, he was a different guy.

I noticed now that other runners were checking him out when we were running. I wasn't sure if he noticed that. Overall, I found him disconcerting.

When he'd told me that he'd missed me, he'd just looked so vulnerable that I hadn't known what to say. And then, he'd said in so many words that he was lonely here in Boston. I think that I knew what he really meant. I had family in the area and girlfriends and guys I had known forever. But I missed that intense depth of having one person who served as the focal point of my life.

And that was the problem. I'd had that feeling of connection only once before, and that had been with David. When Patrick said he'd missed me, I'd felt that connection spring back again and it was too early. And too…similar.

Another orthopod, another fellow at the hospital. It just felt wrong. But Patrick was different from David—more attentive, more interested in me and what I was doing. His presence made me feel comfortable, safer somehow. There was a word for it, but it wouldn't come to me.

Running was the easy part of our relationship. This was the nicest time of the year to run, before the "summer in the city" heat began. All the college students were out, getting a break from studying for finals. The bike path was like a carnival—lots of people, lots of chatter and laughter.

And the weather was blessedly warm. For us year-rounders who put up with snow, sleet, rain, misery, and then blasting heat and humidity, this was payback time. A soft breeze and running in a t-shirt.

Patrick was chatting as we cruised through the warm evening, initially about a couple of Gershwyn's patients with difficult problems who he was spending extra time talking to.

And then, he switched gears. "I just sent my mum some cash to get her house whitewashed now that spring's here. She's got a new job at the hospital in Solway Mills and—thank God—has health insurance now, but I am glad to help her out with the house."

Patrick's family was both different and similar to mine. We had both lost a parent. But my dad had been able to make sure my sister and I had everything while growing up. Patrick had obviously been helping his mum in various ways for years. "What's your mum like?"

"She hates accepting help. But she had such a tough time when dad died, and then my sister's medical bills. It took us a while to dig out from that hole. I will be glad when I finally start making some real income, so I'll be able to help her out more."

My thoughts wandered for a moment, and then the word I was looking for came to me. *Trust.* Patrick's patients trusted him,

Gershywn trusted him, and his mother trusted him to look out for her.

And he was lonely, and he'd missed me when I was away. And to be honest, I'd missed him as well. It kind of pissed me off how we had met. That gallant white knight stuff of punching that guy to protect me. That I did not need. But I did appreciate the strength I felt in him.

And I was starting to feel that maybe I could trust him.

We were coming to my bridge over Storrow Drive to the Back Bay. My hand brushed against my pocket and felt something. I remembered putting two tickets in there absent-mindedly as I'd left the office. Hendricks was a big Red Sox fan and had season's tickets. When he couldn't use them, he usually asked me to check which of the lab nerds would want to go to the game.

Hendricks had dropped them on my desk earlier in the day and I'd put them in my pocket to ensure they didn't get lifted from my office. I would check with the lab guys tomorrow.

And then another thought occurred, and I pulled them out of my pocket.

Chapter 17

Dr. Patrick Maloney
April 22

*I*t was high spring in Boston. As I wandered from my apartment to the older, historical part of the hospital for early morning rounds, the sun was up and the warm breeze convinced me to remove my sweater. Winter was definitely past.

I was enjoying my hectic fellowship with Gershwyn. Our days were a complex tango—sometimes together and sometimes apart. I focused on his clinical responsibilities, assessing new patients, following patients in clinic and in the hospital, and taking them to the OR.

Funny to think of Gershwyn as a dance partner. He was a compact mesomorph, in good shape from his daily workouts, but not elegant by any stretch of the imagination. And his gray springy hair was best covered by a surgical cap. But we worked together like a finely coordinated dance team.

Gershwyn was an absent partner for much of the day, taking care of his multiple responsibilities—the university, the hospital, the residency program, research, and fundraising. I was never entirely sure how it worked, but he had an uncanny knack of knowing the crucial time in a patient's care when he needed to be there.

It would be the moment when I was about to tell a patient and family that the biopsy showed cancer. Just as I pulled up the pathology result on the computer screen, Gershwyn would wander into the consultation room and take over the conversation.

Or I would be working in the operating room, struggling a bit trying to find the right dissection plane between cancer and normal tissue and, sure enough, I would hear the sounds of water running in the sink as Gershwyn started his scrub.

I knew that some of this exquisite timing was Justine. She had been working with Gershwyn for so long she knew how to anticipate the likely progress of his clinical day. But some of it was a deepening partnership between me and Gershwyn as well. I had figured out early on that he and I shared the same values of respect for the patient and wanted our patients to know what was going on with their treatment. And I knew that both the patient and Gershwyn would want him present at important moments of their care.

I easily understood when Gershwyn would want to be present, either in the OR or in the office. And I would simply keep things going until he got there. We had done some remarkable surgeries together in the past two months. Most of the time, he now left the actual operating to me. Surprisingly enough for a guy as intense as Gershwyn, he was an excellent assistant and teacher.

Most of Gershwyn's patients did well, and were likely cured of their cancer. Tomorrow morning, we were going to operate on Randell Prentice's arm. The young man from Manhattan by way of Yale had undergone chemotherapy, but surprisingly, the cancer was not shrinking much. Gershwyn and the medical oncologist had decided that surgery should be moved up. Hopefully, his chances of cure remained very good.

And, over at Sumner Hospital, Philbert had completed three rounds of chemotherapy and was ready for surgery tomorrow afternoon. I had become good friends with Kate Benedict. And Philbert had tolerated Synchro Therapy well. We were eager to see if the treatment had defeated his cancer. Meanwhile, three more dogs with osteosarcoma had been recruited to the trial.

Kate had no difficulty convincing dog owners that their dogs should participate in the Synchro trial. There was really no other good option for the pet or the owner. And Kate just inspired confidence. She was optimistic and cheerful, with a wonderful dry sense of humor that I thoroughly enjoyed.

But outside of work, I really didn't have any friends. I hadn't been able to get any closer to Meredith. I definitely wanted more than a professional relationship, or friendship. I spent more time than needed in Barnes' lab on the chance of meeting her. We ran together frequently. But our conversations never really went beyond work. Except that one idiotic time I'd told her that I missed her. I didn't regret it. I'd wanted her to know she was missed. But I still felt like a dolt.

And then, she had surprised me five days ago. We were running around the path and I'd mentioned something about my mother and how I had helped her to re-paint her house. And Meredith asked me something about my mum and I just went on a bit—too long, I thought—about how we were close because I had tried to help after my dad and sister both died.

We finished up near her place, and I was going to jog back to my place after leaving her. But just as I was about to leave, Meredith grabbed my arm while reaching into her pocket.

To my surprise, she pulled out two tickets. "Hendricks gave me these two tickets to Fenway. He's away on a fundraising road trip. I've used the seats before. They are near the field, just about as good as it gets. Would you like to come with me?"

At first, I didn't say anything, just nodded stupidly. Then, I managed to stutter something stupid like, "Yeah, that's great. I would love to see a game."

So, today was a special day. It was warm, nothing but blue sky, I had a few small cases to do this morning, then I was having lunch with a good friend, and then I was going to Fenway with Meredith.

It was spring, and it just felt like something good was happening.

Chapter 18

Ms. Shanice Brown, RN
April 22

*I*n our hospital OR, there were clearly in-players and outliers, and that was part of why I liked Patrick. And I had plans for him.

I had known Meredith for maybe seven years. When she started hanging around the OR as a grad student for Hendricks, I'd just ignored her as another rich white kid going to get ahead on the hard work we do in the operating room. But she was different somehow. She didn't just make demands about what she needed for her experiments. She genuinely cared about fitting her project into our work and seemed interested in who we were.

So, we got to be good friends, Meredith and me, despite her being a Weston girl and me being from Roxbury. We would go out after work at least once a month and got to know each other pretty well. When I was thinking of marrying Demar, I made sure that Meredith met him. Her opinion and advice were important to me.

And when she got hooked up with that David guy from California—well, I should have warned her. I could see he was no good, I could feel it working with him in the OR. When she called me to come over after her boss Hendricks told her about David, I was not surprised at all.

And now, I could see Patrick making every excuse to visit the eighth floor between cases in the OR. How many times could you forget something in Barnes' office? Patrick clearly loved going up to that research floor.

I knew he and Meredith were running together a lot—and Jesus, the two of them didn't have an ounce of body fat between them. I could think of other activities they should consider. And Meredith needed to understand what I'd been telling her ever since David left: what happened was not her fault.

Besides, Patrick was nothing like David. In our hospital's operating room, there was a big division between the surgeons and nurses. I've heard from nurses who work in smaller centers that this is not always the case. But our surgeons in Boston were just stuck-up big shots. They never knew your name, they barked orders at you like it was the army, and after the case, they just left the room without helping to clean up.

This superior attitude also applied to most of the surgeons who were here for their fellowships. They had usually done their residency in famous hospitals and thought they ruled the world. Nurses and the few surgeons who came from lesser known centers were beneath them.

And they really did not get on with Patrick Maloney. Patrick was from some little training program that no one had ever heard of, and the other fellows treated him like shit. But Patrick was pretty cool. Instead of socializing with other doctors, he gravitated to the OR nurses. When it became obvious that he was a good guy, he just fit in with the nursing team.

On this morning, we were booked in the OR to do a removal of a small benign tumor and a biopsy. While we were waiting for the anesthetist to start putting the patient to sleep, I peered at him through my glasses.

"Hey, Patrick, you know that you are running too much fat off Meredith. That girl is already skinny enough, but I hear you're taking her running around the Charles every night. Now, tell me what's really up."

He blushed which was kind of cute. "Aw, Shanice, Meredith is great. I want to get to know her better. But every time I ask her to do more than run—you know, dinner, a concert—she makes an excuse that she can't make it. But then she invited me to a game tonight and I don't know what to think. So, what's really up, Shanice, is that I need your advice about that girl."

"Well, I hate to gossip—but since you're asking, and me and Meredith are close, and I am pretty sure I can trust you I'll give you some history…"

I looked over to see if the anesthetist needed me, but he was still checking his equipment. I lowered my voice. "Hendricks had a fellow here eighteen months ago from California. A really good-looking, smooth kinda guy. He hit on Meredith, and before you know it, they were a thing. But it turns out he was engaged back in California, and he was lying to Meredith. Hendricks found out and fired the guy.

"Of course, Meredith was heartbroken and humiliated. It was a high-profile romance in the OR, and everyone in the hospital knew about them. And then, everyone knew that she had been duped. She's been feeling awful about it ever since. And some of the staff like to make her feel like she should've known better. So, you can see why she finds it so hard to trust anyone."

Patrick had a surgical mask on, but I had a feeling his mouth was just wide, wide open. "Shanice, thank you. That explains a lot. That must have been terrible for her."

He went quiet. And with that, we got on with our morning work.

After we finished Patrick's two small cases, it turned out that our next case was cancelled. I had a huge amount of time owing built up from doing overtime, and decided that I would do something different today.

I told my super that I was taking the rest of the day off, and she was pleased because she had surplus staff on. After changing, I went straight up to the eighth floor and told Meredith I was taking her to lunch.

"Shanice, I can't just go out for lunch. I have a ton of work I am finishing for Hendricks, and I am going to the game tonight."

"I know you're going to the game tonight, darling. That's part of the reason we are going for lunch." And with that, I grabbed her arm and pulled her to the door. She was a tiny fluff of a woman anyway, and wasn't going to resist me when I had my mind made up.

We found a patio on a quieter street behind the hospital and I took advantage of my afternoon off to order a glass of wine. Meredith stuck to bubbly water.

"Meredith, I hate to bring up that creep, David. I know you worked hard to get over him."

Meredith just looked at me suspiciously over the straw in her water and nodded.

"Well, I should have warned you off that guy. He was so obviously into himself and God's gift to women in his own mind. We should have told you about him before you fell for him so bad."

Meredith remained silent. "But I think that it's time to get past all that. I've been seeing you with Patrick Maloney around the OR, and I hear you've been running races with him most nights."

She put down her glass slowly. I just kept on going. "I know you think that after what happened with David, you shouldn't be seeing anyone from the hospital. But nobody gives a damn if the men in the hospital are seen with their hookups or their dates or their girlfriends or whatever. There's affairs and scandal all over the place. And they try to make you feel bad? It's not right."

Meredith nodded slowly, looking down at the table.

"And I really think this guy Patrick is different," I said gently. "He's not stuck-up, the nurses find him real helpful. And he seems like a really sweet guy."

Meredith pushed her chair back a bit and sat up. "You know, Shanice, it's so funny you are saying this. He does seem different from the other orthopods. We were running together a few days ago and he started talking about his mum. It was just so innocent somehow and so sweet."

"And whenever I talk to him about my work, he seems so genuinely interested. And, you know..." she looked at me with what

I can only call a sparkle in her eye. "He's really cute. And since I met him, he's got into amazing shape."

I reached across the table and took Meredith's hand in mine. "I know you, girl, and I have a good feeling about this Patrick. I heard you are taking him to Fenway tonight—yeah, he told me when we were working this morning."

I leaned back in my chair. "I know it sounds corny, Meredith, but hear me out. I think you should give him a chance to get past first base."

And with that, we both started laughing—slowly at first, and then we couldn't stop.

Chapter 19

Mr. Sandy Spencer
April 22

*I*was meeting Patrick for lunch at 1 p.m., but got to Copley Square thirty minutes early since my speech at the investment conference had finished by noon.

The waiter showed me to a table on the patio. "Will this table suit you, Sir?"

The warm spring weather made the patio irresistible. I just sat back in the sunshine with a fine glass of Sancerre to reminisce about my lunch guest.

Two winters ago, I had been enjoying a quiet Saturday at home when I'd gotten a call from one of my son's friends. He gave me a harrowing account of a terrible injury that Bob had suffered while skiing at Mount Solway. Unlike with most ski injuries, Bob had not fallen or hit a tree. Instead, skiing in a snowstorm in the late afternoon, he had collided with a snowmobile that was cutting across the trail. Fortunately, Bob did not hit his head. However, the snowmobile hit his right thigh directly and then threw him forward and ran over his right arm.

Later, Bob told me that he'd heard two cracking noises as both bones were badly shattered. His ambulance had trouble getting to the local hospital from the hill since the weather was so bad. Bob's comrades stayed with him and kept me updated as I sat by my phone in New York. By the time that Bob arrived in the emergency room in Solway Mills, I was already on the phone to the hospital, demanding transfer by air ambulance to New York City.

The Emergency Department had connected me with the orthopedic resident on call named Dr. Patrick Maloney. He'd checked with the local ambulance people and told me that both fixed wing and rotor wing aircraft were grounded by the weather, and the roads were so bad he did not recommend land ambulance.

Furthermore, Bob's arm fracture was complicated by a wound in the skin that looked like it communicated with the broken bone. Dr. Maloney explained that this meant the fracture was "open" or "compound," and urgent surgical care was needed to clean the bone to reduce the risk of long-term bone infection.

Talking to Patrick, I felt utterly helpless as a father. In New York City, I was surrounded by some of the best health care institutions in the world, and yet I felt that I was consigning my son to treatment by some backcountry rube. I immediately set off by car for Solway, but needed to stop in a motel en route because the roads were closed.

In the car, I called the medical reporter from the major metropolitan newspaper associated with our business journal. The medical reporter checked with his sources and confirmed my worst fears. None of the New York orthopedic experts knew anything about Solway, and all agreed that it was not the right place to get treatment for complex fractures.

I later learned that Patrick had discussed Bob's injuries over the phone with his supervising surgeon. The surgeon himself was skiing for the weekend and was stranded at his chalet; he apparently had confidence in Patrick. Given the fact that the arm fracture was a compound break, there was no question that immediate surgery was necessary.

Surgery started at about 11:00 p.m. Patrick began with the humerus fracture, since it was compound, with the bone exposed to the skin surface. He told me later that he cut away the damaged tissue where the bone had come out through the arm skin and washed the bone with antibiotic solution. He then put the fractured bone back to normal position and held it in place using bone screws and a metal plate that stabilized the entire fracture.

Apparently, the broken thigh bone was quite a daunting surgical challenge.

The femur was badly shattered in its midportion for a distance of about eight inches. Two days later, Patrick explained that he placed a metal guide wire down through the hollow bone canal of the upper half of the femur and threaded it across the splintered part of the bone into the bone canal of the lower half of the femur. He'd then figured out the appropriate length and rotation of the top and bottom parts of the bone and placed a long rod down through the center of the bone to lock the top and bottom parts of the thigh bone in correct position while the shattered center part of the bone could heal.

I learned afterward that if the reconstruction of his femur had not been done right, Bob could have ended up with a shortened or lengthened leg, a very stiff knee, or a knee that pointed east when he was facing south. I was stuck in a motel in the snow, and my son's future was being determined by some guy no expert had ever heard of. It was probably good that I did not understand just how bad the break was.

By the time Patrick got me on the phone in the roadside motel where I was stranded, it was 3:00 a.m. Patrick reassured me that it had been a difficult operation, but all had gone well. Bob was awake in recovery room and I could see him in the morning. I was, of course, polite and thankful—but was also determined to get my son out of that backwoods hospital as soon as possible.

I arrived the next day in the afternoon and was relieved to see that Bob was groggy but essentially okay. After meeting Patrick, I told him in an utterly obnoxious manner, "I have several colleagues who work at the university bone and joint center in New York City, and they will accept my son in transfer as soon as the roads or flights open up."

I asked for the X-rays to send to New York, and Patrick sent the digital X-rays showing the fracture and fixation to my cell phone. He told me that as long as he could keep Bob for a day or two so he knew that there were no major complications, he would be delighted to transfer Bob to New York. I am sure that Patrick was thinking Bob's dad was a pretty high maintenance New Yorker.

I sent the digital X-rays off to my friend from the paper's healthcare section. Three hours later, I received a message back. "Sandy, I sent the X-rays to three of America's foremost fracture surgeons. The consensus reply can be summarized as follows in the report from one of the surgeons:

'This is an exceptional job of fixing a very difficult set of fractures. The surgeon should be commended on the excellence of these results.'"

Reading this message, I realized I had underestimated this young man who had saved my son's arm and leg.

The next day, the storm had passed and the roads had opened. I was at Bob's bedside when Patrick made rounds. He suggested that he could arrange to transfer Bob the following day if I would give him the name of the hospital that I wanted Bob admitted to in New York.

I showed him the message from the New York surgeon my friend had forwarded to me. "Doctor, I think that I owe you an apology and further thanks. It sounds like you did a terrific job for my son, and I would prefer that he stays here under your care until he's ready to go home."

Patrick agreed that he would look after Bob, and wrote physio orders in the chart to start that day. Fortunately, Bob's wounds healed without complication, and he was ready to go home ten days later. However, Bob had confidence in the physiotherapists he was working with in the outpatient department, and we decided he would rent an apartment in Solway until intensive physiotherapy was completed. I returned to New York, but came back to Solway weekly.

Over the next couple of months, I became very fond of the young surgeon. I coaxed Patrick away from the hospital for a few meals and was excited to learn that he was being offered the fellowship opportunity to work with Gershwyn in Boston. I promised to help him set up in New York after his fellowship if he wanted, but Patrick just chuckled and told me that would be way over his head.

Bob continued to do well. At twelve weeks, his leg and arm movements were perfect, and both fractures were essentially healed. Shortly thereafter, Bob returned home with me. But I could not forget the young surgeon from Solway. I loved my son, but Bob, although reasonably bright, lacked my intensity and drive.

And those ambitious features were qualities that I observed and admired as defining characteristics in Patrick. While Bob was recovering under Patrick's care, I got to know the young surgeon better and became increasingly impressed by the enormous workload he was carrying and the grace with which he managed it.

As I finished rethinking that terrible accident that had turned out so well, Patrick arrived at our table in the pleasant sunshine.

"Patrick, you look terrific. You've lost twenty pounds since I saw you last. Boston is obviously agreeing with you."

After we ordered lunch, Patrick enquired about Bob's recovery. He was doing well, I recounted, continuing his physiotherapy, and he had started workouts and weight training. Patrick provided several suggestions, which I carefully noted in the journalist's notebook that was always with me.

Patrick in particular told me to ensure that the therapist paid attention to getting full knee bending and extension in therapy. Patrick knew that Bob was an expert skier and would need that full movement to regain his performance on moguls and in powder.

I was eager to hear about Patrick's initial observations in Boston, and listened intently to stories about Gershwyn, Hendricks, and the other international leaders he was encountering at the hospital. I was particularly interested in Hendricks' work, since I had recently heard rumors about a new investment associated with his name.

"Patrick, have you heard anything about Hendricks raising money for a new company or new product?"

Before he could respond, our lunches arrived—fish for me and a salad for Patrick.

I had to admit that there was some self-interest in my questioning Patrick about Hendricks' work. Although I enjoyed my work as an editor and special projects writer for our business journal, I was also very successful in investing my own book of business. Recently, I had started to focus more on biotech, and had already benefited from the explosion in value experienced in both pharma and medical device companies.

Even though medical devices like hip replacements did not necessarily have the multi-billion-dollar market that some blockbuster drugs enjoyed, it was faster and cheaper to bring devices into the market. I knew that Hendricks had made lots of money for Synvest investors with his current products, and I had heard rumors that something new was coming.

Patrick started to shake his head negatively, but then raised his eyebrows. "Actually, I am going to Fenway tonight to see a ballgame with the woman who leads Hendricks' lab. And she mentioned that we are using his tickets because he is away on what she called a 'fundraising road trip.'"

Interesting, I thought. "What's he up to? Can you give me the layman's version?"

"I'm not entirely up to date with Hendricks' work," said Patrick. "However, I saw a video recently that he uses to raise money for his experimental projects. Hendricks is best known for his work on getting better bonding of artificial joints to the bone. There are more than a million arthritic hips and knees replaced annually in this country, and that number is increasing at about five percent annually."

We had both ordered white wine in honor of the beautiful spring weather, and Patrick paused for a sip. "Total hip replacement works extremely well in most patients, and the current models are effective for most people. But there are two unsolved problems for hip replacement, and these problems are where Hendricks is focusing his energy."

"Patrick, do you mind if I take notes? This may be a valuable lead for an article, or maybe for an investment. Is any of this information confidential?"

"No, Sandy, nothing confidential. I don't know anything that most people in the arthritis world are not aware of. I did see the video in his lab, but it is a video he uses widely to raise money for his dog research."

"Dog research? Is that for dog implants or humans?"

"Well, he does hip replacement in dogs for owners who cannot afford the surgery. And this way, he gets to test new prosthetic designs in animals that need the surgery rather than in experimental animals. It is a brilliant idea for ethical research. And since dogs have much shorter lifespans than humans, it gives him the ability to determine whether a new design is working much faster than he would achieve in human patients."

"I've heard he is a pretty smart guy," I said. "The markets have lots of respect for him. I know that he has made a fortune a couple of times over for people who have invested in his products."

"I don't know anything about his investment success, but I do know how he has influenced orthopedic practice. More than twenty years ago, when he was just starting, he introduced changes to total hip design that improved outcomes for hip replacements in many people.

"He was one of the first people to encourage fixation of the bone to implant by covering the prosthesis with surfaces that resulted in direct bone bonding without bone cement. Hendricks introduced a porous mesh that he attached to the implant to encourage bone to grow actually into the implant rather than just onto the surface of the prosthesis. He patented this mesh, which is used in his 'Bone Ingrowth hip,' or 'B.I.G. hip.'

"The B.I.G. hip has been very successful, Sandy, and I am sure that this is one of the products that has made investors lots of money. In general, the latest model prosthesis that avoids cement can be marketed at about twice the cost of a standard prosthesis. The mesh surface is apparently a bit more expensive to manufacture, but I'm sure that the sale price more than makes up for the extra cost."

I was now very interested. One of the themes successful investors listened for was the opportunity to charge an increased price with minimal increased cost. "What is the market for these new prostheses, Patrick?"

"For many older patients, the standard cemented prosthesis works well enough. However, there are two categories of patients that may need a premium prosthesis. The first target group of patients has undergone a prior hip implant that has become loose in the bone for some reason. This may happen in about 20 to 30 percent of hip replacements eventually."

I opened my notebook as Patrick went on.

"These patients suffer from progressive pain as the prosthesis gets looser within the bone and starts to telescope up and down as the patient walks. In these patients, when we operate a second time, the interior surface of the bone is rubbed smooth by the loose prosthesis."

The sun had moved around the umbrella we were sitting under and was directly in Patrick's eyes. He put down his fork to twist the umbrella to a better position. "It's very difficult to cement a new prosthesis into this smooth surface, and the smooth surface does not have much potential to grow into a bone ingrowth surface.

"The second group are young people who are active and want to remain active despite having arthritis. These patients want an implant that will tolerate forty or fifty years of high-stress activity, and current designs could not be expected to withstand this kind of wear and tear.

"These two unsolved categories—patients needing second operations or revisions and young active patients—are what Hendricks is designing for. This used to be considered a small market, but with the rapid increase in the number of people having hip replacements and the decreasing age of when hip replacement is performed, this market is growing rapidly."

Those were words I liked to hear. Growing markets always interested investors like me.

"And people who need a second surgery or young people with hip pain are certainly willing to pay the extra $2,000 or $3,000 that a premium implant might cost. In fact, when you think about it, if Hendricks is able to design a hip replacement that works better in these two special categories, why wouldn't it be used for everyone needing hip replacement?"

I was carefully taking notes. This was definitely worthy of further investigation for a possible investment or column. I then looked up at Patrick, shook my head, and closed the book. "Apologies, Patrick. I am here to find out how you are doing, and all I have done is to grill you for investment ideas! How are *you* doing? It looks like you have time for fitness in your new job. You look terrific."

Patrick nodded. "You know, I guess because I was enjoying learning about surgery, I never realized how much Solway training took away from the rest of my life. I just had no time for anything except surgery for three years. Since I got here, I've been running just about every evening, and I'm looking forward to hockey in the fall."

"Any women in your life? I know that you were acting like a monk in Solway. Have you managed to get a love life?"

Patrick developed a wry smile. "Well, there is the woman who runs Hendricks' lab and is taking me to Fenway this evening. She is smart and gorgeous, but I just learned she's wary of relationships with orthopods. I was really pleased when she asked me to go to the game with her tonight."

"Did you meet her around the hospital?"

The wry smile deepened. "Well, actually, we were both running on the Charles bike path and a couple of guys started hassling her. I sort of *convinced* them to leave her alone."

I looked at Patrick carefully. In Solway, I had heard rumors about Patrick's hockey career, which had involved lots of minutes in the penalty box. "I suppose that means you went after them with your hockey fighting skills? The intellectual lab leader must have been horrified—or maybe impressed?"

"Not impressed, Sandy, and she's probably right. But it's time for me to leave so I can meet her for the game. Great to see you, and thanks for lunch. Say hi to Bob for me. I am glad he's getting better so quickly."

"Thanks to you, Doc, thanks to you. We will never forget what you did for Bob. Anything you ever need, I am here to help. I am coming back up to Boston in a couple of months. Maybe we can have dinner and I can meet this lab leader."

"I hope so," he said, and strolled away with a bounce in his step I had never noticed before.

Chapter 20

Dr. Patrick Maloney
April 22

*I*t was a 7:00 p.m. start for the Red Sox game at Fenway Park. My lunch with Sandy had extended to nearly 3:30 p.m., and I had made arrangements to meet Meredith at her place at 4:30 to walk to Fenway and get a drink and a bite before the game. Copley Place was close to Meredith's apartment and I could easily walk over.

I enjoyed the warm spring weather as I crossed the shopping intensity of Newbury Street. Strolling with the traffic on Dartmouth, I walked across the Commonwealth Avenue boulevard and entered the Back Bay neighborhood, where Meredith lived near the corner of Dartmouth and Marlborough. I did not understand much about Boston real estate, but I knew that this was a very good address, at the heart of the Back Bay.

I entered Meredith's building and announced my arrival to the extremely polite security desk. The woman at the desk called up to Meredith, and I assumed that she would announce she would be right down. To my surprise, the desk attendant turned to me and said, "Up the stairs and to the right, apartment 204."

I climbed the impressive stairway and wandered down to 204. My knock was immediately answered by Meredith, who was dressed in the workout clothes that she generally wore running—elastic, skin-tight leggings with a tight long-sleeved T-shirt over a form-fitting singlet demonstrated by shoulder straps evident at the neckline.

She peered up at me from her cell phone, eyes looking even greener. "Patrick, I am so sorry. I've been working from home this afternoon and thought I'd be ready by now. But Dr. Hendricks is in New York speaking to investment groups, and he's been calling all day to get our data updated. I haven't had a minute to myself. And my friend Shanice insisted on taking me for lunch, so I just got all behind."

I took in her graceful, slender form, her thick, shining hair, and her unnervingly appealing face—and thought I would be willing to wait for her forever. "Shanice Brown? I worked with her on a couple of cases this morning."

"Yeah, she told me."

I just smiled and nodded. I wondered what else Shanice had told her.

"Patrick, this is your first game at Fenway, and I want it to be special. The game is at 7:00 and we need to get there by 5:45 to see the action on Yawkey Way. Maybe we just grab some street food on Yawkey—would that be okay?"

I thought that it would be fine if someone pulled out one of my fingernails on Yawkey, wherever that was, as long as I could be alone with this incredible woman. I mumbled that whatever Meredith wanted was fine.

She went to her fridge. "Can I offer you a beer while I get ready?"

I nodded and accepted a can, shaking off the offer of a glass.

"I will be twenty minutes."

"Take your time, Meredith, please."

She smiled at me and swept her hair up with both hands. This tightened her T-shirt in front of me and arrested my breathing. "Just wait here. There are some magazines on the table." I looked down and saw recent copies of the *Economist* and the *New Yorker*.

Meredith pivoted and headed to the back of the apartment, closing the door behind her. I sipped my beer and looked around. The high ceilings were complimented at the corners by moldings that looked like they dated to the eighteenth century. The bay windows overlooked Marlborough and were well maintained, but again looked as if they belonged in a museum. The furniture was early American. The couch was formal and firmly padded, but softened by matching throw pillows.

The dining room was separated from the living room by a handsome large bookshelf and completed by a two-pedestal dining table and six ladderback chairs. I felt like I was enjoying a beer in Samuel Adams' home shortly after the Revolutionary War.

The kitchen was a study, in contrast: brushed stainless steel modern appliances, a stone island with surrounding high stools and lights suspended on metal filaments hanging from the ceiling. Cooking utensils hung from orderly fixtures.

I heard the sound of a shower coming from behind the closed door and began to imagine what was happening in the back of the apartment. I let the beer add to the relaxation that I was enjoying from the glass of wine that I'd shared with Sandy earlier in the afternoon. I settled back onto the couch and put my feet on the Ottoman in front of me. I was not certain whether I fell asleep or simply closed my eyes, but somehow, a few minutes were lost. And then, I heard the door opening.

Up to this point, I'd had two images of Meredith. I enjoyed running with her dressed in engineered fabrics that stretched with her like a second skin. I would sometimes watch the sequential flexing of her muscles through the fabric while we ran together.

My other concept of Meredith was in the hospital, dressed like the academic leader that she was in Hendricks' lab. Form-fitting khakis, well-tailored cotton button-down shirts in soft colors that inevitably complemented her green eyes, conservative loafers. On winter days, she would add a blazer, or a sweater sometimes tied around her neck in the New England classic look…and I thought it was all wonderful.

Now, I sensed perfume as the door opened. It was a musky floral aroma that I had never experienced before, and my diaphragm tightened as I drew in the wonderful scent to remember.

And then the door opened more, and a thunderbolt followed. Meredith was offering a new look. Bare legs, high stiletto heels, and a soft dress with spaghetti straps that flowed and stopped above the knee.

"I know it's crazy, but Hendricks' tickets are right by the field and women dress up. The guys just dress for the game, but girls are often on camera and it's a thing to wear a dress on a warm day. That's Boston for you. You don't mind, do you?" She smiled, and I could not imagine objecting to anything that Meredith could wear.

"Should we get going?" I wondered.

Meredith checked her phone. "Dr. Hendricks tells me he's finished for the day. Let's go and enjoy ourselves."

I couldn't agree more. As we locked the apartment door and descended the stairs leading to the entrance, I felt giddy when Meredith linked her arm with mine. We had run together for miles and miles, but she had never really touched me before. For the second time in ten minutes, I was having trouble making my diaphragm work.

It was a stunning, warm Boston spring evening. We wandered back up to Commonwealth Avenue and sauntered along the historic boulevard. Meredith seemed comfortable in the stiletto heels she was wearing, but was leaning against me with each step. I felt like I was strolling on an inclined walkway with each step, pressing against the magical woman attached to my arm.

I felt intoxicated, but really had not consumed much alcohol. I realized I was bewitched by her presence, her perfume and the soft pressure that she was exerting on my forearm. This was an utterly new sensation to me, and I felt unmoored and delightfully adrift.

We wandered through the excessive pageantry on Yawkey Way—the stilts, the bands, the street performers. I could feel myself retreating into a narrow reality with a filter between the two of us and our surroundings. Meredith lifted her green eyes toward me, and I could sense that she was also moving into my slower time zone.

We shared street dogs covered in mustard with a beer and I could not taste anything. I was thunderstruck, oblivious to all sensory elements that were not originating from her.

The seats were exceptional, one row back from the fence, in line with the third baseman. I seated myself closer to the plate, recognizing that I might need to shield her from a left-handed batter facing a fastball. The game passed incredibly slowly. She was attentive to all the details of the game, whereas I was attentive only to her.

By the fourth inning, the Sox were well ahead, and by the sixth, fans were filing out from the stadium. We sat close together, and the video board cameras had indeed noticed her lovely dress, pausing on us for moments at a time.

By the eighth inning, the home team was ahead by nine runs and the seats around us were vacant. "I think that we can go now," Meredith decided. As she stood, I admired her calves flexing in her stilettos. As we walked down the street away from the stadium, she leaned close to my ear and murmured, "If you're still hungry, I could whip up something for us at home."

I put my arm around her shoulders and gently squeezed my approval.

There was a new woman at the security desk who lifted her hand as Meredith opened the front door to her building. As we mounted the stairs, I avoided staring but could not help again admiring her tight calves. Meredith opened her door and spun around as she entered, and I took her in my arms as the door closed silently behind us.

"You don't have anyone else, do you?" she whispered as she brushed her lips against mine.

I could not speak. I simply shook my head and lifted her softly while locking my lips against hers. She wrapped her long legs around my waist, and I moved into the hallway with Meredith locked around me. We glided slowly down the hall and fell together onto her thick mattress and duvet. Her dress was high above her waist by now and my hands were softly molded to her buttocks, which were bare around her thong.

And then, things became intense.

Chapter 21

Meredith McClintock, PhD
& Dr. Patrick Maloney
April 23

*T*he next morning, life had changed for both of us. I had given myself entirely once before and had been desperately hurt. But this man was different—deep, quiet, effective and reliable. I remembered the first time that I'd met him, when he'd protected me even though I didn't need protection. I had heard from Shanice and my friends in the OR how competent he was, and wanted to simply explore his competency and security.

I had never imagined a feeling so deep and encompassing, and my only thought was to keep this intense longing for her forever. I woke at 5:00, knowing that I needed to leave to get to the OR and wanting nothing but to wrap my arms around her.

"I am so sorry—need to go. Gotta get to the OR."

"I know. Can I give you breakfast?"

We decided that breakfast could be bought at the hospital, and elected to enjoy something other than waffles. I jumped in the shower thereafter, and Meredith wrapped me in a thick towel when I was done. She was dressed in a housecoat and held a cup of strong coffee.

"Here, drink this. Do you have a busy day?"

I thought for a moment. "Yup. Got an Ewing's of the proximal humerus this morning, and then a case at Sumner this afternoon. Can I see you tonight? Let me call you when I am finished at Sumner and maybe we can get dinner."

"I have a better idea." I whispered in his ear. "We each get food and then meet up here as soon as possible." I pressed my body against him and felt him rising to the contact. I rubbed him gently and then whispered again. "You better get going."

I literally backed out of the apartment and slowly turned to descend the stairs. I waved at the concierge as I walked out onto Marlborough and left jogging back across the Commons to the hospital.

Chapter 22

Dr. Albert Gershwyn
April 23

I came right from the gym to the hospital the morning of Randell Prentice's surgery and was still feeling overheated. I cooled off, changing into greens and a lab coat, and made quick rounds on a couple of patients recently operated on prior to returning to the pre-op waiting area, where I greeted Randell and his parents. The young man was a bit drowsy from his preoperative meds.

Patrick was already in the pre-op area, talking to the patient and his parents. Randell's father looked gray as he gripped his son's shoulder. Although the cancer in Randell's arm was not terribly large, it had an unfortunate location in the posterior part of the humerus—the upper arm bone. That meant it was uncomfortably close to the radial nerve, which supplies muscle function to the hand and wrist. Patrick and I had agreed that the cancer required us to remove part of the shoulder joint as well as the top seven inches of the arm bone. But with this surgery, there was always the risk of potentially damaging the radial nerve.

I had discussed all this with Randell and his family at our last meeting. I explained the potential tradeoff between saving the radial nerve that powered his hand and wrist movements and the risk of leaving cancer cells behind in the arm.

"In order to ensure that we remove all the cancer, it may be necessary to divide the radial nerve," I'd told them, noticing Randell clenching and unclenching his wrist as though testing to see if it still worked. "If we do need to cut the nerve to safely remove the cancer, it will cause problems for your hand function, Randell. Your wrist and fingers will not be able to extend when laid palm-down on a table, and typing will be difficult without a splint on that hand. Bottom line, if we need to sacrifice the radial nerve, your function will definitely be impacted."

Randell grimaced. His professional life was close to getting started—and he probably couldn't think of a single job he'd land where he wouldn't need to use a keyboard.

"I understand how difficult it is to think about your hand not working as well as it does now," I said. "I also understand how important it is to completely remove the cancer. The reason you are here today is that I am probably the best person in the world to get you the best result possible, and that is exactly what I am going to do."

With that, the nurses arrived to take Randell into the OR, and I promised to meet his parents in the postoperative area immediately after surgery. I then went into the operating room.

"Patrick, I have a teleconference to do with the university and a couple other calls to make. Call me when you have taken down the vessels and the joint and are ready to dissect the radial."

"Got it. Should be about an hour."

I nodded and left for the office, pulling a white coat over my surgical greens. Although Patrick had only been with me for about four months now, I had developed real confidence in the young surgeon's judgment and technical skills. Justine had even told me last week that our fundraising numbers were higher since Patrick started.

She'd scheduled my monthly teleconference with the CEO of the hospital and the dean of the university for the next forty-five minutes. The CEO was a recruit from one of our national health insurance companies. He was terrific at negotiations with the variety of payors that our hospital needed to deal with, but really knew nothing about healthcare. Our dean was a social scientist, and the hospital was an utter mystery to her.

This morning, the only item on our phone call agenda was the upcoming Initial Public Offering that Jon Hendricks was organizing for a company to produce his new hip prosthesis. The dean and CEO were both suspicious that Hendricks was pulling a fast one on them because of the complicated ownership structure for the company producing and marketing the new device. They did not want to offend Hendricks with their concerns (especially since he was a big earner for both of them), but were happy to complain to me as his department chair.

The dean was particularly troubled. "Albert, our lawyers have looked at the corporate documents from the company that is doing the IPO. It looks to us that this new *super-B.I.G.* device is going to be marketed by the same company that sells the B.I.G. device that we receive royalties on today. But then, it gets confusing, and our lawyers are worried.

"Hendricks as well as someone named Kovalov and a company called CellGrow are getting senior voting shares in this new company. Our lawyers are convinced that this is all a ruse for Hendricks to change the royalty structure and decrease our royalty share with what is essentially the same product. Albert, you know that I don't understand these commercial relationships, but I don't want us to lose our rightful share of Hendricks' profits."

The CEO of the hospital chimed in. "Our purchasing department has a different concern, Albert. As you know, this hospital is the biggest user of B.I.G. implants anywhere in the world."

That's true, I thought to myself, *because patients come here from around the world demanding that they receive Hendricks' hip replacement. And, my friend, your finance department is delighted with the premium rates you charge these patients.*

"I understand that even though the federal regulator has approved the *super-B.I.G.* as virtually identical to the B.I.G," the

CEO continued, "Synvest is planning to double the price of the new device. That is going to hurt our margins from your program."

I waited for a moment before responding. The dean and the President wouldn't recognize innovation if they tripped over it in the shower. Our dean had done a wonderful job of renewing the social science program of our university, and the CEO was terrific at negotiating with insurance companies. But neither of them really understood what healthcare was all about. And neither of them understood the years of hard work that Hendricks had expended in preparing this innovative new device.

My job was to remind them just how important our department was to the health of both the university and the hospital. Good relations with both of them were important to me, so I calmed down before responding.

"Jon Hendricks has discussed this with me at length, so let me calm your concerns," I said. "First of all, the corporate structure. It needs to reflect the contributions made to the intellectual property that defines this new device. Even though it is approved by the regulator on the basis of being similar to the current prosthesis, it actually has an additional element, which is going to substantially improve both its performance and its marketability.

"This additional element is a biolayer that is applied to the surface of the current B.I.G. device. And the intellectual property for that biolayer is contributed by CellGrow and one of its former employees, Andrei Kovalov—who, by the way, worked for me some years ago.

"So, as you can imagine, that complicates the intellectual property ownership for this latest model. And, rather than try and solve that issue within the current Synvest corporate structure, they wisely decided to raise money for a new division of Synvest—we are calling it Newco for convenience, but it's just a division of Synvest—that will be in part owned by all of the IP contributors.

"And don't worry. The university and hospital will keep their share of the royalties since Hendricks values his relationship with both of you. He is not trying to weasel out of sharing the proceeds of his intellectual property.

"The university and hospital shares of the royalties may be a bit diluted as your lawyers suggest. However, the increased price and increased sales of this new hip will more than make up for that dilution in absolute dollar terms."

"And, from the hospital's perspective, it's true that the price of the implant will go up. However, I know that you will offer your patients the choice of receiving the old B.I.G. or the new *super-B.I.G.* implant. And when they choose the newer device, as I expect 99 percent of the patients will, then you know that you will recoup the increased purchase price by increasing what you charge the patient. In fact, you will make more profit in absolute terms, because we both know that your increased markup on the more expensive prosthesis will just be money in the bank."

There was silence on the phone. I followed up with a few comments to further soothe them about Hendricks, then left the call to return to the OR. But my instincts told me the conversation was far from over.

As I scrubbed prior to entering the OR where Patrick was working on Randell's arm, I shook off the call and instead reviewed the challenges of this case. The most important issue was whether we could separate the radial nerve from the cancer without damaging the nerve and without leaving cancer cells behind. I expected that Patrick would have already divided the blood supply to the shoulder and the top end of the arm bone.

I had instructed him to open and divide the shoulder joint to allow us to lift the arm bone up away from the joint and identify the radial nerve behind the bone. This was the way I had always performed the operation, and Patrick had seen me do it before.

Therefore, I was surprised when I entered the room drying my hands, and saw that the shoulder was still intact. Instead of doing what I had instructed, Patrick was working at the opposite end of the bone, several inches above the elbow.

"Patrick, for God's sake. What are you doing down there at the elbow? Why haven't you separated the shoulder?"

"Just trying something different, boss. The nerve seems to be separating from the bone nicely. I thought that we could divide the bone at the opposite end above the elbow first, and lift it up with the shoulder intact, providing a fulcrum. I have a feeling that may provide us with better visualization of the nerve."

I grunted in disbelief. "This had better work. You know how I do this operation, and I always divide the shoulder joint first. I don't like voyages of discovery in my OR!"

Patrick nodded, seemingly unperturbed, and worked down to the surface of the arm bone below where the cancer sat, separating and dividing muscles. Placing retractors around the bone to protect normal tissues, he accepted a saw from the nurse and divided the bone at the planned level about eight inches below the shoulder joint. Patrick then applied a bone clamp to the cut end of the bone to lift it forward and offered me the dissecting scissors.

I snorted. "No, you've come this far. Keep going, but I am certainly not convinced this is going to work."

I started changing my mind when the radial nerve fell away from the elevated bone as Patrick dissected behind the humerus. As we approached the spot where the cancer had pushed through the back of the humerus, I warned him, "Slow down here, Patrick. I don't want to take a risk with the kid's life by spilling cancer cells."

I put my hand on his for emphasis. "You know how delicate the membrane is that separates the cancer from the nerve. If you puncture that membrane and cancer cells spill out through the hole, the damage is done—there's nothing you can do. You have probably killed the kid. I would rather give up the nerve."

Patrick nodded. "If you don't mind, I am going to use a knife on the nerve, boss."

"Well, that's unusual, Patrick—but this whole operation is damned unusual."

We were both now visualizing the nerve through the magnifying part of the surgical glasses that we always used. Using a small, sharp knife, Patrick started to divide the sheath that bound the nerve together, exposing the tiny wire-like fibers of nerve tissue within. Having divided the tissue that separated and bundled together the individual wires, he painstakingly pulled each nerve fiber off the cancer surface.

Patrick left the deep surface of the nerve sheath intact on the cancer as a membrane barrier to cancer cells spilling. As he lifted the final nerve fibers up while carefully keeping the cancer containing membrane intact, I slowly elevated the cut end of the bone, relying on the intact shoulder joint as a fulcrum just as Patrick had planned. I knew that most of my colleagues around the world did this operation by dividing the shoulder first, but this seemed like a good modification to our usual technique.

"Well, I'll be damned," I couldn't help but exult as Patrick freed the last millimeter of nerve from the tumor. "If that nerve works postop after all that dissection, this will be a fabulous outcome."

The operation concluded smoothly from there. Working effectively together, we divided the humerus from the shoulder joint and sent the entire specimen to the pathology lab for examination. I went out with the specimen to ensure that the cancer was completely removed. The pathologists assured me after looking at some specimens that no cancer cells had been spilled.

Meanwhile, Patrick brought the bone transplant onto the surgical field and prepared it for implantation, trimming its length and placing sutures through the joint capsule and tendons to attach it to the shoulder joint.

I returned to the room. "It's good, Patrick. The specimen is entirely free of cancer at the closest margin. Now, let's just hope that the damn nerve works." I scrubbed back into the case and we completed the reconstruction of the arm quickly.

Twenty-five minutes later, that very same arm shot up. The anesthetist was pulling the tube from Randell's wind pipe when Randell suddenly woke. He reached up to try and take the tube out himself. I was pleased to see that his left hand grabbed at the tube as quickly as his right hand.

I walked over to his bedside and pushed down on the hand, which resisted with full strength. "Fantastic! He's got full strength." I turned to Patrick, who was entering data into the computer. "You beat the hell out of that nerve getting it off the cancer, but it is working fine. I'm going to speak to the parents and give them the good news. Meet me in my office when you're done here."

Half an hour later, I heard Patrick outside at Justine's desk.

"What's up? The boss told me to meet him here."

"Yeah, he told me to pour you a coffee. He's never asked me to get a fellow a coffee. What do you take?"

"Just black—thanks, Justine." He knocked at my door. I don't think he had any idea of how his life was about to change.

Chapter 23

Mr. James Bailey
18 months later

I blame myself. I'd had no idea how sick Brianna was. Seeing the look on the emergency room doctor's face as he listened to her chest with his stethoscope, I felt my heart sinking. Something was clearly worse than I'd expected.

Thirty minutes later, the same doctor returned to the examination room where Brianna and I sat. The doc looked worried as he explained to us that Brianna's chest X-ray showed multiple areas of cancer in her lungs. I was stunned.

How could my beautiful daughter have cancer? was the first thought in my mind as the doctor explained that she would need to be admitted to hospital for tests. We would fight it together, of course. I'd do anything. Imani would too. But how would we do it without any health insurance?

Imani and I were born and raised here in Gary. My dad left when I was still a baby, and my mom did her damn best to bring up two boys. But school didn't really work for me or Imani, the love of my life since high school. Times were real tough when we started looking for work. We could never get the kinds of jobs that offered health benefits.

I had worked pretty steadily in construction for more than twenty years, but always irregular and for small companies. Imani worked as a waitress. Ironically, our family income exceeded the amount required to qualify for Indiana's Medicaid program. Any child health insurance Brianna received had ended on her nineteenth birthday.

A couple of years ago, things would've been different. In 2015, I felt for the first time that this country cared about me and my family when we were able to register for healthcare benefits. After Obamacare kicked in, for the first time in our lives, we could each go see a doctor and be treated like real patients, not welfare cases. I got a checkup and learned that I had high blood pressure. A nurse explained the risks I was facing with strokes and heart attacks. Imani had her first ever Pap smear and mammogram. Brianna would be covered through college.

Our security didn't last long. As Congress began trying to get rid of Obamacare, most insurance companies stopped offering insurance to folks in downtown Gary. The remaining companies increased the price of coverage beyond what Imani and I could afford. And they didn't cover the medical group that served our community. It was confusing and frustrating, and our coverage ran out.

So, when Brianna complained of knee pain six months later, we had no regular doctor to visit and no insurance. We spent almost eight hours waiting in the emergency department of the hospital before seeing a nurse who told us the pain was tendonitis. "Take an aspirin," he told Brianna, shrugging. "And exercise."

Six weeks later, Brianna started coughing and Imani thought that she had maybe lost weight. I returned to the emergency room with Brianna. And that's where we got the unreal news that my baby had cancer. And it wasn't just in her lungs. The medical team at the hospital discovered that Brianna's knee pain was caused by bone cancer. The cancer had spread through the blood stream from her knee to her lungs.

Cancer specialists at the hospital told us that our only chance was to start chemotherapy and hope that the cancers would shrink.

We already owed the doctors and hospital a lot of money. We took out a home loan and cashed in all our savings to start a payment plan that would require us to pay all our future savings to the hospital for years to come. But we were going to make damn sure that our daughter would get whatever treatment she needed.

Chapter 24

Dr. Albert Gershwyn
April 23

"Come on in, Patrick," I said. "Have a seat."

As Patrick sank into one of the armchairs, Justine appeared with his coffee and another for me.

"Since when do I get coffee for the fellows?" she asked.

"Since the fellow started operating like this guy does."

Justine raised her eyebrows and punched Patrick in the shoulder before she stepped back out.

As the door closed, I savored a sip of the rich, dark roast that Justine kept in the office for me and turned my attention to Patrick.

"That was a hell of a case that you did today, kid. Usually I am pissed when the fellow changes the way we are doing a case without discussion, but that worked out so well it's hard for me to complain."

Patrick simply nodded his head and examined his shoes.

I continued to watch him closely. "Where did you learn to operate like that?"

He looked up. "Not sure exactly, boss. I tended to watch lots of surgical videos in training because we did not have much direct instruction in Solway. We were often on our own. But that case today—well, there are no videos that describe what we did today. I guess that it's just a matter of thinking it through and responding to what seemed the best way to do it at the time."

"What are you planning to do when you are finished here, Patrick?"

He shrugged. "I suppose I'll try and find something around Solway. It's where I grew up and where my mother still lives."

"Well, Justine tells me that I need a partner, and I think you may be the guy. I am fifty-seven. I have another fifteen years or so in this practice, but it would be terrific to have a younger partner that I can rely on to take care of some of the more difficult cases. This is a young man's game, and I am not getting any younger.

"To be honest, kid, I have had junior partners in the past and things haven't worked out well. Supposedly I am too demanding, disrespectful, unwilling to allow my partner to grow his own reputation. So, three of my former partners have left within eighteen months. But I have a feeling you would be difficult to scare off, Patrick."

I have to say the kid had a pretty good poker face. He was listening carefully, but not showing much in return. "What I am suggesting is that you plan on staying here after your fellowship ends and that we become partners. We'll get you a lawyer and they can work out the financial details. You will be hired as an Assistant Professor at the university.

"We would work together in research. You are already started in the work at Sumner, and you could take that IGF Synchro Therapy work as your own. I would, of course, help with fundraising, but you would be the lead on all reports and publications. And if Synchro Therapy works, we'll need two more surgeons to keep up with the referrals."

I could see Patrick reflecting. He had obviously been a little out of place at this hospital when he'd first arrived. Most of the young docs who worked here came from a different kind of background, education, and training than Patrick had received. He'd probably originally felt like a bit of an impostor here. I knew those feelings.

When I'd first come to Boston, appointed as Chief and Chair based on my research and clinical innovation, I'd felt like the selection committee had made a mistake. It was tough for me to feel comfortable to be myself for the first couple of years.

Everyone here was so smooth, especially when they were sticking a knife in my back. But I'd learned once again that hard work and determination generally led to success.

I'd also learned that you could never let them see you sweat. I figured out that if you didn't know what you were doing, you could usually act confident and get away with it. And this was probably a lesson that I would end up teaching to Patrick.

"Boss, this is incredibly generous of you, and I appreciate your offer very much," he finally said. "I might suggest that you think about it and decide in a few months whether you truly want to make me an offer. I am here for at least another eight months in any case, and there really isn't any rush, is there?"

"Patrick," I said, taking a sip of my coffee, "you will understand soon enough that when you are in a job like mine, you need to be constantly planning two years down the road. I could not believe it when that guy from Chicago changed his mind on the fellowship. I have a feeling that fate intervened that weekend to introduce us. But I cannot rely on getting a competent fellow year after year.

"I need someone here full time that I can absolutely rely on, and I think you are the man. If you want to wait a few weeks to think over my offer, that's okay, I guess. But you know that I will start to get royally pissed off if you don't accept."

I smiled as I made that comment, but Patrick knew I was serious. He also knew that if he were to delay accepting my offer, or turned it down, then the rest of his fellowship year would be far less rewarding and pleasant. Patrick would not want to be on my bad side.

But really, I thought, putting down my mug, *this is not an issue*. I had a feeling that despite my demands, Patrick enjoyed working here. My former partners who had left after a short time were highly entitled and could not tolerate the pressure that I felt to perform. Patrick was different.

"Well, boss, if you are sure that you are ready to make an offer, I am delighted to accept it. Nothing would give me more honor and excitement than to be your partner."

I smiled. He was smart, after all.

"If it's all the same to you," he went on, "I will get a lawyer to help work on a contract. Now, I have to run over to Sumner. Philbert has gone through three cycles of Synchro Therapy, and I need to get over to speak to his owners and start surgery."

"Well, okay, Dr. Maloney," I said, standing up. "Let's shake on the offer. We can get you a lawyer." I saw Patrick shaking his head no. "Okay, you stubborn bugger—we will leave it up to you to get a lawyer. And in the meantime, Justine and the hospital lawyers will start drawing up a contract. I have to tell you; I'm delighted about this."

Patrick reached across the desk and shook my hand. "Not half as happy as I am," he said. "Your confidence means everything to me. I will not let you down."

As he left the office, I saw Justine lift her hands and ask, "Sooo…?"

Patrick gave her a discreet thumbs-up sign, and Justine pantomimed rapturous applause. Patrick fist-bumped her and then was out the door.

Chapter 25

Dr. Patrick Maloney
April 23

*A*s I pulled out of my garage in my beaten-up Subaru, I wondered whether I would be able to negotiate an advance with the hospital so I could buy a new car. Things were definitely changing.

I turned onto the road and dialed Meredith's number. She picked up immediately and I could hear voices around her.

"You're not alone, huh?"

"No. I wish I was, though," she whispered.

"Can I see you tonight? I have something I need to discuss with you."

"There's lots I want to discuss with you too. Are you going to Sumner?"

"I'm on my way there now. Can I call when I'm leaving and come over to your place? Or would you rather meet in a restaurant or something?"

"There is only one place I want to see you," she said. "I need to go now. People are going to wonder why I'm whispering. Call me when you're leaving the vet hospital."

I hung up and felt a rush of what I can only describe as longing wash over me. I had never felt that before. I would need to make sure that I didn't rush Philbert's surgery because I couldn't wait to see Meredith.

I dialed Dr. Benedict next. She was excited for her first surgical case of an osteosarcoma in a dog. It was also our first Synchro Therapy trial, and I needed to focus on that for the next few hours. Today was a big day.

"Kate, did the prostheses arrive from the company?" I asked when she picked up. "I asked them to send extra-small, small, and medium. Did they all get there?"

"All here, Patrick. We are all set to go. And I hope you don't mind, but I told the guys from CellGrow that their president could come into the OR to see the first operation. They've been great in getting us various doses of IGF and IGF-Receptor blocker to use in our treatments."

"For sure, Kate. If you want them there, it is your show. I'm the visiting surgeon, remember?"

"Yeah, but you're the operator, and I just wanted to make sure it wasn't distracting to have someone looking over your shoulder."

"Not to worry. When you work with my boss, you get accustomed to someone growling over your shoulder. The CellGrow guy won't bother me. Let's just hope at the end of the day that everything turns out well for Philbert."

At Sumner, I changed into greens and went to the pre-op area, where Philbert's owners were waiting with their sedated pet. I went through the usual discussion about potential risks and benefits of surgery and asked the owners to sign a consent form. They readily signed, thanking Kate and me for our generosity in looking after Philbert without charge.

I headed into the OR area and checked on the setup with Dr. Kate and the nurses. Kate introduced me to a smaller man.

"Patrick, this is Rod Katzner," she said. "He's the CEO of CellGrow. Rod, Patrick is the surgeon from the hospital who will be doing the surgery for the Synchro Therapy program."

"Nice to meet you, Patrick," he said with a mid-western accent, shaking my hand. "We're really excited about this project. I cannot wait to see what Philbert's cancer looks like after three rounds of Synchro Therapy."

"Thanks, Rod," I said, returning his grin. "I understand from Dr. Kate that this has been a huge amount of work for your company."

"Yeah," he said, with a slow, emphatic nod. "We've tried a lot of different formulations of IGF-Receptor blockers to starve tumors. We think we're close to the ideal combination of the blocker and the IGF compound for Synchro Therapy to work. Philbert is the first one to receive it, and we can't wait to see what the effect looks like."

Our team prepped Philbert's leg and draped it off in a sterile field. I had promised to teach Kate how to do the surgery, and it turned out to be a mutual learning experience, because the dog anatomy was unfamiliar to me and second nature to Kate. We quickly isolated the cancer from the surrounding structures, and before two hours had passed, Kate and I had removed our first dog osteosarcoma.

We agreed that Kate would take the cancer specimen out to the pathology suite so the pathologists could figure out how much damage Synchro Therapy had caused in the cancer.

I stayed in the OR to prepare the bones for insertion of the prosthesis. I had inserted the first component into the thigh bone when Kate returned to the OR with Rod, both of them virtually vibrating with excitement. And right behind them, Roland Barnes stepped in as well. I hadn't realized he'd be joining us too. He told me he'd wanted to see the first case of Synchro Therapy and arrived at the OR just in time to look at the pathology specimen with Dr. Benedict and Katzner. I put down my tools and waited for someone to deliver the news.

Chapter 26

Roland Barnes, PhD
April 23

I was running late and knew I'd miss the surgery. But luckily, I arrived just in time to find Rod Katzner, Dr. Benedict, and one of the pathologists examining the osteosarcoma specimen outside the OR. The pathologist literally needed to divide the bone with a table saw that they kept nearby for bone work. There was no evidence of fleshy cancer tissue anywhere in the specimen.

As we headed into the OR, Dr. Benedict led the way. "Patrick, you won't believe it," she said, her face flushed. "There is no cancer as far as we can see. The entire specimen is just a hugely calcified bone. I think that the Synchro Therapy really worked. We will obviously need to wait for pathology specimens to be sure if there is any microscopic living cancer, but right now, it looks like the cancer has been extensively killed."

Rod was also obviously thrilled by what he had seen. IGF and IGF-Receptor were natural compounds and could not be patented. However, CellGrow had developed a variety of receptor inhibitors and had patented the resultant compounds as drugs. They had also modified the IGF molecule to increase its effect on stimulating cancer cell division. The company would be able to sell these patented drugs at a premium price if we could prove that Synchro Therapy worked in dogs and, eventually, in humans.

Five years ago, no company would have staked its future on developing a better therapy for osteosarcoma, which is a rare disease in humans. However, the federal drug regulator was now emphasizing quick approval of drugs for rare diseases, which made creating treatments for bone cancer potentially very lucrative. Plus, other cancers were also potentially dependent on IGF, and this list included more common cancers such as breast cancer. If Synchro Therapy worked, it would create a market value of hundreds of millions for CellGrow. Katzner and his colleagues who had invested everything to keep the company alive during lean times would become wealthy men.

Things have really changed, I thought—and not just because of this new interest in rare diseases. In the old days, pharmaceutical companies had research labs, scientists, and big research budgets. Today, most of the big companies were really investment firms associated with marketing and distribution departments. The big pharma scientists didn't *do* science; they were more like scientific investment bankers. They waited for other scientists in smaller companies like CellGrow to do the crucial early experiments that determined whether a product might work in human trials. Then, they made recommendations for where their big pharma companies should invest.

This meant that over the years, scientists like Rod Katzner who worked in small biotech firms had gradually changed their goals. Rather than dreaming about developing a blockbuster drug, the biotech operators dreamed of a buyout from one of the major pharma companies.

A year ago, Rod Katzner's CellGrow was failing. The company's first opportunity came three years ago, when a well-known venture capital fund agreed to provide four million dollars annually for four years. This seemed like a lot of money at the time, but when the yearly expenses of paying for lab and animal research added up, there was no money left over for paying Rod and his associates, who were basically working for nothing hoping to benefit from the eventual sale of their ideas.

Their first idea in human studies failed miserably. Rod knew that many human cancers produced IGF-Receptor and suggested blocking the receptor with a specialized antibody would work in patients with advanced cancers. Rod's idea worked in cancer cells in the lab, as well as in human cancers transplanted to mice. Encouraged by these results, the venture capitalists agreed to fund a study in human patients, whose cancers produced high levels of IGF-Receptor. These patients had exhausted other forms of treatments. This was their last resort.

This kind of trial in patients with a faint hope of a cure was called a Phase I trial and was designed to test two things: whether the drug was toxic to humans and whether it impacted cancer growth. Albert Gershwyn had helped to sponsor this trial at the hospital, since many of his patients had advanced cancers with high levels of IGF-Receptor. One of Rod's young partners, Andrei Kovalov, had led the study for CellGrow.

The one good outcome of this Phase I trial was that the IGF-Receptor antibody was safe and had no evidence of toxicity in humans. Unfortunately, none of the patients receiving the blocking drug showed any sign of cancer shrinkage or clinical improvement.

At this point, Rod recognized that he was going to go bankrupt unless he developed a new strategy very quickly. His venture capital funder was already talking about stopping any future funding.

I had been very interested in Rod's work and was disappointed when the IGF-Receptor antibody study failed. I helped him look at a number of options for a possible next step. And one afternoon, we had our eureka moment. We knew that dog osteosarcoma was similar to human disease and had a high frequency for IGF dependence. We would use CellGrow's drug to suppress IGF-Receptor for a fairly short period of time, starving the cancer cells of their IGF stimulus. We would then use CellGrow's IGF to aggressively stimulate the cancer after stopping the blocking antibody. And along with massive IGF treatment, we would start simultaneous chemotherapy. And from there, Synchro Therapy was born.

Rod convinced the venture capitalist that this was worthy of funding for another year while he perfected the compounds. And then, we took the idea to Albert and Dr. Nabers, the chief vet at Sumner. The three of us met with Rod to plan Synchro Therapy trials in dogs more than a year ago. It took that long to get the funding in place.

Rod pleaded with his venture capitalist for one more injection of funds. And Gershwyn agreed to commit some of his fundraising potential to support this Synchro Therapy program through grants and philanthropy.

As the funding came together, we realized that our other need was for a talented surgeon who would be willing to work on dog patients and test Synchro Therapy. With Patrick Maloney's arrival, everything seemed to be coming together. And I understood that Albert was considering bringing Maloney on board permanently as a junior partner, so we knew this surgeon would be sticking around.

We had a long way to go, but it felt like we were headed in the right direction. I knew that analysis of dog biopsies in my lab had already identified three more dogs with IGF positive bone cancers who were starting on Synchro Therapy. If we could prove Synchro Therapy worked, CellGrow would be worth a lot of money. It would likely get bought out by a big pharmaceutical company. And since osteosarcoma occurred in young people, a pharma company could charge hundreds of thousands of dollars for Synchro Therapy. No insurance company could refuse to pay for a life-saving drug in a teenager.

Rod and I thanked Dr. Benedict and Patrick, who were finishing up the implantation of the tumor replacing artificial knee joint for Philbert. I announced that we were going for a drink and left them to their work.

"Not to get too ahead of ourselves, Rod," I said as I walked my friend out to the parking lot, "but you should start thinking about how we're going to raise pharma interest in Synchro Therapy."

"We'll see," said Rod carefully, trying to hide his grin. "You and I should obviously follow the next few cases closely. But if they look as good as Philbert's, I think I'm going to be buying a few more drinks."

Chapter 27

Dr. Patrick Maloney
April 23 & 24

*I*finished with Philbert's surgery at 5:45, but by the time I had spoken to the pet's owners and discussed post-operative care with Kate, it was 6:45. I was feeling almost light-headed. Two great surgeries and a new job offer? What a day.

As soon as I started my car, I dialed Meredith. She picked up immediately, but sounded disappointed. "Patrick, I so want to see you this evening. But Hendricks is just back from New York and wants to review some recent results for the analysts that need to be sent on the weekend. He called a dinner meeting for this evening that will start at 7 and probably go on until 9:30. I called my concierge and he will let you in if you don't mind waiting for me. There is no food in the place, but there are several restaurants and take-out places in my neighborhood. I promise to be no later than 10:15. And I also promise that it will be worth the wait. What do you think?"

"Yes."

"You are a doll. Thanks for understanding. You may need a nap. You were up pretty late last night."

"Take your time, Meredith. This project is so important to you and there's no reason you shouldn't enjoy the meeting. I will grab a burger and beer and see you when you get home."

"Listen, the meeting is starting up soon and I need to grab some data. I will confirm with the concierge that you are coming up and that you will use visitors' parking...overnight, I hope."

The last aspect was important to me. I was absolutely beat, and it would be a real luxury to park in Meredith's visitors' lot rather than go back to my own space and walk the couple of miles between our apartments. Two miles and millions of dollars from my tiny bachelor apartment behind the hospital.

Meredith lived in the center of the coveted Back Bay district at the foot of historic Beacon Hill. On the rare instances that I took a leisurely stroll in Boston, this was my favorite route, going through early American history over the hill that was one of the early landmarks of our country. The first homes on Beacon Hill dated to 1625. Today, the area is known for its Federal row houses, gaslit streets, and cobblestone sidewalks. The Hill is quite compact, but it remains one of the most desirable parts of Boston, close to the main hospitals, the universities, and the financial district.

Wandering over Beacon Hill past the landmark Massachusetts State House with its famous gold dome, I would reflect on how many well-known Americans, from Oliver Wendell Holmes to Robert Frost, had lived on the Hill. My usual route led me down the slope of the Hill to the Boston Common and Boston Public Garden. On a warm day, I could sit on a bench and watch the swan boats paddling around the Public Garden ponds with excited children running from the swan boats to the "Make Way for Ducklings" statues.

To the west of the public garden, I would wander onto Commonwealth Avenue—a stately boulevard that ran north-east to south-west and separated the Back Bay residential area from the shopping and restaurants of Newbury Street.

Meredith's apartment was in a classic brownstone that had undergone major updating. I had picked up a burger, onion rings, and a couple of beers, and the smell of the paper bag gave away its contents to the concierge on the security desk.

"Dr. Maloney, I presume?" the concierge asked as I entered. I nodded and handed him my driver's license. "Smells good, Doc," he said as he checked the card. "I can buzz you into Dr. McClintock's apartment from here if you just knock when you go up. She mentioned that you knew which apartment she is in."

Upstairs, I rapped once on the door and a buzzer sounded, letting me in. Feeling a bit like an interloper, I initially restricted my exploration to Meredith's advice to have a bite. I entered the large, modern kitchen and was impressed by the matching crockery. I found a plate and a glass in her sophisticated glass-enclosed cupboards and returned to the dining room, where I ate my meal in hungry silence.

And then, my curiosity overcame me. I went through the rest of the apartment, which I had not really focused on the last time I was here. It was a large three-bedroom apartment with the front bedroom overlooking Marlborough converted to a study with a broad set of windows that would provide considerable natural light during the day. The two full bathrooms were modern, and I remembered showering in a large glass-enclosed tropical stall prior to going to work that morning.

I returned to the living room and sat down on the couch, again admiring the combined living/dining arrangement artfully separated by a beautiful custom bookshelf. I didn't know that much about Meredith as of yet. But it was very clear from her apartment that she was a woman of some means.

I was feeling full and somewhat sleepy after consuming the contents of my paper bag and two bottles of Sam Adams beer. I removed my shoes and lay back on Meredith's comfortable couch. I picked up a *New Yorker* off the coffee table, adjusted the pillow behind my neck, and started to read about the week. I think I must have been asleep within seconds.

Again, it was her smell that first aroused me. She had come home, showered, and was wearing a sheer something that allowed me to feel her nipples on my lips as she lowered her breasts onto my face to wake me. I felt totally grubby and sleepy. I had not showered, and this stunning woman was leaning over me with gardenia smells floating around my weary head.

I thought that I should take a shower—and then it did not matter any longer as she removed my clothes and eliminated any thoughts of a shower or fatigue.

* * *

The wonderful thing about Saturday morning as a surgical fellow was that it was actually different from the rest of the week. For the past three years in surgical training, my Saturday had been the same as any other day: Get up for 6:00 a.m. rounds and then head to the OR for any scheduled cases that had been cancelled or delayed during the week, and any new emergency cases. Sunday rounds started at 7:00 a.m. and only emergency cases went to the operating room. That one extra hour of sleep on Sunday morning was luxury. But more often than not, I would have been operating until the early hours of Sunday morning looking after weekend trauma, so the Sunday morning extra sleep was survival more than restoration.

This Saturday morning was glorious. To this point, I had probably run at least 300 miles around the Charles Basin with Meredith, generally chatting about work, bones, and the hospital as we ran. Now, I had spent two astonishing nights with her.

The first had been adventuresome and athletic, and the night seemed to stretch hours longer than usual. But last night, it had been somehow silky and languorous, with soft sleep separating episodes of pretty wild intimacy.

And now, it was morning. I did not need to get up to go to work or anywhere else, and this astounding woman was lying beside me breathing softly. I moved carefully to avoid waking her, fearful that the moment would disappear. Her brown hair had fallen over her eyes, and I pulled it back to see her face better. And as I lay there looking at her, I had to reflect on the crazy things that were happening to my life.

Thirty-six hours ago, Meredith was my running partner and we were meeting for a baseball game in the evening. Now, I had spent two nights in her bed and was allowed into her apartment in her absence.

A few days ago, I was a misfit fellow with an undistinguished past and uncertain future. Now, I'd been offered the opportunity to work as partner to one of America's premier surgeons.

And my activity at both the hospital and Sumner would provide me with remarkable clinical and research opportunities. For someone who had progressed only by dint of extremely diligent work, fate suddenly seemed to be offering a helping hand and I was not exactly sure how to respond to the good fortune.

But I was certain of one thing, and that was the passion and care that I felt for the woman lying beside me. I wanted to carefully wrap her in her soft duvet and protect her from any of life's imaginable burdens. I knew this emotion reflected considerable chauvinism. Meredith was extremely capable and needed no protection from me or anyone else. However, it was a very real feeling that came from somewhere deep inside me.

Meredith was successful in a highly competitive, masculine world. I certainly respected and appreciated her leadership in her fascinating and relevant work. But as much as I respected her accomplishments, I was even more captivated by her softness and femininity. That night walking to and from the ballgame, I had felt her melting into me. This inspired an overwhelming urge to surround and hold her.

I had been a little surprised by her willingness to accept me into her bed at this point of our relationship. I was aware that the morning might bring a sense of vulnerability, and was determined to maintain a mood of respect and consideration.

Meredith stirred and opened her eyes, covered by a thicket of lustrous hair. "Oh, Patrick, I have been very wicked the last couple of nights, haven't I?"

I lay beside her with our eyes locked, inches apart. "I suppose that I should admit I fed you an enchanted hot dog at the ballgame and this sorcery will wear off for the princess in minutes."

She kissed me deeply. "Then, it's time for another hot dog, you wicked prince," she said, and the enchantment continued.

As I wandered into the kitchen with a towel wrapped around my waist after finally showering, Meredith was draped in an impossibly thick robe and was scrambling eggs while coffee dripped.

I wrapped my arms around her from behind and whispered, "I have so much to tell you this morning. I want to tell you a lifetime of feeling to fill this reservoir you are creating in me."

Meredith raised an eyebrow. "I am not sure what you mean, but it sounds sort of serious for a Saturday morning."

I nodded, "Yeah, it's serious—but let's just follow it and see where it goes. Until yesterday, I had no future to speak of. I come from a little town. My dad died when I was young, my little sister died shortly thereafter and that almost killed my poor mum, who I haven't seen in four months and must see next weekend.

"I came to Boston as a result of someone else's mistake, and I am totally out of place here. It's Saturday morning and you have an impostor in your kitchen."

"Well, you know, I get down to the operating room quite a bit and I know the nurses and team in the OR pretty well. And Shanice Brown is one of my best friends." She handed me two mugs so I could pour the coffee. "I had a bad experience with a doctor from the OR eighteen months ago, and although no one warned me off, they did not say anything positive about him either. Later, I learned that he was an arrogant son of a bitch, and he turned out to be a lying, deceitful asshole.

"But the kids in the OR tell me something different about you. They tell me you are polite and respectful and helpful as hell. They also tell me that you are the best surgeon the hospital has ever seen as a fellow, and despite that, you're *not* an arrogant SOB.

"They also say that you entirely piss off the Ivy League boys who come here for fellowships to set up their seven-figure careers, because they know that they will never be as good as you, and you seem oblivious to their concerns." She paused. "And what did you mean that until yesterday you had no future to speak of? What happened yesterday?"

I told her about Gershwyn's offer, and Meredith looked intrigued. "Well, perhaps Professor Gershwyn ate some of that enchanted hot dog as well." She turned in my arms and wrapped her arms around my neck. "I kinda like the idea of you hanging around here for a few years."

"Meredith, I told you everything you need to know about me in two easy sentences," I said as we carried our breakfast and coffee to the kitchen counter. "Where does someone as smart and stunning as you come from?"

"The short version," she sighed, easing into her chair, "is a ridiculously advantaged country club childhood in Weston. It was idyllic until my mother died of an aneurysm when I was fourteen. Dad was very successful in business up to that time. He ran an investment book in Weston and had done really well for himself and his clients. When mum died, he was devastated and stopped expanding his business so he could be there for my sister Julie and me."

"You seem close with your dad," I said.

She nodded thoughtfully. "Julie married her local sweetheart at twenty-two, and they have two kids and live near Dad in Wellesley. Julie's husband Christopher is an investment guy, and now that we have both left home, Dad has become more professionally active and helped Christopher build his book. Dad seems to be much in demand for investment advice from both private investors and businesses. In fact, he's been helping Dr. Hendricks with structuring the investment he needs for the *super-B.I.G.* prosthesis."

She paused, and her eyes noticeably softened as she continued talking about her dad. "Dad and I always had a thing together. Julie wanted a family and I wanted a career, and Dad loved that one of his girls was going to be a 'worker,' as he called it. He wanted me to do finance, go to Wharton and start off as a banker, but I had something different in mind. My life changed when I got into MIT and was exposed to biomechanical engineering. And getting a chance to do my PhD and coming to Hendricks' lab is exactly what I dreamed of in undergrad."

By now, I was consciously restraining myself from wolfing down the fluffy eggs that Meredith had prepared. I hadn't eaten anything except the burgers in the past twenty-four hours and was ravenous. Meredith looked at me suspiciously and got up. "I think the boy is hungry. Maybe I'll scramble another helping of eggs, huh, Patrick?"

I smiled guiltily and nodded.

After breakfast, we wandered down Marlborough to the Public Gardens and sat in the sun chatting about just nothing for ninety minutes. I eventually needed to return to the hospital to check on Randell and call Kate to meet and check on Philbert. We walked back to Meredith's apartment to pick up my sweater, and made plans to meet later in the afternoon at the Bandstand for a run.

Back up in her apartment, she excused herself for a minute and disappeared into the back. As I waited for her, I noticed her briefcase open on the dining room table. One of the documents sticking out bore the logo of CellGrow, the same company doing Synchro Therapy at Sumner. I began to wonder what CellGrow had to do with Meredith's work. And then, thoughts of CellGrow were eliminated when Meredith came up behind me and began kissing my neck. I turned to meet her, and the starting time for our run was moved back another ninety minutes into the afternoon.

Chapter 28

Meredith McClintock, PhD
April 24

*W*e met in the afternoon in front of the Hatch Bandshell across Storrow Drive. We met casually, each seeing each other from a distance and approaching almost shyly. We touched hands, but did not embrace. I think we both felt that our earlier closeness needed to be regained slowly.

I began to stretch; Patrick had jogged up along the Esplanade and was already warm. He broke the ice, again touching my hands and then gently taking both my hands in his.

"Meredith, forgive me if this is too much too soon. But any time I have been with someone for a day or two, I prefer to get some space—to slow down the intensity, to retreat.

"I went to the hospital to see my patient, went to Sumner to see Philbert, went back to my apartment to change, and ran over here. And the whole time, I was aching for you and missing you. Apologies if I am coming on too strong, but this is very different for me."

I looked down at his hands holding mine. "I told you about the guy that hurt me so badly—the guy that went back to California? I'm afraid of doing that again. I promised myself that I would not date another orthopod from the hospital, and here I am with another orthopedic fellow eighteen months later. I feel something different too. I am just afraid of being hurt and humiliated again."

"Meredith, I would run screaming naked back and forth across Storrow Drive at rush hour rather than hurt you. I just feel so damn protective of you. It's such a powerful feeling. Maybe it has something to do with punching that guy out when we first met? Maybe I have got a white knight syndrome or something."

I was pleased to see that he said that with a smile. But then, he put his arms out and I could not resist curling into his chest as he gently wrapped me into him. It just felt so good to be hugged like that. There was no sense of belittlement. It just felt like an attachment that I needed.

Patrick gently released me to look down at my face. "Hey, next weekend I just have to go to see my mum back in Solway Mills. Would you consider keeping me company?"

"Are you asking me to go home with you to meet your mother?"

"I guess that sounds pretty lame, huh? Yeah, if I want you to meet my mum, that means that I can't wanna hurt you, right?"

I folded even more close and looked up, nodding. "So, should we run?"

He nodded. "Yeah, but let's not motor—I want to tell you what's going on in my life. Things are happening so quickly! And I want to ask you about CellGrow. I saw their letterhead in your briefcase. That's the company that is engaged with us on a new approach to cancer therapy at Sumner."

We started running counterclockwise around the river from the Bandshell along the Esplanade farthest from the road, where it was cooler and quieter. As a newcomer to Boston, Patrick was delighted with the little footbridges that connected man-made islands in the Charles to the mainland along the Esplanade. It was beginning to feel like summer, and running that close to the water was a refreshing antidote to asphalt fever.

Patrick explained that CellGrow was working with Gershwyn on cancer chemotherapy in dogs at Sumner Hospital and asked me what their connection was with my lab.

"Patrick, when I think about it, this all makes sense. Andrei Kovalov is the guy who runs the biology part of Hendricks' lab and designs the IGF biolayer we are testing on the dog B.I.G. hip replacement. Wait a minute…I can't really talk to you about that yet." I stopped, but then remembered that hundreds if not thousands of investors knew about the *super-B.I.G.*

"Oh well, it's going to be public three weeks from now anyway. I just won't tell you enough that I have to kill you, okay, Dr. Maloney?"

He mimed zipping his lips shut. I went on. "Andrei is an okay guy, I guess—although pretty intense for my liking, to be honest. He was working for CellGrow on a Phase I trial with Gershwyn and others at the hospital that apparently was a real failure. While that trial was running, he pitched this biolayer idea to Hendricks, who thought that it was a bit crazy at first. Hendricks staked him for six months' work in the lab, and Andrei developed the biolayer and implanted it in a few dogs, and it just showed amazing results.

"That's when I was just finishing getting my testing protocol up and running with the prototype cutting equipment. Some of the earliest cases we did came from biolayer dogs, and you could see immediately that they were much, much better than any other implant we had ever tested. Andrei continued to improve the biolayer by adjusting the factors, and now, we have a model that is amazing in any bone."

Patrick was obviously slowing his pace as I spoke. He had really improved his fitness over the past couple of months. "And he works for CellGrow?"

"Well, that's complicated. Apparently, he was one of a small group of scientists who started CellGrow, but he had just a small minority ownership of the company. It turns out that the work he has been doing coating hip prostheses for Hendricks uses reagents that were developed at CellGrow. Those reagents are CellGrow intellectual property. However, Kovalov developed the method for applying the agent in the biolayer, and he and Hendricks have the patent for that.

"So, we are testing a product that is incredible, and it has Hendricks' intellectual property in the mesh layer. Synvest licenses the mesh for commercial use in partnership with Hendricks and manufactures and markets the implants. Now, we are adding the CellGrow reagent and Andrei Kovalov's proprietary method for creating the biolayer. It gets complicated."

"Meredith, this feels like corporate espionage. Are you sure that you want to tell me? I was just curious about CellGrow."

"The deal is all inked now and will be announced to the markets in three weeks. I can't invest in it because I'm obviously an insider, although Hendricks has been very generous in giving us stock options. And you just need to promise me that you can keep a secret. I am pretty sure that you aren't planning to play this as an investment, right?"

"Too true, Meredith."

"Okay, Patrick, slow down a bit. You are killing me and if I am going to talk. Let's just jog."

We slowed our pace and I took a couple of minutes to catch my breath. "Hendricks is sharp and realizes that this product is fabulous, but that it's at risk because the intellectual property managed is complex and confused. So, he gets the bright idea that he will create a new company, a Newco, and that everyone will sell their intellectual property to Newco for a share of the profits.

"And since Synvest will be the largest owner of the Newco and manage it for the other owners, it was decided that Newco would be structured as a division of Synvest."

I stopped in the path. It was complicated, and I wanted to be sure I was honest with Patrick, but did not want to break confidentiality. "My dad actually helped with the corporate structuring. The structure has been shown to lots of people. There are two classes of shares. Class A shares belong to the four founders—Hendricks, Synvest, Kovalov and CellGrow, in varied proportions. And, of course, the hospital and university, who always get a share of everything.

"Class B shares are for regular investors. Fifty percent of Class B shares will go to outside investors in Newco, and fifty to the founders. The Class A shares will control corporate strategy through control of the Board. Class B are mainly for passive investors.

"Hendricks and Synvest's marketing group estimate that the *super-B.I.G.* will sell at about a $2,000 increased profit over the current B.I.G. implant, and that it is reasonable to assume that about 50 percent of the prostheses sold around the world will be *super-B.I.G.*s in the next few years. That means a new annual profit line of $800 million for Newco.

"About half of that will go to new investors, so my dad figures that collectively they should be willing to pay at least $2.5 to $2.8 billion for the 50 percent profit share. However, Hendricks is so good at pitching that I understand that we will be raising at least $3 billion.

"The reason I feel comfortable telling you about this is that Hendricks has been on what they call a 'charm show' for the last three months, traveling around to institutional investors and getting them engaged in the sale of Class B shares. So, a lot of people know about it.

"They have all signed non-disclosure agreements, but the circle is now pretty wide. And it's pretty exciting. I am happy to have a chance to talk to you about it, because I think in the end it is going to be huge for patients."

We started running again. "This sounds really incredible, Meredith. And the funny thing is that CellGrow may have another blockbuster product with Gershwyn, although it is much earlier in development. You remember that I told you that we did the first case at Sumner of a dog that had been treated with a new protocol and it looked really good? That was a protocol involving a CellGrow product."

I pulled his arm to slow him down. "Patrick, if we are going to talk, slow down!"

"I am so sorry, a thousand apologies—how's this?"

I reached up to the back of his neck and pulled his head down for a long, slow, sweaty kiss. "Maybe this will slow you down."

I started jogging again, and Patrick was left standing by the side of the track. It took him a minute or two to catch up.

"Okay, you just blanked out all my short-term memory and I can't remember a thing that you told me. When does all this excitement get to be public?"

"Well, that meeting I stayed late for last evening was the final meeting with the investment bankers and a series of institutional investors. Again, Dad helped Hendricks get it all organized. They have become pretty close over the past few months. He has helped Hendricks to meet the right people and it has worked out pretty well. We will be through the fundraising phase very soon.

"Synvest will produce the new implants, and they need to refit one of their existing factories. There is need for capital for their construction cost as well as the industrial scale up of Andrei's biofilm. We have fit out a new lab complex here in Kendall Square, and Andrei says he has worked out how to keep quality high while producing huge amounts of biofilm."

Patrick was watching his speed now, and I appreciated that. "These investment bankers and institutional investors like big pension funds got together, looked at all the data, and figure that with this product—with these early results and this connection to Hendricks and the hospital—we can probably raise a lot of money.

"That's what our meeting was about last night. We were going over data with the investment bankers, who have pretty much guaranteed that the Initial Public Offering will achieve $3 billion for Newco. The partners have hired a CEO for Newco, and he will be leading the IPO that will hit the markets in about three weeks or so.

"But the most exciting thing for me is how far the product can go. We originally thought that these hip replacements might be good for revision surgery, where the surgeon is taking a loose, failed total hip out of a patient and inserting a new component."

Patrick nodded. He knew that getting a new implant locked into a bone that had been damaged by a loose device was a long-standing challenge for orthopedic surgeons.

"You know how difficult reconstruction can be when the bone has been badly damaged by a prior implant. In dogs, the new *super-B.I.G.* prosthesis with Andrei's biofilm can achieve incredible bone ingrowth in revision surgery, even with the worst bone. The bone just regrows like magic into the B.I.G. surface.

"And in younger, very active dogs, the biofilm is so effective on the *super-B.I.G.* prosthesis that we can say it really is stronger than the original hip.

"So, Synvest thinks that if we price the hip properly, we could use the new *super-B.I.G.* prosthesis in just about everyone. And their business case is planned so that insurance companies will probably accept the price of the *super-B.I.G.* for all patients. The insurers like the idea that this hip will reduce or maybe even eliminate more expensive revision operations."

I knew this was the part that always got Dr. Hendricks excited. Doing only one hip replacement for life.

"Even if the insurance won't pay, we figure that most people will be willing to spend the extra money. And with Hendricks' name, as well as the hospital and university promoting it—well, that is about the best marketing any hip implant could get."

Patrick nodded. He knew how valuable Hendricks' name would be. "I hope you're getting your fair share of all this profit?"

"Well thanks to my dad's success and generosity over the years, I don't truly need it, Patrick. I don't really even need my paycheck—it's just a bonus for the great work I get a chance to do. But, like I say, Hendricks has been generous with stock options that vest as soon as the company lists on the stock exchange. So, I suppose that I will be a bit richer, yeah."

"Meredith, that is an amazing story! And we're both working on products from CellGrow. What does this Andrei guy use from CellGrow in his biofilm?"

"To be honest, the biology is a bit beyond me. I know that the problem Andrei solved was getting the product to stabilize in the biofilm so it would be present at the junction of the bone and the implant for more than just a few hours. The CellGrow product's main component is IGF."

Patrick slowed down. "This just gets stranger and stranger. Guess what the product is that we are developing for Synchro Therapy in dog cancers at Sumner? Well, at least one of the products is IGF."

"Patrick, this sounds so exciting. And if you accept Gershwyn's offer, you have a chance to work on this Synchro Therapy in dogs for the next couple of years and see if it could work in humans?"

Patrick nodded. "I think that the dog work is one of the most important reasons that Gershwyn offered me the partnership. He needs someone who can do the surgery in dogs to make sure the results we see at Sumner will be applicable in our patients.

"And, let's face it, working with Gershwyn in the hospital and at Sumner is going to be a pretty hectic program. But it's just fascinating to me. I did some cancer research about IGF in Solway, but never dreamed that I would ever have a chance to contribute to new knowledge like this."

He looked down. "And, to be honest, it means a lot that I'll be working on the same disease that killed my sister."

We both stopped to let other joggers pass.

"You know, Meredith, I've never really talked to anyone about this, but I just felt so helpless and inadequate when she was diagnosed and then when she didn't respond to treatment. There was just nothing that I could do. And she relied on me as her big brother—especially after Dad died. I just felt that I should have been able to help her more. And maybe now, I can do something at Sumner to pay back that debt."

"You are too hard on yourself. But I get it, I guess. I don't have a big brother, but I don't know what I'd do without my sister."

There was silence as we jogged. We had crossed over the bridge and were running west, approaching MIT. We glanced at each other, but Patrick couldn't really say anything. Discussing his sister sounded like a rare event since she had passed away, and he seemed to need some recovery time after mentioning her.

Looking at him, I could see the emotion in his eyes. "Patrick Maloney, you are kind of a special guy. I am enjoying getting to know you."

Chapter 29

Dr. Patrick Maloney
April 28

*T*he following Wednesday afternoon, I was driving over to Sumner to see Kate and Philbert. I had spent the morning in Gershwyn's office seeing new patients. It seemed that Justine knew everything about Gershwyn recruiting me. She'd had a few comments that morning about working together more closely and building plans for the future that suggested she was supportive of me joining the team. That was probably a good thing for me. I wouldn't want to be on her bad side for any reason.

That morning, Kate Benedict had texted me to say that Philbert's pathology results would be available that afternoon and to ask whether I could review the results with her. I figured that I would be finished up at the hospital by early afternoon, and texted Kate that I would meet her around 4:00 p.m.

When I arrived at Sumner, I called Kate and met her rushing down the hall near Philbert's ward. She was obviously excited to see me.

"Patrick, I couldn't resist looking at the pathology. The slides came out a couple of hours ago and I had a look at them. The pathology looks fantastic. Just about 100 percent cancer cell death and a huge amount of recalcification. The whole tumor is full of newly formed normal bone."

I knew how fortunate we were to be using the Sumner Hospital Pathology Department. Dog specimens had been referred to Sumner from across the country for years, and the department had invested in special equipment to encourage other veterinary hospitals to use their facilities.

This was especially true in bone tumors. These cancers were more common in dogs than humans, but still relatively rare. And getting the equipment and lab processes to leach the calcium out of the bone rapidly to allow the specimens to be cut and visualized under the microscope—this was a difficult pathology procedure that Sumner had perfected. Most vet clinics across the country referred their bone pathology specimens to Sumner rather than developing the expertise themselves.

Kate led the way to the pathology suite, where a multi-headed microscope was available that would allow us to look at the pathology slides together. Kate had already examined the slides, so she drove the review, placing the first of thirty or more glass rectangles on the microscope stage and focusing on the tissue section that had been removed from Philbert's leg.

"There are no living cancer cells in this slide at all. And check out that bone growth."

I twisted my eye pieces up and down until the tissue came into perfect focus. And then, I immediately recognized why Kate was so excited. In the chemical staining used to analyze pathology specimens, living cancer cells appeared like blue circles with dense large nuclei. I remembered that Philbert's cancer biopsy had been very cellular, with lots of blue osteosarcoma cells invading between seams of the residual femur bone. Now, the picture was entirely different.

Following the Synchro Therapy, all the blue cells had vanished. The absence of cells was evidence of 100 percent cell death caused by the chemotherapy. This was a sign that the chemotherapy was entirely effective and Philbert would almost certainly be cured of his cancer. Equally impressive to me was the bone healing that had resulted from the recruitment treatment.

Philbert's biopsy before treatment had showed that the cancer cells were destroying his normal bone. This was common in osteosarcoma in both dogs and humans. Occasionally, the bone destruction was severe enough that the patient would present with a fracture through the cancer-weakened bone. But now, following Synchro Therapy, the cancer cells were gone and thick pink seams of new normal healing bone could be seen filling in the spaces in the bone where cancer cells had caused destruction.

I whistled spontaneously. "This is the most dramatic example of chemotherapy impact I have ever seen in dogs or humans. I wish that every post-chemo specimen looked like this. Philbert is a lucky dog."

Kate removed the first slide and focused on the next, which looked identical. Over the next twenty minutes, we reviewed most of the slides and saw exactly the same appearance. There were no cancer cells left after chemotherapy and massive replacement of the cancer damaged bone defects with healthy new pink bone in response to the Synchro Therapy.

"You know, Kate, I really have never seen this much healing bone in a post chemotherapy specimen. I wonder if the IGF we give the dogs to recruit the cancer cells also stimulates the bone to grow more in healing the damage caused by the cancer once the synchronized cancer cells are killed."

"Interesting idea. That may make sense. There are just two slides that I cannot explain. They look entirely strange, almost like they're from a different specimen. Here, have a look."

Kate focused up and down on a new slide and I saw a totally different appearance. There was lots of new pink bone present, but also plump blue cancer cells that had not been killed by the chemotherapy. And these cancer cells were clearly making new bone—the hallmark of osteosarcoma bone cancer.

But the specimen on the slide was different. It was thicker, and at some levels I could visualize normal-looking bone cells lining the surface of newly formed bone. There were normal bone cells mixed in with highly cancerous cells. It *was* quite confusing.

"This doesn't make a lot of sense. To see 100 percent cancer cell killing everywhere with intense new bone healing, and then in two slides see these residual nests of bone-forming cancer cells surrounded by active normal bone—this is really unusual."

"This slide seems different than the other slides from Philbert's surgery," she said. "It seems thicker—you can focus up and down through the slide more than with the other samples."

I used the pointer on the microscope to show Kate something else that seemed strange. "And look here," I said. "There is something really weird here against the normal bone. It looks like metal fragments. I wonder if Philbert had some old injury to his knee with metal shrapnel or something?"

I focused on the new bone surrounding what appeared to be fragments of metal deep in the specimen. I had never seen anything like this in any osteosarcoma or other bone cancer.

But it looked vaguely familiar. These metal fragments were too fine to be shrapnel. And there was new bone tightly aligned against the metal, as if it was growing into the metal fragments or something. And that is when the light went on and I understood what this was.

"Kate, I don't think this is Philbert's bone. This looks like a specimen from a bone ingrowth prosthesis. Those small metal fragments are like the mesh you see on the surface of a bone ingrowth hip. Could this specimen be mixed up with Philbert's by mistake?"

Kate peered down at the metal before removing the slide to examine it. "Bone ingrowth. Is that like the new ***super-B.I.G.*** prosthesis that Dr. Hendricks is using in dogs with arthritic hips? I know that the pathology lab is preparing some specimens for his animals. Maybe they mixed up some specimens with Philbert's cancer."

Kate removed the slide from the microscope and looked at the label on the slide where the pathology technician had penciled the specimen identification number. She then compared the number to another slide and, sure enough, the numbers were different. She sighed deeply. "Well, that is the answer, Patrick. This is a sample from another dog. Maybe it's a ***super-B.I.G.*** prosthesis dog."

This was reassuring. Philbert's cancer had indeed been uniformly 100 percent killed by the Synchro Therapy. There was no residual nest of cancer cells that had escaped the synchronization treatment.

"Well, that's certainly good news for Philbert, Kate. If there were nests of cancer cells in the bone that evaded the Synchro Therapy, then it would be possible for other cells in the body to escape the chemotherapy. But these results mean that Philbert has 100 percent cell death from Synchro Therapy. That is a very good sign for him."

"Good news indeed," answered Kate. "But I wonder where those cancer cells came from. I wasn't aware that Hendricks was using the B.I.G. prosthesis on dog cancers. I thought his lab was focused on hip replacements for conditions like arthritis."

"Yeah, I agree. This is a strange specimen. Let's check it out and see if there are other specimens like it. Let's look in the specimen box first and see if the blocks are marked differently."

When specimens are prepared for analysis, the pathologist cuts them into small samples that are embedded in paraffin wax. The paraffin wax holds the specimen together when it is cut very thin to allow it to be examined under the microscope. I checked the small box that held the tissue specimens that we'd been examining under the microscope. There were about thirty small paraffin blocks and one larger plastic disk. I smiled to myself, thinking Meredith's lab might have produced that plastic disk.

"Look at this, Kate. This must be the specimen from the *super-B.I.G.* prosthesis. They probably embed those specimens in clear plastic rather than wax. They gave us the plastic disk along with the slide by mistake."

"We should let them know," she said. "Let's check on Philbert and then head over to the pathology lab."

We went back to the wards and wandered through the barking animals to the large enclosure where Philbert was recovering from his surgery. He had a large plastic cone over his neck to keep him from licking his wound. Whereas immediately after his surgery he'd been keeping the operated leg off the ground, he was now bearing weight on it, limping but starting to walk.

Kate opened the enclosure and walked in to scratch Philbert behind the ears. The dog whined softly and rubbed his head against the vet's legs. I examined his wound, which was healing nicely, and gently bent Philbert's knee, which was starting to move well. I patted the large, friendly dog. "Looks really good, Kate. I think that Philbert is going to be just fine."

We reapplied his dressing and ensured the cone was well positioned to protect his wound. And then, we left the enclosure to head for the pathology department. Kate had jotted down the numbers of Philbert's specimen that were written on the pathology slides and the other number from the clearly different specimen.

We found Sam, the head technician in the pathology lab, at his desk and explained that we thought his team had possibly mixed up a *super-B.I.G.* specimen with our slides. We handed him the numbers and he looked them up to confirm the two numbers were from different animals. One was Philbert's number, and the other was from a dog that had been previously treated with a *super-B.I.G.* prosthesis and had died. The specimen was from that dog's autopsy.

Sam looked embarrassed. "I am so sorry, Dr. Benedict. You know, since we brought in the faster decalcification process, we are getting lots more bone cancer specimens sent to us—and we lost a couple of technicians to retirement and better pay elsewhere. We have been really short-staffed, and this kinda mistake is what happens when you don't have enough people." He exhaled slowly. "This was a big mistake on our part. Thanks for bringing it to my attention."

"Do you get much work from Dr. Hendricks' team?" Kate asked.

"We get the autopsy specimens here," said Sam. "I understand that the owners get the surgery for a big discount, but they have to agree to return the animal's remains after the dog dies so we can remove the hip and do testing. Most of the testing is done at the hospital, checking for how strongly the implant is attached to the bone." I knew this was the mechanical testing that Meredith's lab performed.

"We also get some specimens sent back from the hospital after the bone and implant have been sectioned," Sam continued. "They grind down the specimens and polish them so that they can do back-scatter electron microscopy to quantitate bone ingrowth at the hospital. Then, they send one or two specimens back to us for routine staining."

He held up another disk similar to the one that had been provided in Philbert's slide box. "If you look at this slide, it is pretty thick for good pathology analysis. It is difficult to cut good slides because of all the bone ingrowth and metal in the specimens. I'm not sure why they do these slides. Dr. Kovalov told me that Dr. Hendricks keeps doing these slides 'cause it's always been part of his protocol."

"Could we have a quick look at the rest of the slides from this dog?" I inquired.

"Well, normally I would need to get permission from Dr. Kovalov. But I guess this is a bit different. You want to make sure that none of your specimens ended up with his?"

"Yes, exactly, Sam," I said. "We just want to ensure that there are no other mix-ups. You guys do such a great job. We'll just make sure that it was just a couple of slides."

Sam went back inside the storage area where specimens and slides were kept and returned with a flat, stiff cardboard container that held the slides from the *super-B.I.G.* dog. There was also a smaller rectangular box. He opened the small box and there were three circular clear plastic wedges, each with a numbered tag applied to the disk. The slides in the bigger box, he explained, each came from a corresponding specimen.

"You can check each of the slide numbers against the three specimens to determine which comes from which specimen," he said, handing me the two boxes. He then showed us into a room where another multi-headed microscope was available.

This time, I drove. I checked the specimen number tagging each of the three plastic discs in the smaller box. I knew these disks had been carefully cut in Meredith's laboratory as thin as possible by her remarkable process that kept the bony detail intact while also dividing the metal prosthesis. Most of these wedges were analyzed in her lab for mechanical properties, showing how tightly the bone had bonded to the *super-B.I.G.* surfaces.

But Hendricks' lab also took these specimens and embedded them in plastic and ground them even thinner. These slides were then examined under a scanning surface electron microscope that would show where the bone had grown into the mesh on the surface of the B.I.G. implant and allow for quantitation of the extent of ingrowth. And then, they sent some slides to Sam for regular microscope pathology evaluation.

There were about twenty slides that I divided into three by grouping the numbers on the slides with the numbers on the tags of the three circular plastic embedded specimens. I first checked the slides from the specimens that were different from the slide mixed in with Philbert's case. These were slides tagged #1 or #2. They looked identical. Normal bone cells, dense new bone growing into the mesh of the B.I.G. prosthesis.

There were three slides from the third specimen tagged #3 that had been mixed in with Philbert's. These were dramatically different and extremely worrisome. There was dense bone ingrowth of normal bone onto the mesh. However, there were also extensive nests of dark blue cells with large very blue nuclei that were producing bone. These cells were clearly osteosarcoma cancer.

Sam joined us and peered into one of the scopes on the multi-headed microscope. "Boy, that sure looks like cancer. I bet one of my colleagues was skimming through these slides rapidly and saw the cancer cells and assumed that this must be one of your slides. He probably just sorted this slide with yours without checking the specimen number."

I agreed. What Sam was saying made some sense. "Kate, I think that we can say for sure that this case was mixed up with Philbert's and we do not need to worry about these cells being cancer cells that evaded the Synchro Therapy."

Kate nodded, but still looked concerned. "But where do these cancer cells come from? I'm not involved in the *super-B.I.G.* work, but I'm fairly certain it doesn't involve cancer."

"It is likely that the dog had a malignancy somewhere else and these cells are showing that the cancer spread to the hip. I bet Dr. Hendricks probably gets a complete autopsy on these dogs done along with the specimens from the *super-B.I.G.* prosthesis. So, the two might not actually be related. Let's just check the records in the pathology office."

We took the slides and specimens back to the office along with Sam and asked him to check whether an autopsy had been done on the dog. Sure enough, a complete autopsy had been done, and the computerized electronic result was documented in the dog's record.

The dog had been entirely healthy for two years after the *super-B.I.G.* hip replacement, but had developed spinal narrowing that resulted in bladder nerve dysfunction and a severe urinary infection. The poor dog had died from the resulting generalized infection. There was no history of cancer and no evidence of cancer on the autopsy.

"Pretty strange, don't you think?" Kate inquired as we returned the materials and left the pathology offices, thanking Sam on our way out. "No evidence of cancer anywhere except in a couple of slides from the prosthesis. Pretty unusual. Is there any way those cells weren't actually cancer?"

"I don't know," I said. "To me, there's no question that those were cancer cells—but I agree that it sure is strange."

Strange enough that I'd slipped the problem specimen disc into my pocket and returned the smaller box with only two specimen blocks, not three, to Sam. Strange enough that I wanted to confirm whether cancer was present in the specimen—especially since this *super-B.I.G.* product was about to be implanted into hundreds of thousands, or even millions, of people.

Chapter 30

Dr. Patrick Maloney
April 28

*W*hen I got home, I logged into the online hospital medical library site to read up on joint replacements and cancer. Many millions of hip and knee replacements had been done around the world, and only a few cases had been reported of a cancer developing in the joint replacement.

Of course, most joint replacements had been reserved for older individuals who were at risk not only for advanced arthritis, but also for cancer because of their age. In the extremely rare cases of cancer developing near a hip prosthesis, it was difficult to tell whether the cancer had been caused by the implant or simply spread to the site of the implant from somewhere else in the body. The chance of developing cancer in a hip or knee replacement was so small that the risk was never discussed with patients considering having a joint replacement.

But there were two issues with the *super-B.I.G.* prosthesis that worried me. First of all, I knew from Meredith that the implant was using some sort of IGF preparation in a biofilm that coated the ingrowth part of the prosthesis, and this IGF had been engineered to have a sustained released long acting effect. It was pretty clear that the biofilm created amazing bone ingrowth. But what if it also stimulated the bone cells to divide abnormally and become susceptible to developing cancer?

After all, that is what really defined cancer: uncontrolled cellular growth. It was clear in dog and human bone cancer that IGF could stimulate exactly that uncontrolled cell growth. What if the IGF biofilm on the *super-B.I.G.* prosthesis caused the same cancer effect on normal bone cells?

And there was another problem with the *super-B.I.G.* prosthesis. It was designed for use in young people who might have only early symptoms from arthritis. The *super-B.I.G.* prosthesis would be marketed as the hip replacement that was stronger than the normal hip and could be implanted in young patients with years of function ahead.

Young people with early symptoms of arthritis might be convinced to have surgery decades earlier than current practice. And it could take decades until it became recognized, if it ever did, that the *super-B.I.G.* prosthesis could be causing cancer. By that time, it would be far too late. If the prosthesis was as successful as Meredith and Hendricks thought, there would be millions of people with a metal implant firmly attached to their bone that was silently triggering incurable cancer.

All this, I realized, brought me to a third problem. I had no idea who to tell about what Kate and I had seen. And I didn't exactly know what I was going to do with the plastic embedded specimen that I had "borrowed" from Sumner to try and sort out this dilemma.

Until I figure that out, I thought, *what the hell should I tell Meredith?* All I had was an unconfirmed suspicion that could interfere with her entire life's research work. I knew from what she had told me that Hendricks' Newco was about to launch for investors in the next few weeks. The deadline was pretty tight.

Before I could mull through anything, I had a call to make. When Gershwyn had offered me the partnership, he'd also offered to get me a lawyer to review my partnership contract. But something about the offer of a lawyer troubled me deeply. I remembered when dad died in the accident at work, the mill owners told my mum not to worry, that they would get a lawyer to look after his insurance and everything else.

My grief-stricken mother was not ready for business decision-making and had gratefully accepted the assistance offered by the company. I remembered that the lawyer had convinced mum that suing the company for dad's accident would just prolong her grief, and that she should get on with looking after her kids. However, the compensation the lawyer negotiated for the family was gone in no time and did not include ongoing health insurance. And then, my sister got sick.

Which was why I wanted my own lawyer to look over the partnership with Dr. Gershwyn. I didn't have a lawyer, but I certainly knew where to get advice. I'd emailed Sandy Spencer late last week, telling him about Gershwyn's offer of partnership, and we'd arranged for a phone call tonight.

Sandy sounded delighted when he picked up. He always said he wanted to pay me back for Bob's care, but up to this point, I had never really requested anything.

"Patrick, I am so pleased for you. Working at the hospital and the university is an incredible opportunity. I am delighted that your talent is getting recognized in the big leagues. No question in my mind that this is where you belong."

"Thanks, Sandy. Can you help me find someone in Boston who will review the proposed contract and not charge me my first year's salary?"

"No problem. I know a great employment lawyer who owes me a favor, and I will be happy to cover any costs associated with his opinion. And actually, I was planning to call you in any case about that new hip replacement that Hendricks is bringing out. We talked about it when we had lunch in Copley Square. There are a lot of investors interested in the new company Hendricks is starting, and I wonder if you have heard anything new about the product. Hendricks is going around saying that it is stronger than your own hip. That sounds like a great marketing approach."

I really did not know what to say.

"Patrick, are you still there?"

"It is kind of difficult for me to discuss that. I assume that you are asking about the *super-B.I.G.* hip replacement?"

"You know about it, huh? Yeah, it sounds like a huge step forward. The prospectus suggests that it can solve problems associated with second operations and can also be used for young people. In fact, I wonder from their investment materials why everyone would not get this implant? It is being priced at a reasonable premium and seems to offer real advantages. Do you think that it represents a breakthrough for people with arthritis?"

"I think I need to be careful answering, because a friend of mine is one of the researchers who have been testing the product. She has certainly demonstrated that it bonds to bone much better than any implant that has ever been tested before."

"She? Patrick, I have reviewed some video pitches that were forwarded to me by clients, and one of the videos included an interview with an engineer testing the prosthesis who is one of the most beautiful women I have ever seen. Is that your friend? I remember you mentioned that you were going to the ballgame with her the day we met for lunch at Copley Square. Is that the woman in the video I saw?"

"Sounds like her. Her name is Meredith McClintock. I do have some information about the *super-B.I.G.* prosthesis from her. But I think the information I have is confidential."

"Understood. There is a lot of public information that I will have access to very soon that is highly technical and will need interpretation. Can I rely on you to help me interpret that public information?"

"For sure."

"Okay. I will make sure you get a message from the employment lawyer this week. And I am coming up to see you in the next couple of weeks for two reasons. The second reason is to review investment information, and the more important reason is to meet Dr. McClintock. It sure sounds like your life is changing, Dr. Maloney."

I was thinking fast after hanging up from Sandy's call. I knew that simply looking at cells under the microscope could not confirm that the IGF biofilm was causing cancer in the dog hip that I had seen that afternoon. That analysis was far too subjective. I was no pathologist, but I had spent lots of time with pathologists looking at possible bone cancers, and I knew the diagnosis of bone cancer depended on many factors.

The patient's history of pain or a new lump, destructive changes on X-rays, the presence of growth in a tumor over a period of time—these were all features that were used along with the pathology appearance to make a diagnosis of bone cancer. And here, I had none of those ancillary elements—no history, no X-rays, and no evidence of change over time. All I had was a couple of slides showing clumps of cells that looked exactly like bone cancer.

In the presence of confirming information, a pathologist would have no difficulty diagnosing cancer from that appearance. But in this situation, in a dog bone treated with IGF biofilm, who knew what impact the sustained release of IGF had on bone cells? In addition to making the bone grow into the prosthesis, maybe the IGF had changed the appearance of the cells to look as though they were cancerous?

My gut told me I couldn't drop this. I did not want Meredith to be associated with a product that was going to be inserted into humans when there was any suggestion that it could cause cancer in the long term.

I knew from Meredith that the *super-B.I.G.* prosthesis had been inserted into around 100 dogs, and about 50 of the animals had now passed away and their implants had been tested. If the changes I saw today were cancer associated with the *super-B.I.G.* implant, then the risk of cancer could be as high as one in fifty.

According to Meredith, they were expecting to implant the prosthesis in everyone that needed a hip replacement. That could mean nearly 800,000 prostheses implanted per year in countries where Synvest sold them. And if the risk of cancer was about one in fifty, that could mean that tens of thousands of patients treated with the *super-B.I.G.* could develop cancers.

I sat in my apartment and thought about next steps. I did not want to alarm Meredith unnecessarily. And I realized there was a lot riding on the *super-B.I.G.* hip replacement. From what Meredith and Sandy had told me, there was a huge amount of money involved that would benefit the hospital, the university, Hendricks, Meredith, and everyone working in the lab, as well as CellGrow and Synvest. I would look like an idiot suggesting that the whole project should be cancelled because of one misplaced slide.

In some ways, it would be easier to just forget about the whole thing. I could make up a story for Kate, say that I was mistaken and the slide was not suspicious for cancer. If I did not say anything, the Newco launch would go forward, the product would be launched, and it would probably provide wonderful long-term results for millions of people.

But if cancer had developed within the two years that the *super-B.I.G.* prosthesis had been implanted in one dog, it would be disaster to implant millions of these devices into people who would be exposed to the prosthesis for twenty, thirty, and forty years.

I decided not to speak about my concerns to Meredith or Hendricks just yet. They would think me a bit crazy. I needed more information about the specimen and had the plastic embedded block that I had lifted from the pathology department. I really wasn't sure why I'd taken it. Something had connected about the plastic embedded bone specimen.

And then, I remembered why.

The great thing about working in the hospital was that everyone was a world expert, and going to regular hospital rounds exposed you to world-class science. Four months ago, when I'd first arrived in Boston, I would religiously go to all presentations about bone because it was a treat to be exposed to the premier thinkers in the bone biology world.

Just after starting at the hospital, I'd gone to a lunchtime lecture given by Dimitri Antonopoulos, a young PhD recruited to the hospital and university from Greece for his expertise in understanding osteoporosis treatment. Dimitri was interested in understanding what genes were turned on and turned off in osteoporosis patients who responded to drug treatment of their weakened bone. Part of the reason he'd come to the hospital was because the specimens that the hospital had collected would allow him to answer this question.

And I remembered that he had described a method for extracting genetic material from plastic embedded specimens that was reasonably reliable. It could help me confirm that what I saw in those slides was cancer. Maybe he could look at the specimen that I had pilfered.

Chapter 31

Dimitri Antonopoulos, PhD
April 29

*I*came to Boston from Athens three years ago. The work that resulted in my offer from Boston was that I had developed ways of extracting DNA and RNA from calcified bone biopsies that doctors used in the Osteoporosis Clinic. Analyzing the RNA from these biopsy specimens allowed us to figure out who was responding to the osteoporosis drugs that were being tested in the Boston clinic.

When Dr. Maloney came to see me, I was quite honored that someone from Dr. Gershywn's program was interested in what I was doing. Dr. Maloney wasn't interested in osteoporosis, but he did want me to do a genetic analysis of a bone specimen he handed me.

"What analyses are you interested in?" I asked, intrigued.

"Dr. Anton—Antopop…" he began, and I cut him off.

"Call me Dimitri, please," I said.

He blushed and went on. "I am interested in confirming whether bone cancer is present in this specimen, and I want to use a DNA marker to test it. The most common DNA mutations in dog osteosarcoma are mutations that result in abnormal p53 protein. If you're able to detect that p53 mutation in this specimen, that'll help me confirm my suspicion that what I'm seeing in the slides generated from this specimen is cancer."

I was nodding my head throughout Patrick's explanation. "I used to work in an oncology lab in graduate school in Athens, and we did analysis of p53 mutations all the time. We have all the equipment necessary to detect mutated p53. We can start doing the extraction right away."

"Thank you, Dimitri. I appreciate your willingness to help out. I will get you the dog p53 primers from the Sumner vet hospital. I do some work there. When do you think we will have results?"

"The thing is, you gotta go slow in dissolving the plastic in the specimen. That takes about a day. And then, extracting the DNA and quantitating takes another day." I drummed my fingers on the desk beside me. "All in all, I would say a week. If the results are positive, we will know right away. I will text you when we've got some results. But remember, a hundred things can go wrong and ruin the process. Do you have another sample in case some step goes amiss?"

"No, this is really the only sample available," he said, handing over the plastic disk. "If this doesn't work, we will never know if the p53 is mutated."

"That is a lot of pressure!" I said. "A difficult process to get right. And only one sample! Well, we will do our best."

Chapter 32

Meredith McClintock, PhD
April 29

*P*atrick called to say he had an hour before he was due to start in the OR, so could he stop in at the lab to say good morning. I had gone to a scientific meeting out of town that started on Sunday, and we had not seen each since I'd left Saturday afternoon after our run. I was really missing him. This was a very new feeling for me, and it felt surprisingly good.

Just after Patrick rang to say he was coming, Andrei Kovalov appeared at my door. He was glowering more than usual and entered without knocking.

"Meredith, I have to talk to you about your damn boyfriend," he said. "Apparently he was at Sumner yesterday asking questions about our *super-B.I.G.* specimens. He has no right to mess around with our experiments. He is not covered by our NDAs, and you know how sensitive Dr. Hendricks is about confidentiality. You have to talk to him."

"Andrei, I have absolutely no idea what you are talking about. But as it happens, Dr. Maloney is on his way here now. In fact, here he is coming through the door right now."

I stayed in my seat, hoping this would be quick. "Hi, Patrick, let me introduce you to Dr. Andrei Kovalov, who runs the biology side of Dr. Hendricks' laboratory. He was just telling me you were in the pathology lab at Sumner yesterday asking to see some specimens from the *super-B.I.G.* autopsy studies."

Patrick reached out to shake hands with Kovalov. I could not help but notice that Andrei, who I knew pumped a lot of iron, puffed himself up as he shook hands with Patrick. I could see him squeezing down on Patrick's hand. I tried not to roll my eyes.

"Maloney," said Andrei, nearly yelling. "One of the pathologists at Sumner told me that you and that vet, Dr. Benedict, were snooping around asking questions about one of our dog *super-B.I.G.* autopsy cases and looking at our slides. I was just telling Meredith that you should not be prying into our business. Those results are private to Dr. Hendricks' lab team."

"Gee, thanks for letting me know, Andrei. Maybe the next time you have something to tell me you should talk to me directly rather than using Dr. McClintock as a messenger."

I started to get a bit concerned that this conversation could erupt into something nastier. Patrick was sounding very polite, but I could hear the challenge in his words.

"The reason we were looking at your specimens," he went on, "was that one of your slides was included by mistake in pathology results for one of our dog cancer patients at Sumner. If you want your slides kept confidential, you should be more careful with them."

Andrei was turned away from me. I looked up at Patrick and surreptitiously wagged a finger back and forth. My silent message was clear. *Don't you go postal on this guy in my office, Patrick Maloney. I don't care how rude he is, he is a colleague and I will be pissed if you're anything but professional.*

I knew that Patrick got my message. He smiled back at me with that angelic choir boy look that accentuated his dimples and freckles. "Look, Andrei, we are just meeting for the first time. You and Meredith are colleagues, so let's not get bent out of shape with each other. Based on the promotional material that I've seen, I think that your work is fascinating."

He glanced at me with a poker face. " I also hear from folks at Sumner that we may have something in common. I am working on IGF Synchro Therapy for dog osteosarcoma with CellGrow. I heard that you used to work for CellGrow before you went over to Dr. Hendricks' lab. I wonder if your current work here is related to the studies we are doing in dog cancer with CellGrow." I then realized he was taunting Andrei, who was pretty easy to tease.

"I don't know what you're implying, Maloney," said Andrei, sounding defensive. "My work here is my own intellectual property and doesn't infringe on CellGrow." Kovalov had looked a little red in the face earlier. Now, he was becoming a volatile shade of purple.

"Hey, relax. I am not suggesting anything that needs a lawyer. I just heard that you used to work with CellGrow. I am working with IGF in dog tumors and it seems to be going really well. I thought that you might be continuing to work on IGF with Dr. Hendricks and we might share results, maybe? All under NDA, of course."

I noticed that Patrick was leaning forward on the balls of his feet, half-expecting Kovalov to come after him. Andrei was clearly not impressed with Patrick and was pondering his next step. I was waiting for steam to come out of the top of his head when Andrei suddenly spun around to leave my office. "You're getting ahead of yourself, Maloney. Stick to your own experiments and don't bother yourself with my work."

Then, he looked at me. "And you should be more careful about who you choose as a friend. You know these orthopods are terrible liars. Look what happened to you before."

That was a bit much for me. I stood up out of my chair, looking straight at Andrei. "That really wasn't necessary, Dr. Kovalov. We're all professionals here. My personal life is none of your concern."

Patrick could see it was time to defuse the tension. "Andrei, I think we obviously got off on the wrong foot. Maybe I will see you again sometime soon and we will share a drink or something."

Patrick reached out and Kovalov suspiciously accepted his hand shake, again trying to pulverize Patrick's hand. This time, however, as Andrei tried to release, Patrick held on and clamped down with pressure of his own. Andrei looked at him in surprise, pivoted, and left the office without a further word.

"Dr. McClintock," said Patrick, "you sure have an interesting colleague."

I broke out laughing. "Oh God, he is such a jerk sometimes. I am lucky that we don't really overlap much in the lab. He designs the biofilm in his molecular lab and gives it to the technicians from Synvest, who apply it to the dog prostheses. I analyze the results of the biofilm in our testing lab and give him the coded results so he can evaluate the changes made in the biofilm. He generally treats me more like his technician than his colleague, but this was the first time he ever criticized me personally."

"You thought I was going to try and punch him, didn't you?" he said, grinning. "I've learned my lesson. But if you ever change your mind, you know my favorite girls are rink rats. They love a good fight on the ice."

"Maloney, you are disgusting. A real lowlife." I pulled down the blinds on my office window and walked over to him. "But I can't resist a hockey player." I loved melting into him, feeling his strength. I put my arms around his neck and kissed him very, very slowly.

"Meredith, either we are going to clear off your desk and use it for a different purpose or you better stop this. You are making me very hot, and I missed you terribly when you were away."

I sat back on my desk and twirled my ankle seductively. Then, I straightened up and remembered what had gone on with Kovalov. "What did go on in the pathology office? Seriously, Andrei was really upset when he came in."

"I'm not sure exactly, Meredith. It was pretty much like I told Kovalov. Dr. Kate Benedict and I were looking at slides from Philbert's surgery specimen. You know, he's the first dog to receive Synchro Therapy. And the results looked absolutely amazing. Every slide showed total cell death and massive amounts of new healing bone formation. Except for a couple of slides that seemed to show extensive osteosarcoma cancer. I guess that may have been why the slide was misplaced in our materials."

"So, what did you do?" I asked.

"We talked to Sam in the pathology lab and he told us that the technicians have been very short staffed recently and a few cases have been mixed up. Sam suggested that one of the technicians probably saw there was cancer present and thought that it belonged in our specimen—not your hip replacement autopsy results."

I literally felt the blood draining from my face. "Patrick, do you realize what you are saying? If there is cancer developing around even one dog *super-B.I.G* implant, this would be an absolute disaster. We could not allow the prosthesis to be implanted into any human patient."

I shook my head. This was unthinkable. "And there is a massive deal underway, probably one of the biggest investments in the history of medical technology in this country, to build a new prosthesis production facility as well as a new lab to produce biofilm.

"You can see why Andrei is nervous. He's very hungry for this investment into his intellectual property. He has spent a lot of very lean years in science trying to make his products work. This must be like a dream to him. He is about to score a very big payday."

The penny dropped for Patrick. Andrei wasn't just generally upset that Patrick and Kate had been checking out the *super-B.I.G.* specimens under the microscope. He was worried that they might be putting his big payday at risk. "So, this payout means a lot to Andrei, huh?"

"Absolutely. He came here as a grad student from Russia with nothing. After his PhD, he had no trouble getting a lab job in this city—there is so much biotech happening. But he got kind of stuck at CellGrow.

"His Phase I trial failed, CellGrow seemed to be at risk of going under, and I think the frustration got to him. He went through a nasty divorce, his wife accused him of physical abuse, and now he can only see his daughter in a controlled setting with a social worker. He is paying alimony and child support that is killing him.

"We didn't know about all this when he first came over to Dr. Hendricks' lab with his ideas for biofilm. His wife and kids had moved out of state, so it took a while for us to find out.

Patrick shook his head. "So, you are three weeks away from a massive investment in a new product that may be the best thing ever for hip arthritis, but it may also cause cancer. Some of the key players involved are motivated by greed. The scientist interpreting the results of treatment may be compromised by his financial difficulties, and Hendricks has been spending all his time raising money rather than checking on autopsy results. It all sounds pretty worrisome to me."

"Well, I know what I am going to do," I said. "First, I am going to call my dad and Dr. Hendricks and let them know everything you just said. My dad doesn't know anything about medicine, but he helped Dr. Hendricks set up the investment strategy and will be as upset as I am if something goes wrong or, God forbid, someone gets hurt by the *super-B.I.G.*"

"Okay, but what are you going to say to them?" Patrick asked. "I suggest that you tell them that you have a friend who saw some slides by accident from a *super-B.I.G.* dog specimen and thinks that he saw evidence of cancer in the bone. And you say that Dr. Benedict was also there and thought that cancer was present. You should get them all to sit down with me and Kate and look at the slides we saw, and probably get a real pathologist to join us. What do you think? Does that make sense?"

"Absolute sense, Patrick."

"Okay, I have to run. I have to operate with Gershwyn starting right now. I will ask Kate to get out the slides from the *super-B.I.G.* autopsy that I was worried about and arrange with one of the Sumner staff pathologists to join us at the end of the day. You get Hendricks and your dad and let's meet at 6:00 p.m. at Sumner, if that works for your boss."

Chapter 33

Mr. Jim McClintock
April 29

*T*o say that I was feeling out of place was the understatement of the decade. I walked into a very tense conference room where Meredith, Hendricks, and Meredith's colleague Andrei Kovalov were sitting uncomfortably with three other people. I was introduced to Dr. Kate Benedict, a veterinary surgeon, Sam, the head pathology technician, and Dr. Nathalie Dempsey, a pathologist who worked at the Sumner Vet Hospital.

I knew that I was getting there late. It was impossible to beat the traffic from Wellesley by 6 p.m. on short notice. I assumed that the meeting would have concluded by the time that I got there. But when I arrived, Meredith immediately mentioned that her friend Dr. Maloney was held up at the hospital and would be arriving soon.

The only person in the room who I knew was Meredith's boss, Jon Hendricks, and I could tell that Jon was furious at being made to wait. I understood from Meredith that Jon was a very significant player in the surgery world. I did not know Dr. Maloney, but imagined that keeping Jon Hendricks waiting was not too smart.

When Maloney finally arrived, just over an hour late for our 6 p.m. scheduled time, he was not a very impressive sight. He was clearly rushing and was still dressed in blood-stained surgery greens and a crumpled white lab coat. Overall, the impression was less than professional.

"So, this must be the Dr. Maloney that I have heard so much about today," said Hendricks, icy irony curling around each word. "Nice of you to finally show up. You certainly inspire loyalty in your colleagues. Dr. Benedict here has refused to allow us to look at these suddenly important pathology slides until you appear."

Maloney pulled out a chair and eased into it while Hendricks went around the table.

"You've met Dr. McClintock," he said, "and I believe Dr. Kovalov is no stranger. Have you met Meredith's father, Jim? And Dr. Dempsey, who we promised would only be detained for fifteen minutes? I apologize, Dr. Dempsey, that your evening appears to be ruined—but believe me, that was not my plan.

"And of course, you know Sam, who works here in pathology. Indeed, it sounds like you and Sam were cooking up mischief trading pathology slides on Wednesday afternoon, which has resulted in everyone gathering here this evening. I suggest that we get underway."

Patrick uttered an apology as he shook hands with me and with Dr. Dempsey, who did not seem quite as upset as Jon was suggesting. He waved at Kate, Meredith, and Sam. At this point, Andrei Kovalov pushed forward the box of slides that had brought us all together.

"Dr. Hendricks, as you know, we use two major measurements to estimate how well our modifications to the *super-B.I.G.* prosthesis are encouraging bone ingrowth. The first measurement is provided by the brilliant Dr. McClintock, who prepares the specimens by cutting the bone very gently with water and then dividing the titanium with a diamond cutter."

I figured that Andrei was overstating his admiration for Meredith for my sake as well as Hendricks'. I had met him on a couple of occasions while I was learning about the opportunities that the *super-B.I.G.* offered. The word that always crept into my mind when I saw him was "smarmy."

"She takes one of these specimens and preserves it for mechanical testing—basically determining how much force is needed to disrupt the bonds between the bone and the B.I.G implant. As you know, we have been achieving mechanical results never seen before. These are extraordinary mechanical results.

"Meredith provides us with alternate specimens, and we place the bone/metal implant in a plastic coating to fill in any gaps between the bone and prosthesis and allow us to do further testing. We use imaging and computer analysis to determine the amount of bone that has grown into the mesh on the surface of the implant.

"Finally, we take one of the plastic embedded discs and polish it further and examine it using routine cellular stains we use for all tissue specimens. This does not add anything major to the testing of the *super-B.I.G.* prosthesis, but it is good practice that we do some routine pathology specimens."

Here, Andrei turned to Dr. Dempsey, the pathologist. "The pathology is not very good because the specimens are quite thick, and I am sure that is what confused Dr. Maloney looking at our specimens on Wednesday. He mistakenly thought that there were cancer cells in one specimen.

"Of course, Dr. Maloney is not a pathologist, and that is why we asked Dr. Dempsey to review the slides this evening with everyone present. Dr. Dempsey, why don't you kindly have a look at these slides," Kovalov said, handing her the slide container, almost with a bow, "and provide us with your considered opinion."

Dr. Dempsey took the flat slide container from Kovalov and sat in front of the main microscope head on the multi-headed unit. Maloney sat down at another head, Dr. Benedict at a third, and Kovalov at a fourth.

As Dr. Dempsey led the review of the slides, Meredith came around the table to stand beside me. By reflex, I put my arm protectively around her shoulders and she squeezed against me. She had called me earlier in the day to tell me about the concerns this Patrick Maloney had raised with her.

I was not certain, but it struck me from a couple of glances between my daughter and Maloney that they might be more than professional acquaintances. Normally I might be supportive of my daughter's interest in an orthopedic surgeon, although she had told me briefly about a bad experience she'd had with a surgeon from California. But I was certainly not impressed with Maloney so far and decided to myself that I would need to talk to Meredith about this guy who kept people waiting and arrived for meetings looking like he just rolled off the OR floor.

Dr. Dempsey appeared very confident and professional as she focused up and down through the specimens. "These sections are really very thick, but the preservation and preparation are superb. The detail is actually fantastic. Congratulations to whoever developed this process. I have never seen such detail in intact, calcified bony specimens."

Meredith appreciated the compliment, as did I. I was entirely proud of my daughter and her work. When Meredith had called me this morning, she'd sounded very conflicted. She wanted the *super-B.I.G.* prosthesis to be a huge success, of course. She knew that it could fill a huge clinical need and would likely become the device of choice for every arthritis patient in the world who could afford it.

If the device were to be implicated as causing cancer, however, then four years of her research life would have been largely wasted. But if the artificial hip joint did cause cancer, it was obviously important to know it now rather than after it was placed in patients.

I had been interested in Meredith's work throughout her time in graduate school. I'd been pleased to meet Dr. Hendricks at a social event twenty-four months ago. We'd seemed to hit it off together, and I was honored when he'd asked me to help him understand the best way to raise money for this new *super-B.I.G.* implant.

Helping Jon develop his fundraising strategy allowed me to use my expertise to help further my daughter's career aspirations and that was a treat. I had never really understood her biomechanics world and it was wonderful to be able to help her in my small way.

"There is a huge amount of bone ingrowth," said Dr. Dempsey, interrupting my thoughts, "but all the bone is mature and there is no evidence of tumor cells or tumor bone."

Maloney silently nodded his head in agreement. "Dr. Benedict and I saw plump round aggregates of very blue cells when we looked at these specimens on Wednesday evening. I am no pathologist, but I have seen many cases of osteosarcoma and I know what we saw on Wednesday. We are not seeing that in this slide."

Dempsey quickly switched slides and began her review of a different section. "Same thing here—great specimen preparation, amazing really given the amount of metal and bone present." She was silent for thirty seconds. "No cancer here. Just lots of healthy bone growth."

She was proficient and economical in her movements and quick in her analysis. Within fifteen minutes, she had looked at all eighteen slides in the box. She looked up at Hendricks. "Jonathan I am not sure what you are doing to stimulate such amazing bone ingrowth but whatever it is, this is incredible. I have never seen so much interaction between metal and bone."

She looked at Meredith. "And the techniques you have developed to look at the bone growing into metal are simply remarkable. Congratulations to you both."

And then, she looked directly at Maloney. "And I have no idea what you were seeing when you looked at these slides, but I can absolutely say that they are no abnormal cells here, no cancer and no osteosarcoma. Whatever you thought it was, you were mistaken. People underestimate how difficult it is to read pathology slides, and I think this is an example of an amateur simply getting it wrong."

With that, she stood up and started out of the room. Dr. Kate Benedict jumped up. "Dr. Dempsey, wait a minute," she said. "I was here with Patrick. I can confirm that we did see something that looked like cancer."

Dempsey drew herself up straight. "Are you a pathologist?"

Kate looked down at the floor. "No, but we definitely saw something different yesterday when we looked at these slides. Sam, you saw those cells as well."

Sam seemed to examine his shoes. "I can't say, Dr. Kate. Sorry."

Dr. Dempsey shook her head. "It takes years of training to recognize osteosarcoma. I am sorry—but my conclusion is that a vet and a surgical fellow looked at some specimens and imagined cancer cells to be present. There is absolutely no evidence of cancer in this specimen."

And with that, she took her leave.

Kate slumped back into the chair she was sitting in at the microscope. Eyes turned to Maloney. He paused and cleared his throat.

"Dr. Hendricks, Meredith, and Mr. McClintock, I am terribly sorry to have wasted your time this evening, and I apologize for the concern I have caused. I honestly thought that I was seeing cells consistent with osteosarcoma cancer cells in the slides we reviewed on Wednesday, but I agree with Dr. Dempsey that we did not see that type of cell tonight. I would suggest that we call it a day, and again would ask your apology."

Dr. Hendricks looked at me. I shrugged and turned to Meredith. "I think that I should take advantage of this evening and buy dinner for Jon and you, Meredith. What do you say?"

Meredith turned back to Maloney. "Patrick, thanks for taking this so seriously. It's important that we make sure the *super-B.I.G.* prosthesis is safe, and I am happy we had this chance to deal with your concerns."

Maloney nodded thoughtfully in response to Meredith's comments.

"Jon, let's get a steak. I am starving," I said. And with that, I led Hendricks and my daughter out of the room. As we left, I heard Kovalov mutter something under his breath that sounded a lot like "asshole" as he carefully took the slides away with Sam, leaving Dr. Benedict and Maloney alone in the room looking at each other.

Leaving, I overheard the vet and Maloney talking. I must say it was a bit disturbing.

"What the hell, Patrick? You know we saw something on the slides yesterday that wasn't there today. Why didn't you say something?"

"Kate, I used to play hockey, and one of the rules I lived by was, 'don't get mad, get even.' I have no doubt that Kovalov probably looked at those slides that we saw, and they will never be seen again. He has a huge financial stake in the launch of this company, and I don't think he is going to let us destroy his chance for a huge payday without a lot of push back. But I am not ready to get even yet. Give me a few more days."

"It just pisses me off to see you put down like that." And then, she left.

Chapter 34

Dr. Patrick Maloney
April 30

I had a difficult night. I dreamed of people getting cancer from the *super-B.I.G.* prosthesis and Hendricks and Kovalov blaming Meredith, and Meredith being placed in stocks in Cambridge Square. It was a strange dream. More like a nightmare.

The next morning, I was in early as usual to see Gershwyn's patients. After rounding on them, I headed back to Gershwyn's office to do the routine billing and paperwork.

To my surprise, Gershwyn was in the office. He was an early riser, but usually used the first couple of hours of the day to exercise and work from home on scientific articles or business necessary to keeping his research program well-funded and well-directed. Most surgeons had left their scientific careers behind long ago by the time they reached Gershwyn's seniority and reputation. Gershwyn was a once-in-a-lifetime kind of doctor—still doing science long after he was expected to stop.

As I entered the office, I had the very real sense that Gershwyn was there to talk to me, and that this was not necessarily a good thing.

"Morning, boss. You are in early."

"You haven't even signed a contract yet and you are already causing me trouble, Patrick."

"Sorry, boss. What's up?"

"Jonathan Hendricks called me late last night. He sounded like he'd had a couple of drinks, which explains the time of the call. He gave me a tale of woe that you have caused him regarding the company he is starting up to produce this new prosthesis. A strange story about you thinking you found cancer in some bone specimens from his new prosthesis? It sounded confused, but he was very pissed at you."

I just wished this would all just go away. "It is a long and confusing story, boss. Do you really want to hear it?"

"Not particularly. You need to know that both the hospital and the university have major stakes in this new company. I have already had calls from the leaders of both organizations wanting to know who Patrick Maloney is and why I am not curbing him. You are not impressing people, Patrick."

I took a deep breath. "Well, I appreciate the warning, Dr. Gershwyn. I had no desire to get everyone so agitated. I am planning to lie very low for a while, believe me."

Gershwyn slapped me on the back. "We will hold up your appointment for a couple of weeks while this thing blows over. Get your lawyers to look at the contract and get it signed, but I will not take it to the hospital or university for a while. Hopefully by then, you will be anonymous again."

He was looking at me intently without blinking over the top of his glasses. "There is so much stuff happening around here that it is easy to get off the radar screen. People will recognize you again for the right reasons, because of your surgery and research. But right now, you are well-known for the wrong reasons."

I thanked Gershwyn and returned to my cubicle at the back of the office. On my way, I passed by Justine. "For Chrissake, Patrick," she growled. "Stay out of trouble until you get on staff at least. Albert wouldn't tell you this, but I know he spent a lot of political capital protecting you from the dean and president this morning."

Sitting in my fifty-square-foot area, I pondered the previous evening. I had not spoken to Meredith since she'd left for dinner with her father and Hendricks, and was disappointed that she had not contacted me. Just then, a text arrived on my phone and my mood brightened when I saw it was from Meredith. *Are you ok? Call me if u can.*

She picked up on the first ring. "Patrick, are you okay? Hendricks was so pissed at you last night that he drank several glasses of wine—more than I've ever seen him drink. I have never seen him so agitated. He thought the deal had smooth sailing ahead and he had worked out all the obstacles. Then, your suggestion of cancer came out of nowhere and really floored him."

"Yeah, I know, Meredith. I felt like such an idiot getting there late last night. Gershwyn ran late in the OR and I couldn't leave, and then I ran out in my greens. As I walked into the conference room at Sumner, I realized that I looked like such a schlump.

"And Gershwyn just told me that I am public enemy number one at the hospital, the university, everywhere. I guess Hendricks is about to make a lot of people a lot of money, and yesterday evening, it looked like I was trying to deep-six everyone's payday. He must have spoken to the university dean and hospital president as well as Dr. Gershwyn."

"Patrick, what the heck happened anyway? I know you would not say anything without reason, and yet you didn't argue with what the pathologist said last evening—that there was no evidence of cancer present. I didn't think it wise for me to say anything, but I wish I'd known what you were thinking."

"I guess that your dad thinks that I am an imbecile, huh? He must have money at risk in this deal too."

"Actually, no, he advised Hendricks on the structure of the investment and the intellectual property ownership shares for the company, but he never puts his own money into an advisory client. And it turned out that he has a different view from Dr. Hendricks. Dr. H. started off dinner with a long diatribe against you—irresponsible, glory-seeking, et cetera.

"But then, Dad said that he really did not really see how you could possibly benefit from suggesting that there might be cancer in the *super-B.I.G.* autopsy specimens. And that it must take courage to suggest that results that are really important to everyone are somehow flawed. He said to Hendricks that he admired your bravery.

"At that point, Hendricks really lost it and told me I should never see you again. I was upset because I had not really said anything to Dad about you and me.

"And then, my dad stopped him in mid-sentence and just said, 'Jon, you are out of line,' and Hendricks sort of apologized to me. It was the strangest evening."

"I am so sorry, Meredith. I have really dragged you into this and I apologize."

"Enough blaming yourself. What are you supposed to do if someone gives you a slide and you think it shows cancer? Like my dad said last evening, you know that you are not going to win any friends, but what are you going to do? How certain are you of what you saw? As we heard a hundred times last night, you are not a pathologist."

"I am certain of what I saw, and whatever it was, someone made sure that the specimen that I saw on Wednesday was gone when we looked at the slides last evening."

"You suspect Andrei Kovalov?"

"Well, it sounds like he had the motivation and the opportunity. If he gets rid of the slide, then I have no proof of what I saw. I should have taken the slide with me, but I really didn't think of someone destroying it."

I knew that the plastic block that the missing specimen was cut from was sitting in Dimitri's lab. I didn't say anything to Meredith about it, however, because it would be a real long shot to learn anything from Dimitri's work.

It would be difficult to extract DNA from the plastic disc, and even if that were possible, only 50 percent of dog osteosarcoma would show mutated p53. I was pretty sure that this was going to fade into the background now that the suspicious slides had somehow disappeared. That was probably best for my future career in any case.

"Hey, Meredith, I have to go home to see my mum and some friends for the weekend. After all this stuff with cancer and Hendricks I could also use some time out of Boston. Would you still be willing to take a road trip to Solway Mills with me?"

"On one condition."

"Of course. What is the condition?"

"We take my car. Your beater is on its last legs, and my little German thing is fun on New England country roads. You can drive. What do you say?"

"That's not a condition—that's a gift! I can't wait."

"I have a late lab meeting tonight. We are completing review of the public material that we will be submitting with our official investment prospectus, and Hendricks wants to go over everything personally. By the way, you saved us one step with that chaos from last evening. We needed to get a pathologist to submit a description of some routine pathology from the autopsy specimens, and Dr. Dempsey has agreed to submit a report for us based on her review of the materials last evening."

"Well, it was a pretty tough way to help you out, but I'm glad that something good came of it. I'm going to be pretty busy the rest of today. Shall we meet at your place early Saturday morning?"

"Sounds good. Let's put this whole mess behind us with a weekend in the country."

I headed up to the operating room for a patient of Gershwyn's who needed shoulder reconstruction after a melanoma had spread through the blood stream to the joint, destroying the bone. It was a difficult procedure, but Gershwyn assisted me doing the surgery while he maintained his usual commentary to the rest of the operating team about my poor surgical skills and how much longer the case was taking because I was operating.

My boss' verbal abuse reassured me that Hendricks' phone call last night and the fracas over the *super-B.I.G.* and cancer had not changed my relationship with Gershwyn.

After finishing the shoulder reconstruction, I headed over to Sumner, where I met up with Kate. Our second patient receiving Synchro Therapy had completed chemo and was ready for surgery.

The patient was a large Doberman with cancer above the knee in the end of the thigh bone, just like Philbert.

Kate had arranged everything to be ready for us. The MRI was on the computer in the OR, and she had had selected a knee replacement metal prosthesis that measurement X-rays showed was the right size for the dog's knee. After reviewing the preparations, I went into the owners' waiting area and chatted with the owners to ensure that they understood the surgery, and then joined Kate at the scrub sink. She was going to be the surgeon on this case, and I was going to assist and teach her.

"I was worried about you at that meeting last night," she said while brushing her fingers and nails. "Those guys were out for your blood. And what the hell happened to those slides we were looking at on Wednesday?"

She shook her head in frustration. "I didn't want to say anything to make the situation worse for you, but we saw something Wednesday that wasn't there last night. I could readily see those blue plump cells were different and they were making cancer bone. To me, it looked like a pretty classic osteosarcoma. And then, yesterday—nothing."

"Yeah, I know. It worries me too. They have done about fifty dog autopsies, with most of the autopsy dogs having the prosthesis for about two years. If we have fifty dogs with two years of exposure before they die on average, that means we have studied about a hundred years of exposure to the *super-B.I.G.* prosthesis.

"If what we saw was an osteosarcoma, that could mean that you will see one osteosarcoma for every hundred years of exposure to the *super-B.I.G.*.

"The average human will have the *super-B.I.G.* prosthesis implanted for much longer than a dog, since the human lives longer after surgery—let's say fifteen years on average rather than two years in dogs. From what I hear, Hendricks is planning on selling millions of that prosthesis.

"The math is easy, right? If what we saw was an osteosarcoma and if the risk of developing cancer is the same in humans as dogs, that could mean that tens of thousands of patients would develop cancer from the *super-B.I.G.*. This would be the biggest disaster in biotech history—much worse than Thalidomide.

"When the federal health regulators approve a new joint replacement prosthesis, they do not insist on proving that it does not cause cancer, because cancer is simply not a problem with hip replacements."

I was finished scrubbing and turned the water of with my elbows. "However, the stuff that Andrei Kovalov has placed on the prosthesis mesh to encourage bone ingrowth—well, that stuff juices up the bone and makes it grow and makes bone cells divide. And any time a slow-growing tissue like bone becomes fast growing, there could be a risk of cell mutations developing during cell division and development of cancer.

"So, despite the regulators not being concerned about showing that the implant does not cause malignancy, finding one case of cancer associated with the prosthesis in fifty cases would likely stop the project."

"I guess that explains why they were so agitated when you were late. They wanted Dr. Dempsey to read the slides before you got there. I felt like Horatio at the Bridge keeping them at bay!"

I laughed at the reference to ancient Rome. "Thanks, Kate, you are a good partner. Anyway, I think it's out of our hands now. I don't think we'll ever see those slides again." I backed in through the OR door and Kate followed.

Kate continued. "Kovalov has a bit of a reputation around here. He is a bully and somehow his experiments always go right—or the results can change or disappear or something. I talked to a couple of colleagues about him. No one would be surprised if he made those slides go missing."

As we looked at the MRI scan defining the surgical case for the Doberman, we stopped talking about the *super-B.I.G.*. We were both excited that the MRI scan had changed dramatically after the dog had completed Synchro Therapy.

Like in Philbert's case, the MRI suggested that the original highly aggressive, expanding cancer had been shrunken down dramatically by Synchro Therapy and had developed a massive amount of healing bone in the cancer. We were eager to get the cancer out and look at it under the microscope. We entirely forgot about Andrei Kovalov as we focused on the surgical challenge at hand.

Chapter 35

Andrei Kovalov, PhD
April 30

I chuckled to myself again as I sat at home replaying yesterday evening's events in my mind. Maloney had looked like such an idiot. And Meredith's father did not seem to know that they were an item. She was probably ashamed of Maloney now, and certainly should be ashamed after yesterday's debacle.

Thanks to God that Sam had called me about those slides. The three prior dog cases of cancer with the *super-B.I.G* I'd seen myself before anyone else had seen the slides, and I'd made sure those slides disappeared. I destroyed the material that Maloney saw, and after yesterday, no one would believe that there was cancer in a *super-B.I.G*.

I immediately cancelled any further specimens with Sam. No point in taking any more chances. I had seen plenty of pathology during my lab career, and there was no question in my mind that the latest specimen had osteosarcoma cancer. Maloney was right about that. If anyone thought that even one animal had developed cancer in a short period after **super-B.I.G** implantation, it would result in a major review of my biofilm work and dramatically delay the IPO.

And if anyone suspected that four of fifty dogs had cancer, the project would certainly be cancelled, *and* the new company would die prior to launch. I would lose the $25 million payout for selling my intellectual property to the new company at the time of the IPO. If anyone thought that the biofilm caused cancer four times in fifty dogs, it would all be over.

Fortunately, the **super-B.I.G.** human prosthesis was already approved by the federal regulator using the 510 (k) clearance based on prior approval for the B.I.G. prosthesis. Synvest and Hendricks had made the case that the new **super-B.I.G.** prosthesis was minimally different from the pre-existing B.I.G. implant. The regulator agreed that doing further experiments to show that the new **super-B.I.G.** was safe and effective was not necessary.

Under the 510 (k) clearance, the stringent, rigorous record-keeping that the regulator required for animal specimens in drug trials was not needed. Synvest and Hendricks did not need to submit any of the dog evidence to maintain the approval for clinical use.

Because of this, I'd been able to easily eliminate the slides that showed cancer.

Of course, it was possible that patients would start getting cancer two or three years after the **super-B.I.G.** was initially introduced to humans. This would be a disaster and the company would be bankrupted by the lawsuits that would follow. But by then, I would have my initial 25 million payout and would also make a point of quietly cashing in my stock options as soon as the company's stock was liquid on the market.

By the time that the association between the **super-B.I.G.** implant and cancer was understood, I would be a wealthy man and long gone from the company—and the country.

I felt bad leaving my daughter. My ex-wife would poison her opinion of me for sure. But I would be rich and independent. If this thing blew over, I might be able to re-establish a relationship with my kid.

On the other hand, returning home with more than $25 million in hard currency, I could enjoy quite a lifestyle. And maybe I would just start a new family.

Chapter 36

Meredith McClintock, PhD
May 1

Solway Mills was about a two-and-a-half-hour drive from Boston. The first ninety minutes were on interstate highway and the last hour on a winding two-lane country road. It was about 130 miles on the road and about fourteen days back toward winter because we were driving north and climbing in altitude away from the sea. Gardens were fully blossomed in Boston and just starting to bloom as we approached Solway.

Patrick was obviously delighted that he had accepted my offer to leave his Subaru behind. It was a beautiful sunny day and we put the top down. My two-seater clung to the road like a go-cart, and Patrick enjoyed his fantasy of Formula 1 performance. I touched his arm several times as he exceeded 80 miles per hour on the speedometer. The car handled so well, and I knew from my own experience driving that its speed could creep up on you.

To a first-time visitor, Solway Mills combined elements of extraordinary natural beauty, the results of industry's impact on nature and a changing approach to economic survival. I knew of course that Solway was a mill town, originally founded by the pioneering Solway family to take advantage of the wild river that provided power to the newly developing lumber industry.

I had read a bit about Solway's history. In days long gone by, the rich forests surrounding Solway had provided old growth wood that was perfect for masts, building lumber, and the hardwoods that supplied the furniture and flooring industry. The state's maples and birches had been coveted everywhere in our younger country, and as the newspaper industry had exploded in America, the abundant pine forests had provided an enormous pulp and paper resource.

On the drive, Patrick spoke to me about his father's life in Solway Mills. It almost seemed as if his concentration on the road provided him with a safe space to speak to me about his childhood.

Patrick's dad had been a mill manager and during busy season in the forestry business was constantly working twelve-hour days, six days a week to maintain productivity while the seasonal markets were booming. He could tolerate that kind of tough scheduling as a young man, but Patrick told me that he could tell in his last year of life that the pace was taking a toll on him.

His dad was a popular man in the community, a former semi-pro hockey player who also coached the local team. He was widely trusted by everyone, who confidently passed their boys over for his instruction on the ice.

But after his fatal injury in the mill, he needed a closed casket. Patrick knew that his death had been a blow to the community. The company he had given his life to was constantly on the brink of insolvency, and within months after his death, they sold the Solway business to a larger company that was owned by New York investors.

And, of course, the new company had vigorously stripped out costs to improve profitability. Part of their "productivity improvements" included reducing commitments owed to former workers, as well as benefits for injured or deceased workers. Patrick's mother found herself surviving on a limited lump sum payment, and when the company's sale was completed, her health insurance disappeared with the transaction. So, as Patrick drove the last twenty miles into Solway Mills, I could feel him expressing a mix of betrayal, melancholy, and warmth that resulted from his homecoming.

The hills surrounding Solway had been reforested. Patrick explained that the new growth lacked the majesty of the original forests that Patrick had seen in photos taken before the first logging. To me, however, the dense green of springtime was breathtaking. The river that had provided power to the original mills flowed beside the road we were following. The spring runoff was recent enough that we could hear the sparkling river over the sound of the engine. It was a gorgeous, warm day—a wonderful day to be running a sports car into Solway with the top down.

As we entered Solway and turned onto Main Street, the evidence of the change that had disrupted the newspaper and forestry industry become evident.

Patrick pointed out a deserted factory just off Main Street with a large sign proclaiming the home of Solway Papers.

"Solway Papers kept a specialty in fine magazine papers that allowed them to stay alive despite the newsprint failure induced by the Internet. Demand for glossy high margin product lasted about five years longer than demand for newsprint. But glossy magazines now, of course, are mainly online publications. Solway Papers closed three years ago."

Main Street was about half a mile long. The most common storefronts were liquor shops and gun stores. There were several vacant buildings along its walkways. Continuing his introduction to Solway, Patrick recounted, "Unlike urban gun stores, there are relatively few handguns on sale in Solway. Most families try and fill their freezers with moose and deer in the fall, and the gun stores are mainly focused on hunting."

Looming over the north side of Main Street was the hulking expanse of Mount Solway, which was providing a new economic advantage for the town. Like many American ski hills, Solway had been developed after the Second World War by a returning serviceman who had seen ski resorts for the first time while fighting in Italy. Mount Solway was one of the highest mountains in the east and had reliable snowfall because of its altitude and latitude.

Patrick continued, "The hill and surrounding lands are now owned by a pretty well-financed corporation that is investing in a four-season resort with golf, riding, tennis, mountain biking, and real estate development complementing ski revenues."

"The real estate construction and property management is becoming a brisk business because we are close to eastern population centers. This development has stabilized the economic downturn in the forestry business.

"Solway is also one of the first rural communities to celebrate a relaxed lifestyle with cost effective housing for retirees. I understand it is developing a reputation as a six-month retreat for retirees who spend the winter in Florida or Arizona. This springtime influx of retirees returning to their summer homes provides a balance for the winter time economic activity related to the ski hill."

Patrick described that these various elements of development had stabilized Solway's population of just above 75,000, including the surrounding hamlets in the hills.

And an expanding element of the local economy was healthcare. The two hospitals in Solway were owned by the county and the Catholic Church. The county hospital was at the east end of Main Street, and St. Anne's was at the west end. Both hospitals had apparently been takeover targets for consolidating health care corporations, but so far had maintained local control as not for profit enterprises with local boards.

Patrick continued his introduction to his hometown, "Taken together, the two hospitals are major employers in town and offer employees the best benefits to be found in Solway Mills. Our surgical training program is essential to keeping the hospitals solvent. The general surgeons, obstetricians, urologists, and orthopedic surgeons who come to Solway for residency receive low compensation for three to five years and help the hospitals to offer good coverage to local patients who often have precarious health insurance."

Patrick pointed down Main Street to the County Hospital as we turned off the main drag. "The more recent arrival of reasonably well-insured retirees who split their year between summers in New England and winters in desert or beach retirement communities have increased hospital revenues and provided much-needed employment to the town. Twenty-five years ago, the most reliable employment was enjoyed by the mostly male forest and mill workers. Today, reliable jobs are focused in the less male-dominated nursing and health professions."

As we entered town, Patrick was obviously touched by the memories and emotions that a returning son would experience after several months away. He lapsed into silence, but I was thrilled by the natural beauty this small town offered.

"Patrick, this is just beautiful. The majesty of that mountain towering over the town, the way that the river crosses back and forth across Main Street, and the well-maintained bridges that cross it. It is just so peaceful here. No doubt, Main Street is tacky. But that drive along the river coming up from the interstate—I don't think that I have ever felt so enveloped by green. And look at this cute neighborhood. It's lovely."

Turning off Main Street, Patrick was traveling to the east end of the mountain. He had already told me that his mother still lived in the frame house that her late husband and father-in-law had constructed to serve as their marital home. It was in in a charming neighborhood that was being renewed by coffee houses, restaurants, and bars that were obviously built for the resort visitors and the more recently arrived retirees.

Solway Mills was the kind of place where locals still built their own homes, and Patrick's dad and grandfather had been justly proud of their skills. The bungalow was obviously solid and boasted a beautiful fieldstone chimney that Patrick's grandfather had completed as a wedding present for the newlywed couple.

Patrick told me that when he'd left Solway, the bungalow had been desperately in need of a paint job. As we approached his home, he smiled. "You remember I told you that I sent money home for mum to hire local help to paint the house?" The little house was now glistening in the sunshine.

As he parked in the driveway, I saw Patrick's mother Leonora—a tall, handsome woman with a brilliant smile—come striding out of the house. Observing her joy at seeing her son, I had difficulty imagining her in the severely depressed state Patrick had described following his father's death. She was obviously delighted to welcome her son home, and her face was beaming.

To my surprise, Leonora came to my side of the car rather than the driver's side. Since the roof was down, she reached directly into the passenger's side and grasped both of my hands warmly.

"Meredith, Patrick has gone on and on about how smart you are, but he has not done justice to how beautiful you are. Patrick, she is lovely. Thank you so much for coming to visit our little town. And what a car you are coming in!"

I opened my door, jumped out, and just gave Patrick's mother a hug. "I am so excited to meet you and see Solway. Patrick makes it sound like the most boring place on Earth, but it's just beautiful. We drove up alongside the river from the interstate and it sounded like a symphony each time we stopped."

Leonora took me by the arm and left Patrick to bring our luggage. As she held me close walking up the path to her house, I felt that I was the one enjoying a homecoming.

Chapter 37

Dr. Patrick Maloney
May 1 & 2

I was experiencing that strange but wonderful feeling that comes when someone you care about meets your mother for the first time, and they connect and proceed to ignore you. I went around the driver's side to the trunk to get our bags, and saw that mum was walking Meredith into the house, their arms locked together while Meredith complimented her on her garden. I just shook my head and wondered what had just happened.

Mum started making tea while Meredith stared out the kitchen bay window that faced up the mountain. Not wanting to interfere with their conversation, I took the bags down the hall to the guest bedroom and remembered that I had never slept with a woman in my mother's house. Judging by how my mother was greeting Meredith, I figured that should not be a problem.

"Patrick, it is so good to have you home. Isn't the paint job lovely? Thanks so much for the help with getting it done."

Before leaving, I had helped mum land a new job as assistant to one of the hospital executives at the County Hospital. The pay was better than the retail jobs she had worked at after dad's death, and the benefits and insurance were the best that you could get in Solway.

"I am so glad you were able to bring Meredith with you on such a beautiful day. First impressions of a place are so important. What are you planning to do while you are here to show her around?"

"We don't have too long, Mum. We want to take you out for dinner tonight. This afternoon, we are going to meet with Larry—I want to show Meredith the hospital. Tomorrow, we will need to head back after breakfast. But it is so good to see you."

"There is no way we are going out for dinner tonight. I have some steaks marinating and we will enjoy a barbeque right here in the yard if it stays this wonderfully warm. I want to show Meredith the best view in Solway—from the backyard that your father created for us."

We took our tea outside to the back porch. My father had chosen the perfect place to build our bungalow. It was at the periphery of the streets that surrounded Solway's town center and backed onto an unobstructed view of Mount Solway. The backyard was bordered by a brook that led to the main mill stream and provided a lyrical accompaniment to our conversation.

And I simply listened. Mum had already described to Meredith how her husband and father-in-law had carefully chosen this spot to build and that it was the first lot on the street to be developed. Meredith heard again how Dad had been a leader in the community as both a manager in the lumber company and a hockey coach.

In return, Meredith described her own mother's sudden passing due to an aneurysm and how her father had struggled and then focused on bringing up his two daughters. Mum was fascinated to hear about how Meredith had been inspired by biomechanics, and listened intently to Meredith's description of the work she was doing. Everyone knew someone who had received a hip replacement, so it was easy for Mum to understand how Meredith's work aimed at producing a better surgical outcome.

While they got to know each other, I simply sat looking at Mount Solway, answering the occasional question. Mostly, I was seeing mum's backyard in a new light through Meredith's eyes. With

Meredith sitting under the umbrella on the porch, the brook burbling, and the mountain glistening in the background, I was experiencing a different perspective—a new sense of peace and beauty.

And I knew that the reason was Meredith. Her warmth in responding to Mum and her willingness to be here with me were starting to sink in. It felt so right to have her here.

As the afternoon wore on, I mentioned that I had promised to meet my best friend, Larry Humphrey. Larry and I had been inseparable as kids and had starred together as hockey players for the Solway Juniors. Dad had started off as our coach and Larry's dad had acted as a second father for me after his death, providing transportation to the ceaseless cycle of hockey practices and games.

Larry's father was still the prominent lawyer in Solway, and Larry had grown up in relative luxury compared to me. But on the rink, differences in affluence were immaterial. Larry had been a talented player who'd won an Ivy League scholarship based on his hockey quickness and goal-scoring touch. I'd been the grinder who'd delivered pucks from the corner to my more talented teammate— as well as protecting him with my fists when other teams tried to intimidate our scorer.

After completing an MBA, Larry had returned to Solway to take a role at the County Hospital as Chief Operating Officer. Shortly after his arrival, the CEO of the hospital had sustained a serious heart attack and Larry had been appointed interim-CEO. He was certainly young for the position, but was well-known and admired locally as a result of his hockey success. His business sense as well as his father's position in town had contributed to the hospital board acclaiming him as interim leader.

That afternoon, Meredith and I met Larry at the front entrance to the hospital. Larry had kept close to playing weight, while I had gained weight through surgical training. I knew he was continuing to stay active as coach of the Solway midget team. He was happy to see that I had lost the extra weight that had accompanied me when I'd left for Boston.

"Hey, man, you are looking good. And I can see why," he exclaimed, shaking Meredith's hand warmly. "Patrick tells me that you two met running around the Charles?"

"Well, not exactly. I would say that I met Patrick after he punched out some guys who were hassling me while I was running."

Larry began laughing and put his left arm around Meredith's shoulder and right arm around mine. "Well then, Meredith, you and I have something in common. This guy spent his entire hockey career in Solway punching out guys who were hassling me. Junior hockey can be a hatchet sport here in the county, and guys like me need guys like Patrick to survive and thrive. It took me a year away at university to get used to playing without him."

Larry gave Meredith a quick tour of the hospital, and then the three of us sat in his office. "Patrick, I hope that I can convince you to return to Solway. Times are changing here. The development at Solway and the new retirement communities are starting to bring a different clientele to the hospitals. And I have a plan to bring County and St. Anne's together. If we merge the two hospitals, we can dramatically strengthen both their balance sheets. We will still keep the faith-based mission at St. Anne's, and integrate most of the clinical services and recruit some new blood to the medical staff.

"With this place becoming a four-season resort and retirement destination and being close enough to Boston, I think there is opportunity to create a new approach here. And, Patrick, I want you to build that medical staff with me."

"What will you do with the clinical services, Larry?"

"The important thing will be the training program. If we can expand the training program to include more surgical specialties and then some medical specialists, we will expand to ensure that nearly all services are present in town."

I loved Larry's enthusiasm as he described his plan.

"My plan is to double the surgery training program to include vascular, neurosurgery, and plastics. After that, we will start an internal medicine program and then expand to medical sub-specialties, including cardiology. That will allow us to move into cardiac surgery and that will make us a full-service center."

He clapped his hands softly for emphasis. "With the number of retirement communities planned for Solway and the region, we will need those doctors to look after the seniors that are moving here.

Expanding the training program is the best way to get good doctors to come here.

"Some of the retirees are wealthier than anyone who has ever lived in Solway. They are here from May to October, and then head to Florida or Arizona for the winter months. When they are here, they are demanding top drawer healthcare."

It was obvious that Larry had lots of practice with this pitch. But I must say it sounded attractive.

"The banks and wealth management houses are realizing that their clients are starting to move to Solway for the spring and summer, and are looking at establishing offices here. Solway is going to be different in the future, and we are going to need you here."

"I leave town for four months and the place is changing," I said. "I knew when you took over at the hospital you would have a bigger plan in mind, Larry. It sounds very interesting. But I just accepted a job at the hospital in Boston. You remember that I went there to work with Dr. Gershwyn? He has offered me a job as his partner."

Larry smiled and looked first at me and then at Meredith. "I am glad to hear that they still recognize real talent in Boston. I am not surprised. Well, if anything changes, Solway will always be home to you."

We chatted about other friends in town and Larry's plans for a family. He and his wife were planning on starting a family soon, and Larry thought that Solway would be the best place imaginable to raise children.

Meredith had been listening to us chatting about medical business and expanding the hospitals with interest. But now, she weighed in. "From what I have seen of Solway Mills, I must admit this looks like a wonderful place to start a family, Larry."

"There you go, Patrick. You listen to this woman. She knows a great future when she sees it."

Shortly thereafter, we left to pick up a pie for dessert with Mum. I had not paid much attention to Solway before leaving for Boston, and seeing the town for the first time in months, I could see what was generating Larry's enthusiasm.

Main Street was still pretty grungy, but there were two signs announcing the future opening of a well-known bank and investment company. You could sense that the town was changing. I was really pleased for Larry. He had always planned to be a leader in Solway, and it looked like his ambition would be rewarded.

That evening, I barbequed the steaks Mum had been marinating, and could hear the two women chatting away in the kitchen like they had known each other for years while I was outside with the grill.

I was relieved and pleased to see that Mum had laid out two towels on the bed, implying her consent for us sleeping in the same room. In the morning, Meredith felt slightly embarrassed, but was warmly greeted by Mum in the kitchen; again the two women conversed like long-time friends.

The next morning, I packed the car for our return trip. Meredith and mum embraced warmly, and I was surprised to see tears in Meredith's eyes as we pulled out of the driveway.

"Meredith, are you okay? Was my mum too overwhelming?"

"Oh, Patrick, she's wonderful. I'm so happy to have met her. It just reminded me how good it would be to have a mother. I miss my mom every day, you know. You just don't know how lucky you are to have a warm person like Leonora in your life."

I stopped the car, put my arms around Meredith, and held her tightly. She had a way of becoming small in my embrace and I enjoyed wrapping her into my arms and chest. Her eyes were even wetter as I gently released her just a bit to see her face.

"Solway is so beautiful. Your mother is wonderful, and your friend has such a good life here. I could be so happy here—especially with you."

The car rested on the side of the road for some time. I knew Meredith was going to complete my life. There was no doubt in my mind. Whether my life continued in Boston or back home in Solway—or on Mars—the only factor determining my happiness was that Meredith must be there forever. And in so many words, I told her just that.

Chapter 38

Dr. Patrick Maloney
May 3

*T*he next morning, I woke up at Dartmouth and Marlborough, and the pleasure in awakening was a novel sensation. For years, I awoke with compelling ideas of what needed to be accomplished that day front and center in my consciousness. This morning, I just looked at the luxurious cascade of Meredith's hair on the pillow and had no thoughts of work. We had made slow love through the evening and during the night, and I felt Meredith was moved as deeply as I was by the weekend.

"Meredith, do you need to be up soon? I need to get in for rounds before clinic shortly—as much as I would rather stay here all day."

She slowly rolled back from my embrace and pulled her phone off the night table. "I have to be in this morning to review this evening's pitch meeting with Hendricks. This is the last meeting scheduled before the IPO launches in the next two weeks. It is already over-subscribed.

"These numbers stagger my mind. But private investors are clamoring for an opportunity to buy in, and tonight is the last night that we will be describing the project for them.

"Plus, this evening is special for me because it's at my dad's office. Dad has helped Hendricks in coordinating opportunities to meet with institutional investors for the last six months. My dad is an interesting guy. I want you to get to know him. He has mainly run retail investments for high net worth individuals in the suburbs over the past thirty years. But through that line of business, he has met and gained the confidence of larger fund managers and institutional investors. Over the last six months, he has been an important connector while Hendricks pitched institutional investors in the *super-B.I.G.* IPO. And tonight, Hendricks has promised to offer an investment opportunity to some of Dad's most sophisticated investors."

She looked at me almost shyly, and I could tell that she was about to ask something important to her. "Would you consider coming with me and chatting with my dad during the pitch meeting, Patrick? The last time you met him was pretty negative. Hendricks was pretty pissed at you, but my dad was impressed you were standing up for your beliefs—even if the evidence eventually did not confirm your suspicions."

I was silent at that memory. I really did not know whether I could or should be doing anything about the *super-B.I.G.* prosthesis. There was way too much momentum behind this major advance in hip surgery. Nothing that I could do would likely derail the launch of this new prosthesis that was going to make a lot of people and organizations very wealthy.

I was pretty sure that Andrei had destroyed evidence of cancer, but it was only one case. And there did not seem to be anything I could do about it.

"Of course, I will come. Where is your dad's office?"

"It's out in Weston. Why don't we meet here after work and drive there together? I want you to have a chance to get to know my dad."

I liked what I was hearing. I decided to run back to the apartment prior to arriving at the hospital for rounds at 6:30. As soon as I left her building, I missed her and appreciated the run to return to the real world of hospital surgery.

I made rounds on Gershwyn's patients and joined the great man for his round at 7:00, then spent the morning seeing new patients in Gershwyn's office. The final patient of the morning had been escorted into the exam room when two texts appeared on my phone.

The first was from Meredith. *Dad is really pleased you are coming to the pitch meeting. See you later.*

The second text was from Dimitri Antonopoulos. *Have some interesting results to show you.*

I had almost forgotten about the specimen I'd left with Dimitri. I was pretty sure that it would be negative for mutated p53. The chance of cancer was uncertain, and even if cancer were present, only 50 percent of dog osteosarcomas showed mutated p53. But Dimitri had said the results were interesting, and I texted back to say that I would come to the lab by 2:00 p.m.

As clinic was concluding, Gershwyn took me aside. "I understand that you are attending Hendricks' pitch meeting this evening. That's a smart move. It'll help me in finalizing your contract."

At first, I wondered how Gershwyn could possibly know about my evening plans. But then, I saw Justine across the clinic smirking at me and realized where Gershwyn's intel came from. Justine knew everything happening in the hospital, and would undoubtedly be figuring out me and Meredith.

Surprisingly, I felt no concern at this invasion of my privacy. I was proud of my developing relationship with Meredith and really did not care who knew about it. I decided that I should be straightforward with Gershwyn.

"Well, boss, I am friends with Dr. Meredith McClintock, who runs the engineering lab for Hendricks. Her dad helped Hendricks with his investment strategy, and he is going to be at the meeting tonight. Meredith wanted me to meet with him."

"I'm glad that you're no longer trying to convince people that the *super-B.I.G.* prosthesis will cause cancer or the black plague or some other damn disaster. From what I understand, Hendricks, the hospital, our department and the university are all about to get very, very rich from this IPO. Questioning the IPO would make you extremely unpopular, to say nothing of unemployable in this town, and maybe in this country."

I nodded and left Gershwyn's office to enter orders on the computer for our last two patients. I knew that Justine would want to quiz me about Meredith and purposefully stayed away from her until I had an opportunity to quietly leave the office and head over to Dimitri's lab.

Dimitri saw me entering his lab and motioned to me to join him in the office, where he carefully closed the door.

"If I understood you properly when you gave me the specimen, we have analyzed the tissue from a dog bone specimen that had undergone implantation of a hip prosthesis, is that right?"

I nodded. I was already impressed. Dimitri had suggested that he would need at least a week to get any results. Generally, with laboratory work and research scientists, that estimate would double or triple in reality. But it had only been four days since I had dropped the specimen off, and already Dimitri seemed to have found something.

"There wasn't very much material to work with, but we still got excellent DNA samples from the specimen you provided. In the end, we used the entire specimen to ensure that we had sufficient DNA."

"So, there is no specimen or DNA left?" I asked.

"That's right—we used up the entire sample to get enough DNA to do three separate approaches looking for mutated dog p53. And in each of three runs, we found a gene mutation that suggests strongly cancer is present in that sample. As you know, if we did not find a mutation, it would not rule out cancer in the bone. But finding mutated p53 is certain evidence that cancer is present."

He looked pleased. "I got really interested in the challenge of working with this small sample. I'm embarrassed to admit it—I was here all weekend doing the DNA extraction and running the gels myself. I guess that I kind of got turned on by the CSI challenge of figuring out what was going on in this sample."

"I'm very grateful," I said. "And you're saying the results are compatible with dog osteosarcoma?"

"I would say yes, that osteosarcoma is the most likely explanation for these p53 results."

I felt my world spinning. Everything had been lining up perfectly: a dream job with a world-famous mentor, the opportunity to immediately play in the big leagues of international surgery, and falling in love with a beautiful woman whom I admired and respected.

Somehow, I had never felt hard done by in my life. I believed that people made their own luck, and despite the difficult circumstances I had suffered as a boy, I'd always felt there were people far more disadvantaged. But as I reviewed the results with Dimitri, I could picture a steep downhill slide in front of me.

"Dimitri, I studied molecular biology like every medical student, and I understand the significance of the gel electrophoresis bands we are seeing here. But I have a feeling that I am going to need to explain these bands to a lot of different people, including some people who have no idea what a gene is. Give me the molecular biology for dummies explanation of what the gels show."

Dimitri nodded. "I know what you mean. This is the universal genetic code we are talking about, and it should be as well-known as the fact that the heart pumps blood to the organs of the body. But somehow, genetics intimidates people. Here is how I describe it to laypeople who want to understand what we do in the lab."

"Genes are located in our DNA, which is made up of chains of four different molecules called nucleotides. The sequence of these four different nucleotides in genes serves as the code, which determines the order of amino acids that make up proteins. So, our body uses DNA coding to make proteins."

Dimitri had obviously practiced this lecture before. "For the most part, proteins provide the cell with its machinery and ability to function—like allowing a muscle cell to contract, for example—so it's very important that gene coding for proteins is accurate. If the DNA is mutated, it can result in a mutated protein. Cancer can be caused by DNA mutations in some genes. So, we can identify some cancers by identifying specific mutated proteins, and p53 is one of these cancer gene mutations."

I nodded. My basic knowledge of the miracle of the genetic coding was re-awakening. "Remind me what happens with p53 mutation."

Dimitri continued. "p53 protein is very important because it controls cell division. Normal p53 protein provides cells with a control switch that keeps those cells from dividing too often. A mutation in p53 can affect the protein's ability to shut down cell division. This allows cells to divide virtually without control. Of course, uncontrolled cell division is the most important characteristic of cancer."

Dimitri's hands were circling in space, mimicking the chaos associated with uncontrolled cell division. "Mutated p53 gene is one of the most frequently observed abnormalities in cancer cells, including osteosarcoma." I nodded my understanding.

"Basically, we test several segments of the p53 gene where mutations are known to occur and create small complimentary fragments of the DNA in question using a technique called PCR. All you need to know is that PCR is great for finding mutations. And I was able to detect mutant p53 gene fragments in the PCR work I did this weekend. That's the gel you're looking at here."

Dimitri looked at me over the top of his horn-rimmed glasses. "If a mutation is present, we get a gene fragment that is a different size and composition from the normal gene and then the electrophoresis gel detects this difference."

I vaguely remembered that electrophoresis gels separated gene fragments because different sized fragments moved through the gel at different speeds.

"And that's what we are seeing in these specimens, Patrick. In each of the gene segments that we tested, we can see bands representing normal p-53 gene sequence. But in certain gels, we not only see normal p53 gene product—we also see extra bands of abnormal gene fragments, which are produced by cancer cells with mutant p53."

I looked at the gels again and could readily see the multiple bands resulting from normal and mutated p53 DNA. It was sinking in that I had strong, unbiased evidence that the dog with the implanted *super-B.I.G.* prosthesis had developed bone cancer adjacent to the implant.

And that evidence gave me a huge problem. For a moment, I tried to tell myself it was possible that the cancer represented a random event and would never happen in human patients. But with a hollow feeling, I realized that I was fooling myself.

I looked at Dimitri. He was obviously puzzled by my silence.

I put my head in my hands. Exposing what I knew might ruin careers, possibly including Meredith's, and would cost my future employers at the hospital and university millions of dollars. But how could I, a cancer surgeon, live with myself if I said nothing about the risk that the *super-B.I.G.* prosthesis could represent?

I broke the silence. "Dimitri, thanks for doing this. Can you get photos of those gels, preserve the gels carefully, and send me a copy of the photos by email?"

Dimitri nodded. "Of course. You don't seem happy with the results, Patrick."

"I can only imagine how hard it is to achieve the clarity of the results that you have provided. You have given me a huge problem by working your butt off over the weekend. But you may also have saved a lot of lives. So, thank you very, very much."

Dimitri was puzzled by my response. "Do you mean that I have saved dog lives?"

"No, Dimitri. I do not just mean dog lives. I wish I did."

Chapter 39

Dr. Patrick Maloney
May 3

*I*finished the day back in Gershwyn's clinic, examining patients who had undergone previous treatment and surgery. Justine provided me with a latte from the machine in the office. "It's great that you and the boss get along so well, Patrick. Your presence here allows him to be more efficient, and that makes it much easier to schedule him for the important jobs he does. And, of course, it's all about making my life easier."

I knew that she was only half joking. Justine was one of those power assistants who absorbed their boss' life goals into their own and lived by their boss' success. "Justine, some docs might think that the most important job is looking after the patients."

She punched me in the ribs. "You know what I mean. You guys will make a great team. You are good with patients, and the nurses from the OR tell me that Gershwyn already trusts you to operate. With you running the clinical practice and lab work at Sumner, the boss will be freed up to do the other things that only he can do—like raise money to support the amazing things we do here."

And with that, she opened her arms expansively to indicate the fullness of her empire, pivoted, and marched back to her desk. I was pretty sure that I would eventually need to deal with Justine when Gershwyn and I became partners. She would always remain committed to the professor, and I would likely always be the chore boy in Justine's world view. However, this was a secondary issue.

Joining Gershwyn's practice as a partner would provide me with instant entry to a very small international community of special surgical expertise. I knew Gershywn liked me. I expected that he was probably at the age and stage of his career when promoting a young surgeon as his successor would be a pleasure.

I was pleased to see two patients on the clinic list who we had recently operated on. Sarah had recovered well from her knee osteosarcoma surgery and was ready to leave Boston for her home in California following this check-up. Her physio had gone extremely well, and her knee motion lacked only the last twenty degrees of flexion compared to the normal knee.

I explained to Sarah and her parents, "You need to remember that your knee will never be entirely normal. The prosthesis that we used to replace the cancer is not designed to provide exactly normal knee movement, and you have already achieved all the movement that you will likely ever get out of your knee."

I checked the pulses in Sarah's foot and was delighted that the two blood vessels in her foot were pulsating normally. Her cancer had grown immediately adjacent to the main blood vessel in the back of her knee, and I remembered the difficulty I'd had in freeing the cancer from the vessel and the bleeding that had ensued. I had needed to repair the artery during surgery, and this could sometimes restrict blood flow through the repaired artery, resulting in a weak pulse in the foot. Fortunately, the repair was working well in Sarah's case.

I also went over the pathology report with Sarah and her parents. The pathology examination was an important indicator of the impact of chemotherapy on Sarah's particular type of osteosarcoma. It reported that cellular death within the cancer was substantial, but not complete. Sarah had undergone chemotherapy prior to surgery, and the chemotherapy would be ranked as moderately effective based on this pathology report.

I always found this aspect of patient care rather surreal. Sarah was an intelligent and optimistic young woman. She saw nothing but a bright future ahead once this unexpected bout of illness was behind her. This bland pathology report told me that she had a good chance of cure. But not a great chance.

I remembered the agony that had followed when my sister's cancer had returned shortly after the amputation. Without benefit of chemotherapy, the cancer had returned rapidly in multiple spots in her lungs, and I could vividly remember the horror of watching her breathing become more and more difficult over the three months before her death.

Those memories fueled my enthusiasm for the Synchro Therapy we were testing with Kate at Sumner. If providing IGF synchronization of cancer cell division increased effectiveness of chemotherapy, then I would feel that we were honoring my sister's memory in a very special way.

I described the follow-up care that would be needed and agreed that Dr. Gershwyn would be happy if Sarah's care would be provided in California. She would continue with chemotherapy for another three months and would continue with physiotherapy for the knee. I promised to send electronic copies of her various records, scans, and X-rays to her surgeon, physiotherapist, and oncologist in California, and these doctors would keep Dr. Gershwyn informed of her progress.

As they got up to leave, Sarah and her parents had tears in their eyes and Sarah hugged me tightly. Cancer surgery is a fragile and intimate enterprise, and surgeons either need to achieve inspiration from emotional engagement with their patients or choose to be purposefully disengaged.

I knew that it would be difficult to be close to a patient when the cancer returned. However, I felt I could manage the loss of a patient I felt close to better than the isolation of being emotionally distant from a vulnerable person. I wondered how this would feel twenty years into practice.

The next patient was Randell from New York, who had undergone resection of the upper arm for Ewing's sarcoma. His pathology report was better than Sarah's in that most of his cancer had been killed by chemotherapy prior to surgery. The peripheral margins of surgery were negative for cancer cells, and I was encouraged that Randell's chance for cure was excellent.

Randell's reconstruction would not be as functional as Sarah's. The shoulder is a more complex joint than the knee to reconstruct. The shoulder is stabilized and activated by the small muscles of the rotator cuff, and these muscles were necessarily damaged during surgery to remove the cancer.

However, Randell's lower arm and hand worked normally since we had been able to preserve the radial nerve while removing the cancer. Gershwyn had pointed out this area to the pathologist following the surgery and the pathologist had taken multiple specimens to search for residual cancer cells.

I looked at Randell and his parents as I finished reading the pathology report. "The results of the pathology are really very encouraging. All the cancer was removed for sure and the chemotherapy has been very effective. This is about as good as it gets."

Randell's dad had been the quiet one of the three when we'd first met them. Randell and his mother started hugging and crying when I told them the pathology results. His dad started by shaking my hand, then threw his arms around me. He had tears running down his face when he leaned back and simply said, "Thank you, Doctor. Thank you very much."

I worked through the rest of patients in the clinic and left the hospital after 5:00 p.m. I returned home to get a sports jacket and tie, then Ubered to the Back Bay to join Meredith by 6:00. In rush hour, it would take an hour to drive to Weston, where the pitch meeting was scheduled to begin at 7:00.

Meredith welcomed me with her arms around my neck, lips softly against mine and her body folded against me from knees to shoulders. I felt her firm pressure and thought that I could stay in this position forever.

We were both panting slightly as we separated, and Meredith raised her eyebrows. "Do we have time?"

I checked my watch and shook my head sadly. "Not unless you want to be notably late for your Dad and your boss. After my last experience with them, I think that I would like to avoid notable lateness." I kissed her again. "A promise for reconsideration later tonight?"

Meredith's tongue protruded slightly from the corner of her mouth and she looked down coyly. "Well, I suppose if we get home early we could consider."

She smiled and kissed me again. "I want you right now and I want you forever I think, Patrick Maloney."

"We better get going or I am not going to be able to leave."

Chapter 40

Mr. Jim McClintock
May 3

*E*ven though I had lived in Weston most of my nearly sixty years, I was always struck by the wealth of the community. The houses I passed on my drive to the office were enormous and set on large wooded lots. The retail stores included all the up-fashion brands, but you still had the sense of a small village where people knew you.

The final pitch meeting for the **super-B.I.G.** was held in my firm's office building. My investment management business occupied the bottom three floors of the four-story building that I bought years ago. Most of our business was related to managing the financial affairs for high net worth individuals living in west suburban Boston. About 75 percent of our clients were professionals—doctors, lawyers, dentists—and the rest were successful business owners.

I had been in business for nearly thirty years, and was always proud to tell people that most of my company's first clients were still with us. Over time, we had expanded our offerings, which now included comprehensive accounting, tax, estate, and investment advice.

I'd also had a great deal of luck or success investing in my own book, and my family's wealth derived equally from the business and investment results. I directed most of my clients to lower risk, diversified investments, and my business was known to fund managers along the Eastern seaboard.

I had learned about the *super-B.I.G.* prosthesis through Meredith and had met Dr. Hendricks as the surgeon was beginning to develop an investment plan for this promising new approach to hip arthritis. Hendricks had already selected Synvest as his main partner for the prosthesis. Synvest knew that production of the prosthesis would require an extreme antiseptic environment for assembly and packaging. Synvest needed funding to refurbish an existing plant to produce the *super-B.I.G.* product.

I'd considered the strategy with Hendricks and advised him that a collaborative approach to fundraising with investment bankers would be a secure way of achieving relatively low-cost funding. I helped Synvest and Hendricks run an audition for several investment banks eager to help with the fundraising, and we negotiated a good low-cost partnership for raising the money.

I had tried to coach Hendricks on how to approach the fundraising task with the investment bankers, but soon found I didn't need to; the surgeon was an absolutely natural pitchman. The demand for hip replacements increased every year, and this prosthesis was a disruptive offering with strong patent protection. Hendricks knew he had a good product on his hands, and his crisp, polished appearance only gave the whole venture more credibility.

The cost of any hip prosthesis was actually a small part of the total cost to insurance companies for total hip replacement surgery, and the *super-B.I.G.* prosthesis would be readily marketed for twice the cost of the B.I.G. implant that it would supplant. The profit margins and the potential volumes of sales would be remarkable, and we anticipated in our business case that the *super-B.I.G.* would capture 50 percent of Synvest's American market for hip replacement within two years. Within four years, it was reasonable to assume that half the hip prostheses sold around the world would be **super-B.I.G.** implants.

Synvest was a large, well-respected company with an established sales force, and the opportunity for success was obvious to the institutional investors that the bankers and Hendricks initially approached for funding. Competition to get into the program was intense and the bankers raised their fundraising target to $3 billion from $2.6 billion.

The increase in the IPO to $3 billion would mean a large windfall for Synvest, CellGrow, Hendricks, and Kovalov, as well as the hospital and university, which shared in any intellectual property commercialized by their faculty. Because of my daughter's involvement, I had refused a profit share. In return for my advice, I only asked that I might be allowed to offer the opportunity to invest to a small number of my most sophisticated investors. This was why Hendricks was concluding his fundraising tonight in our offices in Weston.

When Meredith and Patrick arrived, seven of my earliest and best clients were enjoying a catered meal in our boardroom, chatting with Hendricks, who had arrived a bit earlier. These clients had all signed non-disclosure agreements, partly to protect any proprietary secrets that Hendricks might mention, but more importantly to ensure that my other clients did not learn I was being selective in offering only these seven the opportunity to invest in this remarkable product.

As I took my seat, Hendricks was explaining the advantage of the **super-B.I.G.** "Hip replacement began sixty years ago as an option for elderly people, who had the operation as an alternative to life in a wheelchair," he said as my clients dug into their prime rib. "As the surgery and the implants grew more reliable, the operation was offered to people with less crippling diseases. And now we are at the point where we can make the promise that our new **super-B.I.G.** *will be the only hip replacement the patient ever needs.*

I loved watching Jon speak to an audience. His sincerity was palpable, and people just wanted to believe him. "We have implanted the **super-B.I.G.** in more than a hundred dogs with arthritis. Using remarkable technology developed by Dr. McClintock, we have evaluated these prostheses by removal after fifty of these dogs passed away."

The investors smiled at Meredith. Most of them had known her since childhood, and they shared my pride in her accomplishments.

"The bottom line is that the *super-B.I.G.* prosthesis attachment to bone is a quantum leap in mechanical stability enabled by a novel biological stimulation of bone growth. It eliminates the need for all other hip operations in younger people. I will also be happy to give patients permission to do any activity—running, basketball, aggressive skiing—no restrictions."

The potential investors asked several questions of me and Hendricks about the business case. How much would insurance companies cover of the increased prosthesis cost?

"The cost of the prosthesis is really a small part of the total cost of hip replacement. And insurance companies will be happy that we're reducing the risk of a very expensive revision operation. They have said that they will cover the full cost."

Had the federal regulator approved the prosthesis? "This is a relatively small change to existing implant design, and the regulator has approved the new *super-B.I.G.* based on prior approvals for the existing B.I.G. implant."

Were there any potential complications associated with the new prosthesis? Before answering that question, Hendricks glanced at Patrick. Meredith had told her boss that Patrick would be attending the meeting at my invitation, and I was relieved to hear that Hendricks had not raised an objection.

"We expect no complications using this new design. Patients have been treated for years with Growth Hormone therapy, which increases their own body's IGF without any adverse effects. IGF is a naturally occurring substance, and we are simply taking advantage of its impact on bone by applying it directly to the prosthesis."

One of the potential investors had a question for me. "Jim, as you know, I decided to invest in Synvest several years ago after I had a total hip replacement. The stock has been a steady gainer for the past ten years, but suddenly it has taken off and more than doubled its stock price in the past six months. Is that because of the *super-B.I.G.?*"

I nodded in affirmation. "Some investors are increasing their exposure to the *super-B.I.G.* by buying Synvest since it is the only partner in this IPO that is currently publicly listed. CellGrow is privately held, and you cannot buy shares in Dr. Hendricks or Dr. Kovalov, the scientist who developed the biolayer from CellGrow's product. As you know, Synvest will be the majority owner of voting shares in the new company."

One of the investors had taken interest in Patrick's presence. "Jim, I understand that we have another orthopedic surgeon in the room. Dr. Maloney, I believe? What do you think of the *super-B.I.G.* prosthesis? Are you going to use it in your practice?"

I watched Patrick and was concerned to see his face twisting. "I don't really do much hip replacement surgery in my practice. I am here in Boston studying bone cancer surgery. So, I do not expect to use the *super-B.I.G.* prosthesis in my practice."

But the investor would not let up. "But given that you're here today, I'm sure you must have learned a lot about the *super-B.I.G.* prosthesis already. If you were doing hip replacement surgery, would you recommend the *super-B.I.G.* to your patients?"

Patrick looked noticeably uncomfortable. I felt the tension in the room begin to mount as he struggled to figure out what to say. "I am sure that the *super-B.I.G.* will do just what Dr. Hendricks says it will. No doubt about it. But I guess that I might wait for a couple of years to see what results in humans look like before deciding."

Meredith and I looked at Patrick with concern and Hendricks had turned red. The investor kept at it. "You mean that you wouldn't use it immediately. Do you think that other surgeons should delay advising their patients to use the *super-B.I.G.?*"

All of the investors in the room were now staring intently at Patrick.

He was obviously straining to answer the question positively. His discomfort was palpable. "Every surgeon will make his own mind up. I expect that most will follow Dr. Hendricks' advice about the *super-B.I.G.* He is one of the most respected hip surgeons in the world."

The meeting broke up shortly thereafter. The investors went away with information about the IPO, and I told them that if they were interested in investing, they would need to confirm that they wanted to be part of the deal by the end of the week.

A couple of the investors looked at Patrick quizzically as they left. They were not sure why he was there, and certainly did not feel he was confident in the *super-B.I.G.*

I heard Patrick quietly mention to Meredith that he thought they should leave. I took my daughter aside as they were on their way out.

"Meredith, what's with this guy? I know you care for him, but he does not seem to have much concern for your work. The first time I met him, he was trying to convince us that the project you are spending your life on causes cancer. And today, I assumed that you wanted him to have a chance to make up for that first meeting. I must say that he acted very strangely. He just about said that he would wait forever before using the product. I get the feeling that he may be jealous about you having a huge success as part of the *super-B.I.G.* team."

"I know, Dad, I don't get it. Patrick is not like what you have seen in these two meetings. He is very supportive about what I do, and I don't think that he is jealous at all. To the contrary, he seems to be very proud of my work. There is just something about either Hendricks or the *super-B.I.G.* that is making him very nervous. I'm going to ask him on the way home and I'll let you know."

Hendricks pointedly ignored Patrick as he marched past us and out the door.

Chapter 41

Meredith McClintock, PhD
May 3

*W*e walked out to the parking lot and drove the first five minutes in silence.

"Meredith, I am so sorry," Patrick finally said. "I know that I screwed up again with your dad and your boss. I was not expecting those guys to ask me what I thought about the *super-B.I.G.*"

"Patrick, you were not there to provide a testimonial, but my goodness—you almost said that you would never use it. Is it Hendricks you don't like? Why do you have such a problem with the *super-B.I.G.*?"

Patrick lapsed into silence and stared ahead into the evening traffic as I drove. Then, he started talking non-stop for more than fifteen minutes. I was astonished by what he told me and increasingly concerned. I kept having to remind myself to watch the road. He finished by saying that he knew just what he needed to do.

Chapter 42

Mr. James Bailey
21 months later

*T*hree rounds of chemotherapy resulted in severe side effects for our daughter, including the loss of Brianna's beautiful hair. The doctors repeated her chest CAT scan and provided me and Imani with the horrible news that the lung tumors had continued growing despite the toxic chemotherapy.

I received this news while sitting with Brianna and Imani in a clinic room. I could not believe what had befallen my little girl. She was dying in front of my eyes. "So, what are you telling us, Doc?" I asked, not knowing where to look. "What can we do now?"

The doctor replied that the oncologists had already tried the most aggressive drugs available for this cancer. There was no further standard treatment he could recommend.

"Mr. Bailey, the team has looked at all options. We think the only real hope is to refer Brianna to Boston, where a new form of experimental treatment called Synchro Therapy is being offered for young bone cancer patients when all else has failed."

"You know we will do anything for our daughter," Imani said steadily, putting her hand on my arm. "But we just don't have the money to go off to Boston. I lost my job taking time off to look after Brianna the last two months, and our savings are gone. I don't think we will be able to borrow any more money. I have no idea how we are going to pay your hospital's bills, let alone pay for treatment out of state."

"Mrs. Bailey, we found one piece of good news since we started looking for options for Brianna," the doctor replied. "They have set up a fund at the hospital in Boston that pays the costs of experimental bone cancer treatments to include patients who do not have health insurance. And when I explained your situation to the surgeon this morning, he said that they would also cover your transportation and living expenses in Boston."

I just wasn't used to this kind of good news. "This sounds too good to be true."

"I checked the website, Mr. Bailey, and it seems that Brianna's expenses can be covered by what the hospital calls its Emily Fund. There's some information about the fund and Emily, the young woman it's named after, on the website. Apparently, she was quite young when she developed bone cancer. Emily's family did not have health insurance either. Unfortunately, she passed away from the cancer, and this fund was set up to try and save patients who have not responded to standard treatment. It almost seems like this fund was set up for someone exactly like Brianna."

I rubbed my chin thoughtfully. "Don't get me wrong, Doc. I am grateful if Brianna can get help from this Emily Fund. It just sounds miraculous, and I don't usually believe in miracles."

A few days later, as Imani and Brianna prepared to leave for Boston, I found myself praying, despite my lack of faith in miracles, that this experimental Synchro Therapy might offer hope for my girl.

Chapter 43

Mr. Sandy Spencer
May 4

*W*hen Patrick called last evening, I was happy to chat for more than one reason. Since the last time Patrick and I had talked at Copley Square, I had followed the increasing hype around the ***super-B.I.G.*** story. I'd figured that Hendricks' big new project accounted for the fact that Synvest stock had more than doubled over the past six months. When Patrick broached the topic at the start of the call, I assumed he was calling me to advise taking a major position in the IPO that was coming. But what Patrick told me was shockingly different from what I expected.

After talking to Patrick for more than an hour, I hung up and dialed another number, waking a colleague who covered biotech for our investment journal and telling him that I was sending him some images of something called a p53 gel—whatever that was. Patrick had tried explaining it twice, but it was still over my head. Twenty minutes after my call and email transfer of the images, my colleague called back and confirmed that the gel showed evidence of mutated p53 in one DNA fragment that was indicative of cancer.

I asked him whether this would be typical of dog osteosarcoma. "That's bone cancer," I told him, trying to be helpful. My colleague told me that he would need to check and called me back fifteen minutes later with confirmation that yes, that type of p53 mutation was frequent in dog osteosarcoma.

The next morning, I flew to Boston on the first flight and headed straight to Sumner Hospital to meet Dr. Kate Benedict. The morning was warm, and after meeting in the surgery offices, we strolled outside.

"Kate, I am here to listen to your story about the slides that you looked at with Patrick last Wednesday afternoon. Can you describe to me what you saw?"

"Mr. Spencer, I assume you are writing a story about this and I am happy to talk about what we saw, but I do not want my name used. Will you agree to that?"

"Yes, I sure will. Patrick knows that if I am going to write this story, I need to test his commitment by naming him as a credible source and he has agreed. I need your statement in corroboration of Patrick's story, but I can describe you as an unnamed professional who confirms Patrick's version of what happened.

"Rather than ask you questions, I want you to describe what happened that afternoon when you examined the slides with Patrick. That is the best independent confirmation I can get of what Patrick is telling me. And, Kate, can I tape our conversation? I promise that no one will hear it but me. I will use the tape to transcribe our conversation."

We sat on a deserted bench at the back of the vet hospital and Kate quietly recounted what happened the afternoon she and Patrick had examined the slides. "We were looking at specimens from a dog that had received treatment called Synchro Therapy for his cancer. The treatment seemed to have killed all the cancer cells in the tumor and we were seeing amazing bone healing, which seemed to have occurred everywhere the cancer had previously been present. We probably looked at thirty slides from various parts of the cancer and they all essentially showed the same thing. We were extremely pleased with this outcome."

I was sitting quietly, taking careful notes in a notebook. I checked periodically to make sure the recorder was on.

"But there were two slides that seemed entirely different. There was plenty of new bone formation, but in the center of the slide there were densely packed cells—plump, very blue—demonstrating abnormal bone formation on their surface. To both me and Patrick ,they looked like abundant residual osteosarcoma cells that had not been killed by the Synchro Therapy."

I looked up from my notebook. "Dr. Benedict, do you have training in veterinary pathology?"

"No, not at all. But I have been specializing in treating dog bone cancers for the past year, and I have seen lots of osteosarcoma pathology specimens. To my eye, this slide showed classic dog osteosarcoma."

"Was anything else different about this slide?"

"As we scanned around the slide, we saw fragments of metal. Obviously, there would be no metal expected in a cancerous tumor, so this captured our attention.

"And Patrick suddenly realized what we were seeing. It was mesh from the surface of the *super-B.I.G.* prosthesis that had been implanted in the dog. There was bone growing around all the metal fragments, which was evidence of dense bone ingrowth into the mesh on the prosthesis."

"And this slide was different from all other slides from the surgical specimen?"

"Oh yes. There were about thirty slides that had been taken at various areas of the dog osteosarcoma, and these all showed similar complete cancer killing by the Synchro Therapy and massive new bone formation throughout the cancer. And then, there were these other two slides that were entirely different."

"How do you think these aberrant slides came to be placed among your slides?"

"The technicians will scan the slides from all the specimens they receive for testing and then label and store them. They likely were not expecting to see cancer cells in dog hip prosthesis specimens. Our patient was labelled with osteosarcoma as a diagnosis, so when the technician who sorted through these slides saw osteosarcoma, they must have placed it with our materials by mistake."

"Did you only have slides to look at? Was there other material available to you?"

"It is typical that the technicians keep the embedded specimen stored with the slides so if the pathologist wants to order more sections taken from a particular area, the embedded specimen block is readily available for further sampling."

"Were embedded specimens accompanying these slides that you were reviewing?"

"Yes. When we checked, most of the slides were accompanied by paraffin wax blocks. Following bone cancer surgical removal, the specimen is decalcified—"

"Decalcified?"

"The calcium is leached out of the tissue," she explained, smiling. "So, the decalcified tumor tissue is embedded in paraffin wax, and then very thin slices are cut from the tumor to be analyzed under the microscope. But the unusual slides were accompanied by a different type of specimen block. Instead of paraffin, the tissue was embedded in plastic. This technique is used in looking at bone ingrowth results in the *super-B.I.G.* prosthesis."

"How do they label the specimens? Is there an identification code?"

"Each of the paraffin blocks have a paper attached to the wax with a number that represents the dog number that the specimen was taken from. In this case, all of the paraffin embedded specimens had the same number. But the plastic embedded number was different."

"Did you return the slides?"

"We returned them to Sam, the head pathology assistant who looked at the numbers on the slide, and confirmed that it was a different number from the other slides we were examining. He said that he would need to let Dr. Kovalov know that we were asking about the specimens."

"What happened to those slides you looked at?"

"Well, to our endless embarrassment, those slides have never been seen again. Patrick and I suggested to the Hendricks team that there may be cancer in one of their *super-B.I.G.* dogs. We were invited in to review all the slides from the dog in question with a pathologist present and there was absolutely no evidence of cancer in any of the slides. But I know what Patrick and I saw. I definitely don't want you to quote me as saying this, but I suspect someone got rid of the incriminating slides."

"That last part is off the record, then. Did Patrick return all the slides and specimens to the pathology assistant that Saturday morning?"

"No, sir. He returned the slide, but kept the plastic embedded specimen so he could test it in other ways."

"Do you know what 'other ways' he was planning to use?"

"I'm not sure. I would imagine that he was thinking about doing genetic testing on the plastic embedded specimen. I also know that there was probably little chance that we would be able to get an accurate analysis of genetic material from the plastic blocks."

"Dr. Benedict, I know that you are not a people doctor. But if this dog specimen showed that cancer was present, what impact would that have on the *super-B.I.G.* prosthesis and its use in humans?"

She seemed to understand what I was really asking. "The *super-B.I.G.* prostheses that were implanted in dogs were expected to last between one and six years, since dogs live much shorter lives than humans. The dog that we are discussing now had the prosthesis in place for two years. But the *super-B.I.G.* prosthesis in humans is designed to be implanted for decades—ten to forty years or more. And the number of total hip replacements undertaken in people is huge compared to dogs.

"So far, *super-B.I.G.* prostheses have been implanted in about a hundred dogs, and fifty have been tested after death. If we are right that this dog developed cancer, then one in fifty of the dogs developed cancer. That's two percent. Just imagine if the *super-B.I.G.* prosthesis was used in half of the 400,000 hip replacements done annually in this country. If two percent of those developed cancer each year, that would be 4,000 new cases of osteosarcoma in people who otherwise were not at risk of malignancy."

"Is it logical to expect that the *super-B.I.G.* prosthesis may be more likely to cause cancer than other hip replacements?" I looked at her directly. This was an important aspect of my questioning.

"I understand that the breakthrough the *super-B.I.G.* offers is that the mesh on the surface of the prosthesis is saturated with a slow release form of a protein called IGF. We know that IGF sensitivity may be associated with the onset of bone cancer, both in dogs and in humans."

"Dr. Benedict, bottom line—would you advise anyone to have a *super-B.I.G.* prosthesis implanted?"

"I am not a people doctor, as you said. However, I am knowledgeable about bone cancer and hip arthritis. Based on our suspicions that one in fifty dogs has developed bone cancer with a *super-B.I.G.* prosthesis, I would advise that no one should have this operation." Kate looked somewhat defiant, but also very, very convinced.

My next interview was with Dimitri Antonopoulos. Unlike Dr. Benedict, he was more than happy for me to use his name in the article.

"Dr. Antonopoulos, why would Dr. Maloney come to you for analysis of the specimen to determine whether the dog had cancer in his bone?"

"Patrick knew that I had developed special expertise in extracting genetic material from plastic embedded specimens of bone," he said. "My understanding is that he had only one specimen available."

"Was the testing that you undertook on this specimen terribly difficult, and are the results reliable?"

Dimitri nodded. "Great questions. Getting DNA from plastic embedded material is not rocket science, but you need to be very careful with your techniques. I have a lot of experience isolating genetic material from plastic embedded bone biopsy specimens that are used to quantitate osteoporosis. Typically, I am looking to analyze different genes in my experiments. However, the hard part is getting good quality DNA or RNA for analysis, and my lab is very expert with that step."

"Have you done cancer gene analysis in the past?"

"Yes, I did my graduate work in a cancer lab in Greece, where we were looking for a variety of cancer genes in human tissues."

"And you used the DNA you isolated from the plastic specimen Dr. Maloney gave you to determine whether the p53 gene showed evidence of mutation?"

"Yes. I have learned that p53 is mutated in about 50 percent of dog osteosarcomas. So, it made sense to look for mutation of p53. If there was no p53 mutation present, we could not conclude that there was no cancer. However, showing p53 mutation is pretty clear evidence that cancerous change has occurred."

"Can you show me the gels and why you are certain about the p53 mutation?"

"Of course," he said. "The abnormal gene is shown in this gel," the scientist continued, comparing the bands of normal and mutated DNA on the gels he was showing me. "The presence of the p53 mutation is a very powerful indicator of the presence of cancer."

I thanked Dr. Antonopoulos for his straightforward description of his work on the embedded specimen. Then, I headed to a coffeeshop to review my notes and consider the story.

With Patrick's and Kate's consistent independent testimonies regarding the description of the microscope slides and Dimitri's description of the gels, I knew that I had a strong rationale to publish concerns about the *super-B.I.G.* Patrick's willingness to put his reputation on the line by allowing me to use his name certainly helped. Of course, I'd have to disclose that I knew him previously. That's where Kate's willingness to corroborate Patrick's story, even though she was not comfortable with allowing her name to be used, was also important.

I had wanted to meet her and test her story in person, and I'd asked Patrick not to tell her about the p53 results until I spoke to her. She'd offered exact collaboration of what I had already heard from Patrick.

I knew his story would have very detrimental effects on the business case for the *super-B.I.G.* prosthesis and the IPO that was due to be publicly announced shortly. The *super-B.I.G.* prosthesis had been approved by the federal regulator. But the fact that a case of bone cancer had been associated with the *super-B.I.G.* within two years of implantation would likely result in revocation of the regulator's approval for the *super-B.I.G.* And even if the regulator for some reason did not revoke their approval, the suggestion that the *super-B.I.G.* was not safe would definitely impact its marketability and the major fundraising that was planned.

Sadly, I also realized that the story was going to ruin Patrick's career. I had always been impressed by this young man and was pleased that Patrick's talent had been recognized by Gershwyn so quickly after arrival at the hospital.

However, I knew that Gershwyn would not be able to protect Patrick from the response that this story would create at the hospital and university. Hendricks was one of the most influential voices at the hospital since he raised enormous amounts of philanthropic donations and ensured that well-insured patients attended the hospital from around the country and the world. As soon as this story was published, Hendricks would be implacably opposed to Patrick coming on staff at the hospital.

I knew from my contacts in academic medicine in New York that Gershwyn and Hendricks respected and generally supported each other. In this case, however, Hendricks would have the influence to blackball Patrick. Gershwyn would be too savvy to waste political capital protecting his young fellow if he was attacked by Hendricks.

In addition to Hendricks, both hospital's and the university's administration would also be losing a big payday if the IPO failed. With all these powerful forces impacted by the story, Patrick's fate would be sealed when the article was published.

The *super-B.I.G.* prosthesis promised the hospital and university a stable source of funding for years to come. I knew from reviewing the investment documentation for the IPO that Synvest planned to market the implant at a premium, and patients would likely clamor for the implant.

Since Hendricks was a faculty member of both the university and the hospital, he was required to share royalties from any intellectual property developed with the two institutions. The proceeds from the IPO would provide the institutions with funding that they would be furious to lose. Patrick would be extremely unpopular once my story broke.

I thought about this for a moment and focused on how unfair this was. Patrick was only trying to protect future patients, as well as shield the hospital and university from future lawsuits. However, his commitment was going to earn him immediate animosity from very powerful people.

And then, I had a thought.

I pulled out my phone, locating a junior reporter at the journal. I knew that the revelation of the *super-B.I.G.*, with all its intrigue and impact on the powerful interests of academic medicine and corporate medicine, would be an irresistible story. It could even lead to a series of articles about the risks to patients from conflicts of interest for industry, hospitals, universities, and leading doctors. This series could have Pulitzer potential.

I almost didn't want to give it up. But I had broken a number of blockbuster stories in the past, and maybe now it was time for me to play a different role.

Chapter 44

Dr. Patrick Maloney
May 4

I was surprised that afternoon when Sandy asked me to repeat the entire story to his junior colleague at the paper. Theresa Branton was obviously highly intelligent, understanding the impact of the story on the IPO and eager to learn about the clinical aspects and genetic issues at hand. Dimitri was always willing to talk about his science, and Theresa told me subsequently that she'd had to remove herself from his lab with the PhD still lecturing. She'd thought Dimitri's discourse would never end, but she certainly now understood the significance of the DNA extraction from the plastic embedded bone and the methodology of using PCR and gel electrophoresis to compare regular and mutant fragments of genetic material.

Theresa finished the afternoon interviewing Kate and me. We now understood she planned to post her article on the paper's website at midnight. I was uncertain as to why Sandy had suddenly given up authorship of the story, but Sandy reassured me the reason would become apparent soon enough.

On the way home from her father's office the night before, I had told Meredith about my plan of sharing my concerns about the **super-B.I.G.** prosthesis with Sandy. I was not surprised that she had at first been confused and then concerned.

"But isn't it possible that this is just a random event? Maybe the cancer just developed in the dog bone by absolute coincidence. Why are you so sure that the cancer is caused by the prosthesis?"

"Meredith, there are a couple of issues to think about. First, we know that IGF causes bone cell division and growth, and Andrei's sustained release product creates bone cell growth and division that results in amazing bonding of the bone to the prosthesis. We know from your mechanical studies that the prosthesis bone bond is really strong. However, we also know from our human and dog cancer work that high IGF levels can be associated with bone cancer. So, there is a plausible biological connection between IGF and cancer risk.

"Secondly, if there is any risk that Andrei's IGF preparation may cause cancer, surely that needs to be worked out to understand how big the risk may be. I am pretty sure the regulator would not approve the **super-B.I.G.** if they knew about what we saw under the microscope. They would at least demand more studies.

"And letting the prosthesis go to market when I know what I saw is impossible for me. After all, my sister died of bone cancer. I work treating patients with bone cancer. I know the pain and suffering that bone cancer can cause for families. How could I possibly know what I know about the risk associated with the **super-B.I.G.** and not say anything?"

"But when we met at Sumner with you and Kate, you looked at so many slides and did not see anything suspicious for cancer. Both you and Kate and the dog pathologist all agreed that there was no cancer present—and you looked at a lot of slides."

This was the hard part for me. Until this discussion in her car, I had not told Meredith that I had kept the plastic embedded blocks from the dog specimen, or about the work that I had asked Dimitri to undertake. "There is something that I haven't told you about, and I feel bad about only telling you now.

"The slide that Kate and I saw from the B.I.G. was accompanied by the plastic block that the slide was cut from. When I returned the slide, I kept the block. I don't know why. I guess I just had a feeling that the slide might disappear."

She was driving, and it was difficult to see her face. I felt terrible about not telling her about keeping the block. "I think that Andrei likely destroyed the slide after he heard about my concern for cancer. I didn't say anything about keeping the block, because I doubted that it would show much of interest.

"However, I gave it to a genomic scientist who is one of the world's experts in extracting DNA from plastic embedded specimens, and he was able to get some DNA. And he then showed that the DNA had a p53 mutation that is just diagnostic of osteosarcoma bone cancer."

I looked at her while she drove to see if this revelation was making an impact. It was hard to tell for sure. "Am I certain that that dog developed bone cancer because of the *super-B.I.G.*? Well, not 100 percent certain. It would be nice to have an expert review the slides that Kate and I saw, but I am pretty sure they are destroyed. But I know what the expert would say if the slides were available.

"Along with the DNA results, I would say that I am 99 percent certain that the *super-B.I.G.* implant was associated with cancer in that dog. And when your boss is getting ready to implant that device in millions of people around the world, I think I need to say something."

At this point in the conversation, we had just pulled into Meredith's parking spot off Marlborough. Meredith was obviously rapidly processing all of the outcomes that my going public with this story would entail. Her job, her relationship with her boss who knew that she was close to me, her father and his investment future, my future career prospects in Boston—there were so many elements tied up here.

"Patrick, I know this is a dilemma for you and I respect that. You need to understand that my career and my family are deeply affected by your decision to go public. Right now, I just don't know how to process that. I'm going to call my father right now to warn him. Apart from that, I just don't know what to say."

"I understand. I'm going to contact Sandy tonight and expect that he will break the story in the next day or two. At this point, I'm not sure what to say to you either. Other than I really care for you. In fact, I love you."

"Well, this is a hell of a way to tell a girl that you love her, by giving her the biggest headache of her life." She kissed me softly on the cheek and looked at me pensively. "Let's connect tomorrow after I have a chance to speak to my dad, okay?"

I left the conversation there and went back to my apartment. I spoke to Sandy that evening and arranged to meet him when he came up on the first flight the next morning. Fortunately for me, Gershwyn was away on a speaking date on the West Coast the next day, and nothing was scheduled in the office or operating room. I had plenty of time to speak to Sandy and then to Theresa, who had arrived that afternoon.

I had hoped that Meredith would call, but there had been nothing from her as yet. Just as I thought about Meredith, my phone rang, and her name appeared on my screen.

"Patrick, I have had several long discussions with my dad, and he wants to talk with you. I know it's getting late in the day, but would you be willing to go out to Weston with me right now?"

"Of course. Where are you now?"

"At my apartment. I will pick you up."

Sixty minutes later, we were sitting in her dad's boardroom. Jim McClintock had a notebook open in front of him. "Patrick, thanks for coming so soon. Meredith and I have been puzzling over what we should do next, and I thought that it might be useful for me to speak directly to you."

"Please realize that neither of us understands the clinical or biologic aspects of the situation we are facing. I understand only too well the financial impacts, and Meredith understands the impact on Dr. Hendricks' program, but I wanted to hear directly from you why you are so concerned about what you have learned."

I started from the beginning and described my concerns for the fourth time in twelve hours. Jim McClintock took copious notes and asked several probing questions. Ninety minutes went by quickly.

At the end of the story, Jim pushed back from the boardroom table and put his hands behind his head.

"Well, Meredith, I don't know where you found this guy."

I could feel the start of the negative response I expected would be aimed at me consistently and repetitively over the next few days. Meredith's father, Hendricks, Gershwyn, the hospital, the university, the investors—they would all be furious with me. I knew Gershwyn would not be able to protect me, even if he wanted to help, and my short-lived career in Boston was finished. Furthermore, the influential people I would be alienating in Boston had a long reach and influence. It was likely this story would follow me my entire career and would be detrimental to getting any job that I pursued.

"Meredith, there must be so many reasons why Patrick should have just dropped this story, why he never should have asked this Dr. Antonopoulos to run these p53 gels or whatever they are called, and to just forget about and cover up his concerns. What the hell? No one would ever criticize him if he just shut up. And speaking out like this—he puts your career and especially his career at major risk.

"Now, Patrick, I am going to talk like Meredith's father for a moment. I know without her saying anything that she cares for you. At risk of sounding old-fashioned, can I assume that your intentions toward my daughter are honorable?"

"Absolutely, sir. I am so sorry about the impact this could have on Meredith's career. I would never otherwise do her any harm. I care about her very deeply."

"So, young man, why are you damaging both of your careers, causing unbelievable financial complications, and creating a situation whereby you will be treated as a pariah in New England forever?"

I could not help but gulp. I realized Jim McClintock was describing the reality that would likely face me in the next twenty-four hours and for years to come. But the answer to his question was clear and unavoidable.

"Mr. McClintock, I am first and foremost a doctor, and I swore an oath that I would do my best to help people and first do no harm. I cannot know that something may cause terrible harm to people and say nothing. I know that what I am doing is very disruptive, but it is my sworn duty to simply tell people what I know if it can possibly help them."

Jim looked at his daughter and shrugged. "I'll say again that I don't know where you found him. Patrick, I know you must feel like I am part of the forces of evil aligned against you right now. However, I'm impressed and grateful for what you have done, and for your insistence on speaking out."

Meredith gave her father a hug and then came around the table to hug me in that special way that turned me into jelly.

"Mr. McClintock," I managed to say, "I can't tell you how much I appreciate your comments. But what about all the investors who you have lined up for the *super-B.I.G.* investment?"

"Call me Jim, Patrick. If you had held onto this news for the next three weeks until after the IPO was accomplished, it would have been a disaster for investors. Don't get me wrong—it still would have been the right thing for you to do, but for us financial guys who have been recommending the deal to clients, we would have lost them an awful lot of money. However, as I understand it, the story will be coming out in the next twelve hours."

I nodded. "I called Sandy Spencer last evening and gave him the full story early this morning. He has also interviewed my colleagues the vet surgeon and the gene scientist, and then decided to get another journalist involved. She has completed re-interviewing everyone and is likely writing her story now. She said it would be published online by midnight and be in press for the morning edition."

"Patrick, I have mainly been involved in advising Jon Hendricks on how to do this deal and maximize the revenue that he would generate with Synvest and the other partners for this IPO. And I must say that he and I have done a pretty good job. He exceeded his fundraising target, and the issue will be over-subscribed. A lot of people were going to get rich from this IPO, including to a certain extent my daughter."

Meredith looked over at him and shrugged.

"Meredith can afford to be nonchalant because she understands that she doesn't really need any more money. My company has done very well, and our family is very secure. And actually, I am not one of those people who will be losing potential riches. I helped Jon out because Meredith convinced me to believe in her work, but I personally have nothing at stake in the IPO but reputation. I have advised a few clients who would be very minor players, but that is it."

"So, you won't be one of the investors who gets hurt by this, Dad?"

"No one is really going to lose money. With Sandy Spencer's story, no matter who writes it, this IPO is going to be cancelled. No money has been transferred yet, so no one gets hurt except the owners of the *super-B.I.G.* intellectual property who were expecting a massive payday. The investors will have lost a *super-B.I.G.* opportunity—pardon the pun—but they will not have lost money.

"I'm sure that is one reason why Sandy wants to get the story out now. I know him by reputation and have met him at several investment events. He is known both as a good reporter and a very shrewd investor on his own account. He has done extremely well in the markets, often through his own careful research, some published and some not published. It's interesting that you say he is handing this story off to a colleague, Patrick."

"Yeah, that was a surprise to me as well."

"Well, young man, I am sure you are very concerned about what the next twenty-four hours will bring. Meredith told me that you'd hoped to stay at the hospital with your mentor. I guess you know that will be unlikely now?"

It was my turn to shrug, although I was probably less sanguine than Meredith about my likely loss.

"Despite all that, I have huge respect for your decision to put patients ahead of any of your personal concerns. And now, I think that there is only one thing left to say. Let's try and forget about this story and the consequences that will unfortunately be very evident for Patrick tomorrow morning. I am very afraid that this will be one good deed that will be punished forever. But since my daughter seems to be very attached to you, and since I cannot imagine a more honorable individual, why don't the three of us just go out for a late dinner and let me get to know you better?"

And that was the start of a pleasant evening. It turned out that Jim had played some hockey in university, and Meredith felt enjoyably left out while her dad and I traded rink war stories through dinner. Following the dinner, I returned to Dartmouth and Marlborough, where we continued to make history in our young relationship.

Chapter 45

Dr. Alfred Gershwyn
May 4

*I*had just finished a very successful dinner with San Francisco area alumni of our residency program and was in my hotel room getting ready to pack for my morning return flight to Boston. I was on the West Coast for a scientific conference, and Justine had organized a meeting with about twenty of the hospital's orthopedic graduates who had established their practices in Northern California.

I was very experienced in taking a low-key approach that would nonetheless remind the graduates about the debt they owed to the residency that had prepared them for their successful and lucrative practices. These evenings inevitably started with jovial toasts to absent professors and anecdotes exchanged about the personalities that made our residency program well-known in surgical communities across the country.

I enjoyed this opportunity to lampoon my colleagues along with the graduates during the first part of the dinner. But I would inevitably lead the discussion to the challenges we faced in maintaining an international center of excellence at the hospital that could remain a source of pride for its graduates. I emphasized the high cost of recruiting and resourcing surgical leaders, and by the end of the evening, all the graduates at the dinner would be proud to renew their contributions to their surgical alma mater.

Justine would inevitably follow up the next day by sending the dinner participants sincere thanks from Gershwyn. This well-practiced methodology to keep the orthopedic alumni engaged with the residency program ensured several million dollars of donations annually through our Alumni Fund.

I had just taken my suit jacket off in my hotel room when my phone rang. I recognized with alarm the number of the university dean. It was 9:30 in San Francisco and past midnight in Boston. As I picked up the call, I saw that a message had just arrived with an attachment from the president. "Albert, for God's sake—have you seen the article I just sent you?"

"It just arrived. What's going on?"

"I think that's for you to answer. My team just woke me up to warn me. It's this Maloney guy again. But this is unbelievable. Hendricks' IPO is being denounced as causing cancer. It's at the top of the *Journal's* website, and I bet it will be above the fold on the front page in the morning edition. And we are being accused of conflict of interest! It's unbelievable, Albert. This is just a disaster!"

I promised to get back to her after reading the article. And what I read entirely eliminated the satisfaction I was feeling from the fund-raising dinner.

The byline was from Theresa Branton, and the article opened with an attention-grabbing headline.

"Multi-Billion-Dollar Innovation May Cause Cancer in Hip Replacement Patients."

"Potential Conflict of Interest with Industry, University, Hospital, Surgeons, and Patients"

Branton's story then continued.

The Journal *has learned that a revolutionary innovation in hip replacement may put patients at risk of developing a dangerous bone cancer. A new prosthesis, called the **super-B.I.G.** implant, has been developed by medical giant Synvest in collaboration with famed*

Boston surgeon, Dr. Jonathan Hendricks. It will be widely marketed as "stronger than your own hip," and promises patients decades of use out of the prosthesis. But recent testing shows the **super-B.I.G.** *implant has caused cancer when implanted in dogs.*

Dr. Patrick Maloney, a cancer surgeon at Sumner Veterinary Hospital where Hendricks also works, identified the risk late last month. While Maloney is not involved in the development of the **super-B.I.G.***, he undertakes cancer surgery on dogs at Sumner Hospital, which is where the* **super-B.I.G.** *hip replacement has been extensively tested in canine experiments.*

"While reviewing pathology slides related to our dog cancer surgery, my colleague and I identified a dangerous bone cancer in a pathology slide that had been included with our material in error," said Maloney. "We discovered that it came from an arthritic dog that had received the **super-B.I.G.** *biofilm hip replacement two years previously." He alleges Hendricks dismissed the concerns he raised about a potential cancer link.*

Last year, more than 400,000 Americans underwent hip replacement for arthritis, and most had a dramatic improvement in their quality of life following surgery. Hip replacement is one of the most successful operations offered in American medicine, and the number of hip surgeries undertaken worldwide is increasing by about 5 percent annually.

This is big business for hip implant manufacturers in an increasingly consolidated market place. Synvest, a major manufacturer and international distributor of equipment and devices for bone surgery, has the largest international market share, with nearly 50 percent of hip replacements sold around the world bearing the Synvest brand.

In recent months, the medical device world has been buzzing with anticipation about an upcoming announcement from Synvest that some predict will change the field of hip replacements forever.

Hendricks and Synvest, along with a small privately-held biotech company called CellGrow, have designed, tested, and achieved regulatory approval for a new prosthesis called the **super-B.I.G.***, which adds an active biolayer to the surface of the metal implant. Studies in dogs have shown the biolayer allows the prosthesis to* *attach itself completely to the bone through the effect of a natural hormone, making it the most effective model of hip prostheses to date.*

But news of a possible cancer link threatens the IPO to fund the new company and calls into question the effectiveness of the new product.

"It also raises difficult questions about unethical behavior and scientific misconduct for individuals and organizations associated with this research," said Dr. Jane Bergin, a medical ethics professor at Birch Arbor University.

The slides that both Maloney and a colleague identified as showing evidence of cancer have disappeared, and so far, attempts to recover them have failed.

Maloney obtained the source specimen for the pathology slides where he had identified cancer and provided this material to Dr. Dimitri Antonopoulos, an internationally leading bone biologist. Antonopoulos isolated genetic material from the dog specimen and has been able to show that a reliable cancer marker known as p53 mutation was present in the dog bone implanted with the **super-B.I.G..**

Antonopoulos has provided electrophoresis gels, which demonstrate the p53 mutation, to the Journal*. The* Journal *has shown this scientific evidence to three independent cancer scientists from other institutions who have no prior knowledge of the work. All three scientists confirmed that the presence of p53 mutation is strong evidence that the dog had cancer.*

Dr. Andrei Kovalov, who is responsible for the biofilm development on the Hendricks team, has denied in an email responding to the Journal's *questions that any evidence of cancer was present in the pathology slides recovered from dogs who received the* **super-B.I.G.** *prosthesis. He offered no further comment.*

I skimmed the remainder of the article, which discussed the financial implications for Synvest that would result from cancelling the IPO. I was furious Patrick had gone to the press without consulting me. At the same time, I realized that Patrick had brought his concerns about seeing cancer in the specimen to Hendricks and had been attacked and told to forget his observation.

I returned the call of the university dean, who remained incensed. I then called Justine despite the late hour in Boston. As usual, when she saw it was me, she answered the call promptly. "Yeah, boss, what can I do for you? How was dinner?"

"Dinner was great, but we have a real problem with that damned Maloney. Get me a ticket on the red-eye. I am coming back tonight. And get Maloney in my boardroom at 2:00 p.m. tomorrow.

"And you better call Jack Albright first thing in the morning. I will stop for a shower at home and will be in the office by 10:00. And I need to talk to Hendricks and then Albright."

"What has Patrick done, boss?"

"Have a look at the online *Journal*, Justine. I better get to the airport. See you in the morning. Damn Maloney. I hate the red-eye."

As I packed to catch the limo to the airport, I heard myself muttering angrily about Patrick's nerve in going public. But as I got into the limo to catch the red-eye flight that I'd sworn to give up years ago, I was surprised to find myself chuckling. *No doubt about it, that kid has balls. Hendricks must be ready to kill him.*

And as the limo pulled out for the airport, I found myself softly singing the lyrics of the Boss' "Born to Run."

Chapter 46

Dr. Patrick Maloney
May 5

I was deeply unconscious at 1:30 when my phone went off for the first time. It was Gershwyn calling from a limo en route to the San Francisco airport.

"What the fuck, Patrick? I thought that you had given up on this cancer thing with Hendricks' hip prosthesis. I just read the online *Journal* article sent to me by the dean of the university, who is plenty pissed at you. I don't know why Hendricks hasn't called yet—oh, there he is now calling my cell. Patrick, I have never seen anyone undertake career suicide like this.

"You were poised to be a star, and I am afraid that you are now going to have trouble getting a job anywhere in this country. I am on the way to the airport just about to get on the red-eye because of you. We will meet in my office at two o'clock tomorrow, and I suggest that you have a lawyer with you."

It went downhill from there. Meredith got a call forty-five minutes later from Hendricks, who wanted to know who this guy Maloney was, and did he realize how much trouble he was in, and

Meredith better stay far away from him because he was going to be very toxic.

I could hear Hendricks on Meredith's phone as she lay close to me in bed. Hendricks was yelling, and I felt terrible for her. However, my spirits were revived when she rolled over to face me, put her phone on mute and murmured with a sly grin, "I think Dr. Hendricks may be upset at you, Patrick." She turned the phone back on and said, "Yes, Dr. Hendricks, I will be at Dr. Gershwyn's office at two o'clock."

The next call came from Andrei Kovalov, and he was absolutely livid. His dreams of financial reward from the IPO were vaporizing, and he was blaming Meredith.

"Your fucking boyfriend has screwed us totally. When I see that son of a bitch…"

Meredith ended the call, silenced her phone, and turned to me. "Since everyone is so angry with you, I suggest that perhaps I should punish you a bit. But first, turn your phone off." And what followed resulted in both of us forgetting about the chaos I was creating.

At 8:00 a.m., I called Sandy. I was surprised to learn he was still in Boston. I had assumed that having turned the story over to Theresa, Sandy would have returned to New York.

"How are you doing, kid? Have you seen Theresa's story?"

"I read it online. Reads well, it is certainly accurate, and the picture of the gels turned out well, I thought. Meredith doesn't know much about electrophoresis gels and she certainly understood the captions."

"It is unusual to see a picture like that above the fold on the first page of America's premier financial journal, believe me. This story is causing immense interest and Theresa is getting lots of messages from whistleblowers who want to talk to her about medical devices, conflict of interest between industry and doctors, and the regulator's 510 (k) clearance process. I think that there may be some awards waiting here for her, which is terrific—she is a great talent and this story will make her career."

"I'm delighted for Theresa, but I'm afraid my career is in tatters. I have been summoned to Gershwyn's office for two o'clock and he told me to bring a lawyer. Do you have any advice as to what lawyer I could ask to represent me?"

"Patrick, you do not need a lawyer. I will be there with you, and believe me, that is all you need. Except you need to delay the meeting until about 4:30."

"Sandy, I don't think you understand. Gershwyn is my boss and he set a meeting for 2 p.m. He is coming back on the red-eye for that meeting and he told me bring a lawyer. I think I need to be there when he told me to arrive whether you are available or not."

"Wait a minute. I am checking something." I could hear the sound of activity on Sandy's phone. "Yeah, we are in good shape. Delay the meeting until 4. I will be there by 4:30. Let them rant for the first half hour and then I will be there."

I called Justine, who answered with an oath. "Shit, Patrick, do you have any idea how much trouble you are causing? Do you know how crazy it is here right now? The boss moved his flight up to get the *red-eye*, which he never takes anymore, and we have the hospital and university leadership and a bunch of lawyers coming to crap on you at 2 p.m. Patrick, I really would not want to be you today. If I wasn't so pissed at you, I would feel sorry for you. Your career is about to just disappear."

"Justine, call everyone back and tell them I will not be there until 4."

Justine literally screamed at me. "Patrick, what are you doing? The most powerful people in our Boston medical world are coming to meet you and you want to tell them to cool their jets for two hours? They are going to lynch you if you keep this up."

"Just tell them that my representative will not be available until 4:30, so I will not be there until 4. See you then, Justine."

Meredith was putting things straight in her room. "I guess we have the day to ourselves, Patrick. I am certainly not going to go into the lab this morning, and you just told some very important people that as far as you are concerned, they can take a powder until you are ready to see them. What do you say we go for a run?"

I had left a set of running gear at Meredith's place and readily agreed to work off some anxiety. Just before we left, Jim McClintock phoned to say that he had been asked to come to Gershywn's office at 2:00, but just received a text telling him to delay until 4:00.

Meredith almost giggled. The phone was on speaker. "That's because the man of the hour, my Patrick, told them that he could not possibly change his schedule to make it before four."

"Meredith, I really like Patrick, but is it wise for him to show that kind of disrespect?"

"I am not sure what's going on, Dad. His friend Sandy said it was important to wait until after 4 and that he would join everyone at 4:30. I don't know why he can't be there until then, but he said to Patrick that the time was essential."

There was a thoughtful silence on the phone. "Four o'clock, huh? That's interesting. I guess that I will see you at the hospital. At least Patrick will have a couple of friendly faces present."

We went on a long leisurely run and whiled away a pleasant but anxious afternoon. Meredith was worried for me, but I had become resigned to my fate. "Meredith, I came to Boston with nothing, and now I have a chance to invite you into my life. I am already a winner no matter what happens today."

"But you have worked so hard for this, and now you may lose your opportunity in Boston."

"Any opportunity I had in Boston is pretty well shot. But I will figure something out. When you come from where I come from, everything kinda looks up."

It was a beautiful early summer day and we walked to the hospital hand in hand. As we got off the elevator on Gershwyn's floor, we encountered Andrei Kovalov, who was pacing back and forth in the corridor.

"Patrick, he looks furious. Should we call security?"

I thought for a moment, then took Meredith's cell phone and started its video recording running on mute. "Not to worry. This challenge I can look after. Just keep the video lined up on Andrei."

"Patrick, remember where you are! This isn't a hockey rink or boxing ring."

Meredith's words echoed in my head as I walked straight down the hall toward Kovalov. He stood three inches taller than me and was probably twenty pounds of muscle mass heavier, but I was not particularly worried. Andrei looked slow and uncoordinated and I anticipated that he could be provoked into carelessness. I walked directly at him, and when I was about five feet away, I said something softly.

Kovalov was already violently red in the face. Hearing my words, he grimaced, and then shouted back at me in Russian. As expected, the big guy then lunged forward angrily, swinging his right fist at my temple. But I wasn't there. I took two quick steps toward him while crouching to my right so Kovalov's right fist passed over my left shoulder.

Rather than retaliating with fists, I pivoted on my left foot and put my right foot out as I had extended my skate many times when I'd thought the ref was looking elsewhere. Lunging forward as he missed my head, Kovalov tripped and landed heavily head first on the floor.

As he lay dazed on the floor, I leaned down to grab the back of his jacket and pulled it over his head. I then reached around him for Meredith's hand and continued down the corridor to Gershwyn's office.

"Patrick, I heard you say something in what sounded like Russian. Do you speak the language?" Meredith asked.

Despite our situation, I couldn't help but chuckle. "Tell you later. Make sure that you save that video. I am pretty sure we will need it."

Justine greeted us right inside Gershwyn's office door. "Man, are you screwed, Patrick. You are just totally finished. They are all in the boardroom wanting several pounds of your flesh."

"Thanks, Justine. Nice to see you too."

As we entered the boardroom, Jim McClintock got up immediately and came around the table to kiss Meredith on the cheek and shake my hand warmly. I could see that this surprised Hendricks, who was glowering at both of us.

Gershwyn was sitting at the head of the table, and I sensed that he would chair the inquisition. He was accompanied on either side by the dean of the university and the president of the hospital. They were both checking their watches, obviously wanting to dispose of this minor player and get on with suing someone.

I recognized the hospital lawyer, Charles Schwarzman, who was sitting next to Hendricks, and Rod Katzner, the principal scientist in CellGrow. On his other side were six well-dressed men and women who Gershwyn introduced as lawyers representing the hospital, university, CellGrow, Hendricks, Kovalov, and Synvest. Gershwyn did not explain who was representing whom, and I decided it would likely be bad form to ask.

Chapter 47

Mr. Jack Albright
May 5

*T*he team of lawyers that I had rapidly assembled in response to Albert's message had been in the room since noon, plotting the strategy for the meeting. I was senior counsel. Our firm had managed delicate issues and litigation for the hospital for more than a hundred years.

The annual retainer that we received from the hospital was substantial and important in identifying our firm as a major player in the Boston legal world. In this case, we were continuing to primarily represent our client, the hospital.

However, after we'd reviewed the case early in the morning, the hospital had accepted our advice that we should also offer to represent the other members of the consortium planning the IPO. Following brief consideration, Hendricks, the university, Synvest, CellGrow, and the other contributors of intellectual property to the start-up agreed that we should take carriage of Maloney's interview today.

Naturally, I was pleased. The multiple clients would allow us to triple our fee.

I had been a senior partner in our firm since our representation of the hospital had been threatened almost twenty years ago. I'd managed to keep the hospital on board at that point, and thereafter I was identified as the relationship manager for the hospital in our firm. Bottom line, despite the short notice, I was determined to get a good result for one of our most important clients in this very unusual situation.

Over the past four hours, I had been leading the discussion between the lawyers in our group, determining what we would try and accomplish in this meeting. On my right hand was a younger man who personified the aggressive, hard-hitting litigator. Roger Hamilton was lean as a whip and dressed in a tapered European suit with an Egyptian cotton shirt and vivid silk tie. His closely cropped hair and stylish spectacles were consistent with his role as the leading corporate litigation expert in our firm.

We had decided that he would cross-examine Patrick. The other four colleagues were more junior lawyers from the firm who would be keeping notes and managing follow-up. The presence of six lawyers would undoubtedly be intimidating to this young doctor and would also help in justifying the fee that I was planning to charge the hospital and the IPO partners.

Forty-five minutes prior to Maloney's revised arrival at 4:00 p.m., I asked the other participants in the meeting to gather and listen to our advice regarding the conduct of this meeting. Unfortunately, the hospital lawyer Schwarzman was late arriving and didn't hear much of the direction from our firm. But in concluding, I was very clear.

"Gentlemen and Dean, there is really only one reason to meet with this Maloney character this afternoon, and that is to introduce reasonable doubt into the story that he has told the media. Hopefully by reason, and by letting him know the impact this story will have on his future career, we will convince him to recant and damage the credibility of the false and libelous story that Theresa Branton published today.

"The only hope we have to keep this IPO on track is to destroy the credibility of Branton's story, and that means getting Dr. Maloney to consider repudiating what he told the journal.

"You have met Roger Hamilton from our firm. I have asked him to hold nothing back in cross-examining Dr. Maloney in order to destabilize him and get him to realize just how much trouble he is in. Having seen Roger in action on many occasions, I have no doubt that Dr. Maloney will soon have considerable regret about his role in this debacle. I expect that he will then be amenable to our suggestions as to how he can help us to resurrect the IPO."

I leaned forward and took off my spectacles to slowly look each of the meeting participants in the eyes.

"Let me re-emphasize that our only goal for this meeting is to save the IPO. This meets the hospital's goals, the university's goals, and the goals of the various contributors of intellectual property to the start-up supported by the IPO.

"This means undermining and eventually destroying Maloney's credibility. When we stack up the reputations of the people in this room against this unknown fellow, I think we have a good opportunity to get this investment back on track." I then leaned back and put on my glasses. "Any questions?"

Mr. McClintock, who I understood had helped Dr. Hendricks in his fundraising strategy, started to protest, but was cut off by Dr. Hendricks.

"Jim, I know your daughter is close to this fellow. But we cannot let him destroy all the work we have done with these absolutely unfounded allegations."

Just at that moment, Maloney entered the room accompanied hand in hand by a lovely young woman. She took a seat next to Mr. McClintock at the boardroom table and gave McClintock a warm hug. Checking my notes, I realized that she must be Meredith McClintock, the biomechanics PhD who worked with Dr. Hendricks.

She seemed to have a relationship with Maloney that I had not recognized. Maloney was attacking Hendricks' research but was involved with a member of Jon's team? This was the first of several surprises that I would experience this afternoon.

Maloney seemed to purposefully separate himself by sitting at the opposite side of the table from Gershwyn. I had another moment of concern. He chose his seat deliberately, with no sense of indecision as to his place. He looked anything but intimidated at present and waved with confidence to Mr. McClintock. He seemed confident in setting himself apart. I had not expected that lack of doubt or indecision.

Gershwyn looked around the table and started off. "I guess that I am chairing this fiasco." With that, he glared at Patrick, and I knew that my message about unsettling Maloney had been received. "The only invited participant who is not here," Gershwyn continued as he looked at his meeting notes, "is Dr. Kovalov. Has anyone seen him? Is he coming?"

Maloney seemed to smile across the table at Dr. McClintock. "Dr. Gershwyn, I saw him outside in the corridor. He seemed rather unwell, and I expect that he may be late."

I was again surprised by Patrick's equanimity—and for senior counsel, surprise is not an enjoyable sensation.

"Maloney, will you have a lawyer representing you?" asked Gershwyn.

I had known Albert Gershwyn for years. He was probably the most creative and valuable member of the hospital's staff and frequently came to our firm for advice. I knew that he had considered hiring Maloney. It was good for him to make this young man realize his future career was in severe jeopardy.

Maloney shook his head and looked at his watch. "No, Dr. Gershwyn. My friend Sandy Spencer will be here in about twenty minutes, but you are all very busy people and maybe we should get underway."

I was surprised but delighted that he was not represented by counsel. Our mission at this table was to rock Maloney's confidence, to create chinks in his armor. If we could introduce just a small element of self-doubt, his story would likely start unravelling like a sweater. I hoped this could lead to a complete disavowal of the journal story.

And, of course, while we were working on convincing this young surgeon to withdraw his story, our firm would be Maloney's best friend, showing him how he had been manipulated by the unethical reporters working for the journal. And then, as soon as the story was discredited, we would probably sue him for good measure.

Whether Maloney was unable to afford a lawyer or whether he just did not realize the seriousness of the situation, giving up counsel for this meeting was a terrible mistake for him. A good lawyer would fight tooth and nail to prevent a seed of doubt being sewn in Maloney's mind. A good lawyer would interrupt, natter, bicker, and prevent us from intimidating his client.

Allowing Roger Hamilton to cross-examine this young surgeon with no lawyer present to defend him would be like staking a lamb in front of a wolf. It would not be very pretty, but it would be exactly what we needed to start Maloney down the road to a retraction.

Just then, Andrei Kovalov entered the room, glowering at Maloney. He appeared pale and distressed and was holding a wad of tissue over his eye. Gershwyn waved him to one of the empty seats at the table.

Gershwyn then gestured down the table to Roger Hamilton. "Maloney, this is Mr. Hamilton, who along with these other gentlemen is representing the hospital and the IPO partners. He is going to lead off for us. There is no record being taken of this conversation, but we will undoubtedly have some strong suggestions for you as the discussion proceeds."

Hamilton cleared his throat. He briefly consulted his notes and then closed his briefing binder, giving the impression that he had all the information he needed to show this young surgeon that he was in deep trouble.

"Dr. Maloney, you have been working with Dr. Gershwyn at the hospital and at Sumner Veterinary Hospital for the past five months, am I right?"

Maloney nodded. I was again a bit troubled in that he appeared entirely calm and unaware of the risky situation he was in. I almost felt pity for him.

"Answer my questions verbally, doctor. Your nod is not sufficient for these proceedings." Here, a good lawyer would have accused Roger of intimidation and aggressive cross examination.

But Maloney, being unrepresented, could do nothing but humbly respond, "Yes."

Hamilton leaned in toward the young surgeon. "Yesterday, you provided highly confidential information to Theresa Branton that was published online last night and in the print *Journal* this morning. This accusatory, unfounded story will have enormous financial consequences for all the parties represented in the room. Do you understand that?"

Maloney nodded and then responded, "Yes," again.

"Doctor, the information that you provided to the *Journal* was gained through your work at Sumner Hospital, correct?" Again, the young man responded in the affirmative, and for some reason, I felt concern rising.

"Dr. Maloney, do you remember that on February 16 of this year, you signed a non-disclosure confidentiality agreement following a discussion with Mr. Schwarzman?"

Maloney nodded.

I now anticipated my partner beginning the destruction of one Patrick Maloney. Whether Maloney's accusations were true or false, he was prevented by his confidentiality agreement from disclosing what he knew. Roger was about to make this sound like the crime of the century, a real hanging offense.

Of course, if Maloney had enlisted a lawyer, his counsel would have started vociferously objecting at this point, declaring that the confidentiality agreement was not relevant if patient safety were at risk. And we would argue back that there was no immediate risk to anyone, and this matter could have been brought forward without bringing the media into the discussion. And Maloney's lawyer would have responded that Maloney had tried to bring information forward before, etc. etc.

But this was a moot point. If Maloney had brought legal representation, this afternoon would turn into a donnybrook and we would likely have left this room without resolution after hours of acrimonious lawyerly back and forth. Without counsel, Maloney was about to be destroyed.

And Gershwyn had suggested that we might offer a carrot along with the stick. According to the confidentiality agreement, Maloney should be fired immediately for his breach. However, Gershwyn suggested that if he would agree to withdraw his story today, the hospital would allow him to finish his fellowship training.

Hendricks had initially objected to this strategy. He wanted Maloney horse whipped. But he'd finally muttered his agreement seeing that immediate withdrawal of the journal story might save his IPO.

"Just keep him away from me and my people," Hendricks had snarled, looking at Jim McClintock. McClintock started to say something in response and then remained silent.

"And, Dr. Maloney, do you understand that the story you provided to Theresa Branton was prohibited by your confidentiality non-disclosure agreement? You are in breach of that agreement, and the penalty for breaching the agreement is immediate dismissal from employment. And according to the agreement that you signed, the hospital and university are able to pursue damages against you for any financial losses caused by your irresponsible action."

Maloney remained silent, and tension in the room started to climb.

"Dr. Maloney, I interpret your silence as agreement with my statements about confidentiality. You have put a three-billion-dollar investment in jeopardy through your reckless disclosure of your employer's confidential information. Do you realize that the IPO partners will be immediately taking action against you to recover their loss?"

At this point, Maloney surprised me by smiling and leaning forward to comment. "Mr. Hamilton, the only thing that I own is a reliable but well-used Subaru Legacy. I think you may have difficulty getting the three billion you are looking for from my assets."

"There is no need for insolence," Roger snarled as he removed his glasses for emphasis. "You need to understand, Dr. Maloney, that the cause of action that you have created for these partners will not go away just because you have no assets today. A judgment against you as a result of your defamatory confidentiality breach will follow you for your lifetime whenever you look for further work."

Roger continued staring at Maloney for emphasis, and then replaced his spectacles to pick up a document at the side of his briefing binder. "And believe me, doctor, we have clear documentation of the billions of dollars in financial harm that will result from your irresponsible and negligent commentary reported by the journal."

He held the document toward Maloney. "We will have no difficulty whatsoever establishing the damages suffered by these fine organizations when we bring you to court."

Hamilton was certain that the ultimate way to get Patrick to recant the article was to convince him he would be unemployable forever and subject to the IPO partners claiming whatever assets he might accumulate in the future. I knew there were legal limits on the ability to encumber future assets, but that was not important at present. We simply planned to intimidate, whether the threats were real or not.

Surprisingly, instead of responding to Roger, Maloney turned to face Charles Schwarzman. "Mr. Schwarzman, you haven't shown Mr. Hamilton the NDA that I signed, have you?"

I could see beads of sweat appear on Schwarzman's forehead. "I have not had a chance. I was late for the pre-meeting."

Roger started to interrupt. But Maloney lifted his hand and held it in Roger's direction while he continued, "Mr. Hamilton, when you review the NDA ,you will see that I modified the standard confidentiality form, which I found much too broad, and wrote in that the NDA would only apply to work done for Doctors Gershwyn and Barnes. The microscopic cancer that I identified in the *super-B.I.G.* dog specimen had nothing to do with their work."

Hamilton attacked. "Just because you wrote some silliness on the standard NDA, Dr. Maloney, does not mean that your signature does not bind you to the terms of the full NDA. You did sign the agreement, did you not?"

"I am no lawyer, Mr. Hamilton. But what if the hospital counsel counter-signed my changes agreeing to the limitation of confidentiality that I just described?"

The entire room now stared at Schwarzman, who seemed to be shrinking in his seat. Gershwyn was the first to speak. "Did you agree to the limitation of confidentiality that Patrick is describing, George?"

Schwarzman silently nodded, and Hamilton seemed nonplussed.

I realized that things were suddenly going south. Why hadn't Schwarzman told us about this issue? The NDA was fundamental to intimidating Maloney. One of our junior lawyers had ensured earlier that the hospital had an NDA on file for Maloney. No one had said anything about a modified document.

With the momentary silence in the room, Hendricks could not resist interjecting. "You have no proof that this cancer, even if it exists, has anything at all to do with the **super-B.I.G.** prosthesis. I am going to sue you for libel for suggesting that my years of research showing that this is the best implant ever created should be disregarded just because you dreamed up a cancer."

Now, we were really getting off agreed strategy. This was turning into a free-for-all rather than a carefully planned attack.

Maloney, however, remained calm—and my concern increased as a result of his composure. "Dr. Hendricks, I am truly sorry that I am causing you this dreadful difficulty. But we both know that you really cannot sue me for libel if I can prove that what I am claiming is true. I will swear under oath that I saw cancer cells in a pathology slide that seems to have gone missing. My colleague at Sumner will support me under oath. As you now know, there is also evidence of p53 mutation in the specimen, which is clear evidence that this dog had cancer."

I felt a real sinking feeling. This kid was going to be very difficult to discredit. I could see the hope for a big bill that my firm would submit after rescuing the IPO was fading. Even though this kid was too naïve to get a lawyer to represent him, we were not going to easily intimidate him into withdrawing his allegations about the **super-B.I.G.**

Just then, there was a knock at the door and Sandy Spencer entered. I knew Sandy by reputation, and we had met at a financial advisors conference. He nodded to me, introduced himself to the room, and listened intently as our lawyers introduced themselves.

Sandy certainly looked the part of a successful investor. His bespoke suit was tailored and fit him perfectly. One suit button was closed as he stood before the table. His polished shirt was a bright periwinkle blue. Being the only man at the table not wearing a tie somehow gave him a sense of self-assurance.

He walked over to where Maloney was sitting and put his arm on his shoulder.

"Gentlemen and ladies…" Sandy bowed shortly in the dean and Meredith's direction. "I am here to talk about two things. The first will determine the future reputation and legacy of four people in this room. And I am not referring to Dr. Patrick Maloney." Sandy paused and looked dramatically at Gershwyn, Hendricks, the president, and the dean.

"The first thing to talk about is the next story that Theresa Branton and I will write together. I expect that this next story may be part of a series about the relationship between industry, hospitals, universities, scientists, surgeons, and what is good and safe for patients. That next story can have two different endings, but it will definitely have this beginning."

Turning toward Patrick, Sandy continued. "It will start with how I met Dr. Patrick Maloney when he was training in a little-known surgical residency in Solway Mills. How my son was skiing at Mount Solway and got smashed by a snowmobile and could not be evacuated because of a blizzard, and how this young man saved my son's life and his arm and leg.

"The story will go on to describe how Patrick overcame his father's and sister's deaths to get through university on a hockey scholarship and then surgical training in Solway to come here, to the center of the surgery world to train as a fellow."

He paused for a moment and looked carefully into each of the faces sitting around the table. "And how, from what I have learned, he turns out to be one of the best young surgeons to show up in Boston for some time. Despite the fact that he is previously unknown, he gets offered a job with America's best orthopedic surgeon."

Gershwyn leaned forward to protest, but Sandy cut him off. "Dr. Gershwyn, I know that there is no paperwork yet, but I will find witnesses, including some in your office, willing to tell me you offered him a job."

Sandy paused and then turned to the young doctor. "And then Patrick Maloney screwed it up, didn't he? Through no fault of his own, he became aware that a major advance in hip surgery also might be associated with a risk of a very dangerous cancer. And then the evidence that caused his concern about cancer in the **super-B.I.G.** dog implant mysteriously disappears, Dr. Hendricks."

In a reasonably theatrical move, Sandy pivoted to point his hand at Jon Hendricks, who nearly jumped out of his seat in protest. "No, relax, Dr. Hendricks—I am not accusing you personally, but there are plenty of people on your IPO team who will benefit from those slides disappearing. When the slides showing cancer disappear, Patrick creatively seeks out further scientific evidence that shows clearly that the **super-B.I.G.** implant is associated with a risk of cancer.

"And he does all this with no hope of reward. And with the recognition that powerful people who can make or break his career are going to be furious with him. And that a close friend may suffer a career setback because of him." Sandy offered a subtle bow in Meredith's direction.

"So, is he crazy? Does he have a self-destructive streak? Why does he persist in telling this story when he knows that he will be very badly hurt by it?

"And the first part of the story that Theresa and I plan to write in the next two days will conclude with absolute certainty that he refuses to eliminate this risk to his promising career for only one reason."

Here Sandy paused again, searching out each pair of eyes around the table. "And that reason is simply that he is a highly ethical and brave young man who believes his first duty as a physician is to ensure that no harm will occur to patients. And letting the **super-B.I.G.** prosthesis get implanted into millions of patients is a risk that Patrick could not allow to occur.

"That is the first part of the story that Theresa and I will be writing. The second part will go down one of two ways. The first option is that the leaders at the hospital and university who have a financial stake in the **super-B.I.G.** implant try to intimidate our young surgeon into retracting his story. That would be a huge mistake, because he is very difficult to intimidate and extremely cool under pressure."

At this comment, I noticed that Gershwyn could not help but nod in agreement.

"The second reason this intimidation approach is a mistake is that Theresa Branton and I will stop at nothing to destroy the reputation and legacy of whoever tries to hurt this fine young man, since he has acted in entirely ethical fashion at enormous risk to his own career."

Looking again at Gershwyn, Hendricks, the president, and dean, Sandy continued, "And believe me, nothing will ruin the reputation of a respected academic more"—and now, Sandy leaned forward on the table with both fists clenched—"than the accusation that they attempted to destroy evidence of a risk to patients in order to benefit financially."

Here, there was a very long pause. He then repeated, "Destroying evidence of a risk to patients to benefit financially." The words hung in the air.

I was impressed. He could deliver a great address to a jury. "And make no mistake: Theresa and I will be delighted to allege that Dr. Maloney's academic future and freedom is being assaulted by leaders who should support him, not attack him, for exposing a risk to the health of millions of Americans."

Here, Sandy looked carefully at the dean. "Dean, you know how universities must protect academic freedom. It appears to me that Dr. Maloney's freedom to report important scientific observations is being infringed by the university."

As the dean struggled to respond, Sandy waved his hand at her and continued.

"Now, the other way this story could conclude is that the outstanding leaders of this fine department, hospital, and this great university recognize that Patrick has acted ethically and prevented them from potentially harming patients. In recognition of his honesty and bravery, they immediately appoint him to faculty."

Hendricks started to protest, but Sandy cut him off. "And there is another reason why you should consider appointing Patrick to faculty immediately, and this relates to the second thing that I am here to discuss today. To explain this, I will need to bring in Mr. George Bartholomew, who is waiting outside."

Sandy opened the door and welcomed a portly gentleman in his sixties, well-dressed in an old-fashioned way with vest and bow-tie, peering at the room over the top of his wire rimmed glasses. George and I, as well as the president and dean, knew each other well and nodded.

Sandy continued. "Allow me to introduce George Bartholomew, whom I have retained to represent me in the next aspect of our business here today. As many of you know, George specializes in developing gift agreements for high net worth individuals who wish to donate to your hospital or university."

George nodded to the room, and Sandy went on. "And this comes to why we needed to delay our meeting today. As Jim McClintock has probably figured out, I wanted to wait until the markets closed before coming to this meeting.

"It also explains why I gave Theresa the byline for this story rather than writing it myself. Because as soon as this story was posted online as public information, I completed writing put option contracts on $300 million of Synvest stock."

Meredith's father gasped, but the rest of us just looked puzzled.

"I started developing the contracts the day before and could accomplish this large short position because Synvest is listed on several exchanges and derivative markets around the world."

I looked at McClintock, who seemed to be the only one understanding what Sandy was saying.

"As you might imagine, Jim, writing puts on 5 percent of Synvest stock required breaking up the short position up into smaller contracts with various brokers in Europe and Asia, as well as at home, so I would not spook the markets. By about three o'clock this morning, I had the $300 million short position I was looking for. As you know, Jim, that is a pretty intense short play.

"By close of market today, Synvest is off by a third, and I have already partly covered the short play and made $50 million free and clear. I expect to double that in the next few days, because Theresa will be doing another story confirming that the IPO is cancelled and the entire doubling of Synvest stock over the past six months no longer has the legs to stand on.

"I expect the stock will likely be tumbling back to where it started six months ago, and I will be up more than a hundred million dollars."

He paused to allow the room to consider what he just said. We did not entirely understand put options, but we did understand a hundred million dollars.

"And you will note that I took that short position not on the basis of any insider information, but on the basis of the public information that became available when Theresa posted the story online at midnight. At one minute past midnight, I started completing the put contracts, and all $300 million was placed by 3:00 a.m."

"You need to remember that my background is social science, not finance." The dean looked bewildered. "What the hell is a put option contract and what relevance does this have to the IPO?"

Sandy nodded. "Writing a put option contract means that I have contracted to sell Synvest shares at yesterday's market value of about $100 per share any time over the next twenty-one days. These contracts are written with current institutional holders of Synvest shares who were willing to provide this put option contract for a non-redeemable fee. These options can be bought on derivative exchanges around the world, and I spread the $300 million purchase quite broadly so no single holder would realize that I was accumulating a substantial position.

Here, Sandy unbuttoned his suit coat and spread his arms for emphasis. "With the publication of Theresa's article and the likely cancellation of the IPO, I expect that Synvest shares will return to about $45 a share within the time that I can exercise my options. That number represents the value of Synvest stock prior to the IPO being developed.

"This will be a substantial gain for me, probably equal to one-third to one-half of the value of the contracts. I do not really need another hundred million dollars. And that is where George Bartholomew comes in."

At the mention of his name, George sat up straighter in his chair. I was beginning to see where this was headed. *Interesting.*

"I have instructed George that I want to make a gift to the university and the hospital, as well as to Professor Gershwyn's and Professor Hendricks' programs. I estimate the total gift will likely be more than $120 million when the short position is fully wound up.

"I have instructed George to draw up gift agreements to provide $15 million in discretionary grants for both the university and the hospital, to be managed at the direction of the dean and the president."

The president and the dean looked at each other with interest. That kind of discretionary philanthropic funding never occurred. This might be turning out differently than they had feared.

"And I have instructed Mr. Bartholomew to split the remaining funding, likely at least $45 million each, to the Gershwyn and Hendricks labs. The Gershwyn funding is to be used for furthering bone cancer research at Sumner, investigating Synchro Therapy. The fund will be used to continue dog research with Synchro Therapy and start human trials as soon as possible, if the dog work is promising.

"The other $45 million will go to Dr. Hendricks' program and will be used to investigate a method for application of IGF in the *super-B.I.G.* prosthesis that does *not* cause cancer. I would expect that CellGrow will be delighted to participate in this funded research pursuing further use of their product."

Sandy looked down the table at Rod Katzner, who raised his hand in affirmation of Sandy's assumption.

"All these gifts will be contingent on two factors. First, that the university and hospital immediately appoint Dr. Maloney to faculty for a minimum ten-year term. If he leaves faculty before ten years, the entire funding will be returned to me. After ten years, he will have demonstrated his value and I predict he will be appointed to your position, Dr. Gershwyn."

"The second contingency is that the Gershwyn gifted program for bone cancer research and all papers and research developed from the program must recognize this fund in honor of Patrick's deceased little sister, Emily Maloney. It will be called the Emily Fund."

I could feel the mood in the room relaxing. Everyone was getting something they wanted, although the big IPO payday was going to be put off, at least for a while.

Except for me. The opportunity for our firm submitting a big fee had faded. However, the fact that everyone was making much more than they feared meant that a substantial but reasonable fee submission from our firm would likely be paid to put this issue behind them.

I looked around the table and ended up looking at Gershwyn. "Mr. Spencer, may we have a moment to confer with our clients? Perhaps Mr. Bartholomew could stay in the room to answer any questions. I would suggest that you do not wander too far."

Sandy, Patrick, Meredith, and her father left the room and waited outside. I could see Gershwyn's assistant Justine standing outside the door and wondered if she had been listening to our conversation. She was undoubtedly surprised to see that some people in the room were smiling.

After a brief discussion with George Bartholomew, it was obvious that everyone would agree to accept the funds offered by Sandy Spencer. I opened the door and asked them to return.

"I think the terms described are agreeable to all. George and I are going to work on the paperwork for the gift agreements, but I expect no difficulty coming to resolution." I activated my phone to show the future quotes on Synvest to Sandy. "Synvest stock is plunging on heavy trading in futures markets. I expect that your short play will be even more lucrative than you mentioned."

Gershwyn walked around the table to approach Maloney and Meredith McClintock. Gershwyn was beaming and put his arm around Patrick's shoulder. "Well, partner, we will get your paperwork done and present you to the partnership at our next meeting. With both me and Hendricks supporting you, and Sandy's generous gifts, there should be no trouble welcoming you to our hospital and university faculty—right, guys?"

The president and dean smiled, thinking about the discretionary grants, and Hendricks managed a nod. "Yeah, I guess that's right."

There was one very angry and dissatisfied participant in the meeting who now lurched to his feet. Andrei Kovalov was obviously furious to see his IPO payday disappearing while everyone else got money from Sandy Spencer.

"This guy stole the specimen from my lab without permission. He cannot just take my specimen to test without telling me. He is costing us a lot of money through his theft. We need to stop him. We need to sue him or fire him, but we need to stop him."

I looked up from the folder where I was writing notes that I would use to complete the memorialization of this rather extraordinary meeting. "Dr. Kovalov, I think Mr. Spencer has satisfied many of the IPO partners, but not you. However, it appears to me that you will have some other questions to answer regarding your research methods. I expect those questions will be asked and answered in another venue."

With that comment, participants began leaving the boardroom. I saw Justine standing outside the door as we all filed out, and her face betrayed utter confusion.

Chapter 48

Meredith McClintock, PhD
May 5

*L*ater that evening, Patrick and I were reviewing this remarkable day, enjoying the end of a meal on my balcony, when Patrick's cell rang. He smiled when he saw the number was the Boston Police Department. After a brief conversation, Patrick agreed to meet with officers at my apartment.

The two officers arrived within fifteen minutes. After introductions, the lead officer described the reason for their visit reading from a notebook, where she had obviously recorded material from an earlier interview.

"We have a complaint from a Dr. Andrei Kovalov. Dr. Maloney, he states that you attacked him without provocation at the hospital this afternoon just before 4:00 p.m. As evidence of the attack, he showed us a cut over his left eye that he says came when you pushed him onto the floor. He stated that he was simply waiting outside an office to join a meeting when you advanced on him and tripped him without warning.

"When asked for a possible motive for an unprovoked attack, the complainant said that you are very jealous of his scientific success and you have recent disagreements with his research results."

Patrick looked at me with concern. "Hmmm, this is really distressing. Meredith and I were in the hospital heading to a scheduled meeting that Andrei was also attending. When we stepped off the elevator, Andrei was standing in the hallway between us and the office where the meeting was being held. I understand that he has real anger management problems, so I asked Meredith to video him as we walked past. I was worried that he might try something like this."

"You have a video showing an altercation?"

"Yes, we uploaded it to Meredith's computer. Would you like to watch?"

I turned the screen toward the officers and started the thirty-second video. It clearly showed an angry-looking Andrei Kovalov in the hallway. He appeared to be yelling. The officer asked me, "Can you turn the sound up so we can hear what he is saying?"

Patrick responded, "Unfortunately, Meredith seems to have hit mute during the recording. There is no audio recorded at all."

"I understand. Looking at Dr. Kovalov, I can imagine that you were quite apprehensive. He seems very upset," the officer suggested, and I nodded my assent.

Returning to the video, the officers watched as Patrick walked toward Kovalov. As he came within five feet of Kovalov, the man seemed to literally erupt, yelling and reddening even more than he appeared earlier in the recording.

I guess that Patrick's behavior might have seemed unusual. Most people would have stopped and backed up with a very angry, big man standing in front of them. But Patrick kept moving forward with his hands still at his waist. The officers looked carefully at Patrick on the video and in person. They were obviously wondering about his seeming disregard for Andrei's apparent anger.

Then, the video started bouncing around as I obviously had difficulty keeping focus on the action in front of me. But the officers could see readily that Kovalov yelled something at Patrick and swung his right fist at his head. Most people would have ducked or stopped or retreated, but Patrick stepped forward into Kovalov's swing, which resulted in his fist passing harmlessly over his shoulder.

The officers then saw Patrick pivot, and suddenly Kovalov was falling onto the floor. As he hit the floor, Patrick grabbed the bottom of the bigger man's jacket, pulled it over his head, and left him immobilized in the corridor. The officers saw his head connect with the hallway, which is likely how the cut over his eye originated.

The second policeman pointed to the screen. "Hey, that almost looked like a hockey fight where guys pull the jersey over their opponent's head to immobilize them."

"Officer, I played hockey in junior and college. I guess I might have been involved in a couple of fights on the ice."

The lead officer played the video back and forth and stopped it seconds before Kovalov swung at Patrick. "It's strange. Right here, it almost looks like the guy heard something that made him go off the deep end. Did you say something to him right here?"

Patrick played the video back and forth. "Officer, I cannot really remember saying anything that I can relate. Maybe something like, 'Hey Andrei, what's up?' I'm really not certain. And then, he just launched at me."

"Okay, Doc, thanks for this. Can you send me a copy? It seems pretty clear from this that Kovalov was the one who started an unprovoked attack. It's too bad that we don't have audio to be sure, but the video is pretty good evidence against him."

She handed her card to me. Copying the officer's email address into my system, I sent the video off to the officer's account. "Of course, officer. I'm sending it as an attachment right now."

Patrick assured the officers that he had no plan to file a complaint against Kovalov and would be happy to let the matter drop. The officers left shortly thereafter.

As I closed the door behind them, I looked at Patrick slyly. "Well, Dr. Maloney, that video certainly served your purpose. And I seem to remember you saying something to him in what sounded like Russian to me. Now, you come clean. What did you say?"

"Well, I really only know one phrase in Russian. When we played Russian visiting teams in junior tournaments, my job was to get in a fight with their best player and get the two of us sent off for major penalties. Needless to say, their team's relative talent was diminished when their best player accompanied me to the penalty box."

"What does that have to do with what you said?"

"I am not exactly sure what the words mean, but it has something to do with carnal relations with your mother and something about a barnyard. It never failed me to get the Russian player taking a swing at me, and it just worked again.

"I knew that Andrei was going to hold us up in the hallway to scream at me about stealing his samples, and I just wanted to get inside Gershwyn's office and get things over with. I figured that the phrase might come in handy."

I shook my head in astonishment that Patrick had had the foresight to start videoing on mute as we stepped off the elevator. But I was learning that I usually enjoyed being astonished by this hockey guy.

Chapter 49

Dr. Patrick Maloney
22 months later

I was reflecting on how our lives had changed as Meredith and I drove north to Solway Mills. Meredith's sporty two-seater used for our initial trip to Solway had been traded in on an SUV to accommodate the car seat in the back for three-month-old Emily. Emily had been born fourteen months after our October wedding and was the center of my world.

We had asked Sandy to serve as our daughter's godfather and he was taking the role very seriously. He dropped in at least monthly to visit his goddaughter and had established an educational fund with a substantial donation shortly after the christening. Of course, I left the fund in Sandy's hands to invest, and figured that Emily would be able to afford several Ivy League degrees by the time she was old enough to go to college.

Sandy's shorting of Synvest stock had worked out to everyone's advantage, excepting investors who had run the stock up in anticipation of the ***super-B.I.G.*** IPO. In the nine months prior to the cancelled IPO, Synvest stock had gone from a price of about $45 a share to about $100 a share.

Sandy's wisdom in shorting Synvest became evident when the cancellation of the IPO was announced two days after Theresa's first article and the stock rapidly fell to its earlier range of $40 to $45 per share. Sandy carefully covered his put contracts over the next three weeks, and by the time he finished, he had achieved more than $150 million in profit as Synvest's share price cratered.

Sandy's signing of put contracts starting minutes after Theresa's article appeared online attracted attention from securities investigators. After discussion with Sandy, however, the investigators agreed that he was acting on public information available to all investors.

Following the cancellation of the IPO, Hendricks made major changes in his research program. He started by firing Andrei Kovalov and, at my suggestion, hired Dimitri Antonopoulos to run the biology program in developing a new B.I.G. strategy. Hendricks also ordered a review of pathology in all fifty dogs who had undergone autopsy to date in order to determine whether any other slides had gone missing.

Hendricks' team identified three other dogs where slides could not be located. Dimitri was able to locate the plastic blocks associated with the missing slides and again undertook genetic analysis, identifying a variety of cancer gene mutations in the specimens with missing slides.

Hendricks was furious. Kovalov had obviously known that cancer was present in all these dogs and had eliminated the slides in order to ensure his payday from the IPO. Hendricks considered bringing civil or criminal action against Kovalov. But Andrei could not be located, and everyone assumed that he had left the country.

Hendricks had the good grace to admit to me, "We were sitting on a time bomb with that IPO. I can only thank you for saving me from myself and that Kovalov."

Dimitri was working hard with CellGrow to identify a new IGF product that stimulated bone in-growth in the lab without causing genetic changes. The resultant compound was now being implanted as a new biofilm in dog prostheses and in initial studies, Meredith was finding very effective bone ingrowth. Dimitri was hopeful that they might be ready to start a major study in dogs within six months.

With Sandy's investment expertise, the Emily Fund was constantly running a surplus despite the financial demands that Kate and I made on the grant pursuing our work on Synchro Therapy in dogs. I remained closely involved with Kate at Sumner Hospital, and dog Synchro Therapy was proving remarkably effective. It was already obvious that our dogs' survival was much better than what was previously achieved with standard chemotherapy.

With the positive results in dogs, I was increasingly interested in introducing Synchro Therapy to our patients. Starting a new treatment in humans required evidence that the treatment caused no harm in Phase I clinical trials.

To start testing the treatment in people, we established a Phase I protocol for use of Synchro Therapy in patients with advanced osteosarcoma who had failed standard therapy. The first patient enrolled was a 21-year-old woman from Gary, Indiana. Brianna Bailey had presented to her local hospital with cancer that had already spread to the lungs from the primary cancer site in her knee. The lung tumors had failed to respond to standard chemotherapy, and she was referred to Boston for consideration of experimental therapy.

Her family did not have health insurance and were virtually bankrupt from paying Brianna's bills for treatment in Indiana. I was so pleased that my little sister's fund could help this family access the best care despite their financial straits.

It was exciting that Brianna's biopsy from Gary, prior to treatment, showed high levels of both IGF receptor and IGF production. After careful discussion with Brianna and her mother Imani, Synchro Treatment with IGF-Receptor blockade was started, followed by intense IGF stimulation and provision of chemotherapy.

We ordered a new chest CAT scan three weeks after the first round of Synchro Therapy. It was very encouraging to see major shrinkage of all the cancers in Brianna's lungs. Brianna's father had flown in from Indiana to hear about the results of the CAT scan with his wife and daughter. I sat with James, Imani, and Brianna, giving them the good news—and was not surprised to see quiet tears running from James' eyes.

I took care to tell them that Brianna was not out of the woods by any means, and suggested that we should provide two more courses of Synchro Therapy followed by surgery if the excellent response continued. James was obviously not entirely comfortable with strong emotions, but muttered his appreciation. "Doc, I cannot thank you enough for helping my daughter."

I could not help thinking about how eighteen years ago, my little sister had succumbed to a very similar situation.

I looked up at James. "James, I think I understand how you are feeling, and you have my promise that we will keep on doing everything possible to help Brianna."

James could see from my eyes that this was personal for me.

Chapter 50

Dr. Patrick Maloney
& Meredith Maloney, PhD
22 months later

*A*s we pulled into the driveway of Mum's home, she rushed out to the car to greet her granddaughter. Inside the house, I smiled as Meredith and Mum passed a giggling Emily back and forth. At the same time, I remembered my little sister and how helpless I had felt watching her demise almost twenty years ago. Silently, I pledged that my primary professional goal would be helping Brianna and others like her to avoid Emily's fate.

A pickup truck pulled up in the driveway, and Larry Humphreys yelled in the front door. "Get your gear, Patrick. We have the ice in thirty minutes."

I looked at the happy scene in the living room where my wife and mother were enjoying Emily. Meredith had just told me this week that she was pregnant again, and we planned on telling Mum at dinner that night.

But first, it was ice time. I called out to Meredith, "We will probably get a beer after the game. I will definitely be back for dinner," and winked broadly at her.

I smiled as Patrick grabbed his hockey bag from the SUV and threw it in the back of Larry's pickup. My husband might be an increasingly celebrated surgeon and a future medical leader. But I loved him most for the man he had grown into from that brash young hockey player I first met on the Charles River bike path.

About the Author

Robert Stuart Bell, MDCM, MSc, FRCSC, FACS, FRCSE (hon). Professor of Surgery, University of Toronto

Dr. Bob Bell received his medical degree from McGill University in 1975. Following internship at McGill, he worked as a General Practitioner outside Toronto for three years. Bell returned to surgical residency at the University of Toronto and received his fellowship in Orthopedic Surgery in 1983.

Bell then spent two years as a surgical and research fellow at Harvard University, Boston Children's, and Massachusetts General Hospitals in Boston. While in Boston, he gained clinical expertise in arthritis and cancer surgery and worked in cancer research. His love for Boston is evident in the setting of *Hip* in this Massachusetts center of medical excellence.

Recruited to the University of Toronto's Faculty of Surgery, Bell worked as a cancer and orthopedic surgeon for 19 years. During that time, he trained more than 30 surgical fellows in principles of cancer surgery, and these former fellows are now surgical leaders on five continents. Bell collaborated with dedicated expert basic scientists throughout his surgical career and published more than 200 peer-reviewed, scientific, and clinical papers—mainly on bone and muscle cancer. He has presented his research at scientific meetings around the world.

In 2005, Bell stopped performing cancer surgery when he was appointed as President and CEO of University Health Network (UHN), Canada's largest research hospital network. Toronto General Hospital, one of the hospitals in the network, was recently named the seventh best hospital in the world by *Newsweek* magazine. During his nine years as CEO of UHN, Bell led a massive expansion of clinical and research programs.

In 2014, Bell was appointed Deputy Minister of Health in Canada's largest province of Ontario. For the next four years, Bell was responsible for the operations of a health system serving 14 million people.

After resigning as Deputy Minister in 2018, Bell has focused on charitable activities and providing commentary on Canada's publicly funded health system. This commentary can be found at www.drbobbell.com and @drbobbell. Bell and his wife Diann divide their time between homes in Toronto and on Georgian Bay.

All profits from this book will be donated to serve bone cancer research at Princess Margaret Hospital, one of the world's premier cancer hospitals and a member of University Health Network.

Connect with the Author

Website:
drbobbell.com

Email:
docbobbell@gmail.com

Social Media:
Twitter: @drbobbell

12890936R00157

Made in the
USA
Monee, IL